THE ACCIDENT

DAWN GOODWIN's career has spanned PR, advertising and publishing. Now, she loves to write about the personalities hiding behind the masks, whether beautiful or ugly. Married, she lives in London with her two daughters and a British bulldog called Geoffrey.

THE ACCIDENT

Dawn Goodwin

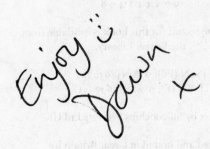

HEAD
ZEUS

An Aria Book

First published in the UK in 2017 by Head of Zeus Ltd

This paperback edition first published by Head of Zeus in 2021.
An Aria book.

9 7 5 3 1 2 4 6 8

A catalogue record for this book is available from
the British Library.

ISBN (PB): 9781838930721
ISBN (E): 9781786699633

Typeset by Siliconchips Services Ltd UK

Printed and bound in Great Britain by
CPI Group (UK) Ltd, Croydon CR0 4YY

Head of Zeus Ltd
First Floor East
5–8 Hardwick Street
London EC1R 4RG

WWW.HEADOFZEUS.COM

For my girls, Paige and Erin

Veronica

'It's me, Veronica. Open the door.'
The letter box rattled. I stood at the top of the stairs and pushed the curtain of lank hair out of my eyes.

'It's a beautiful day – open the curtains and see for yourself.' Felicity's voice was shrill.

I lowered myself onto the top stair and wrapped my arms around my legs. If I sit quietly, she will go away. She always does eventually.

The letter box rattled again, already with less force.

'Has Tom gone to the hospital? Come on, open up.' She paused. 'We could go out? Do something together? I'm going into town with Zara tomorrow to get Tabitha's new school uniform for next week. Come with us. A change of scenery will do you good.'

She really didn't have a clue sometimes. Begrudgingly, she had a point though; I should get that organised too. The summer was over; I hadn't even noticed.

I lowered my chin to my knees and breathed in the

familiar smell of worn flannelette. When last did I wash these pyjamas? When last did I take them off? My mind tried to grasp onto yesterday, last weekend, last week.

'Okay, fine. I have to go. The cleaner is coming. But this isn't healthy, Veronica. It's time to start picking yourself up.'

The letter box rattled one more time for punctuation, then lay silent.

I buried my face in my thighs and sat a moment longer before slowly making my way back to bed.

My phone vibrated on the bedside table, but I hid behind closed eyelids for a minute before reaching my arm out of the warm cocoon of the duvet and feeling around for it. I pulled it back under the covers, the artificial blue-white of the screen assaulting my eyes.

Home soon. I'll sort dinner. T x

I sighed. It was a twenty-minute journey from the hospital, enough time for me to pull on some jeans and force a toothbrush around my mouth. I stretched, feeling joints creak and muscles groan. Then, with more effort than required, I pulled myself out from under the duvet and sloped to the bathroom.

With yesterday's jeans hanging low on my thin waist, I made my way into the kitchen. Dust speckles danced in the sun's rays streaming through the glass doors to the garden. It was a warm August evening, but I felt cold and shivery. I flicked the kettle on, then retreated to the lounge to open the curtains before Tom got home, maybe straighten a cushion or two on the couch, make everything look like it should. I tugged back the heavy curtains and stared into the street. It was empty except for a little girl on a scooter, who whizzed past, her ponytail flying behind her. A short distance after her, a woman trotted to keep up. I could see her mouth moving, making large shapes of outrage, probably shouting for the girl to slow down – that's what any responsible parent would do.

I followed the girl with my eyes and saw Tom's car pull around the corner just as the scooter reached the end of the pavement. I raised my hand in slow motion, but the child stopped safely on the kerb and waited as the car drove past. It pulled into the driveway, the gravel crunching familiarly, followed by a door thudding closed. Out of the corner of my eye I could see Felicity striding over from her house next door to intercept Tom. I noticed him glance across to our window and I retreated into the shadow of the curtain. Felicity was talking at him, her hands illustrating every word. He reached out and stroked her arm, saying words I couldn't hear. He looked around again.

When he pulled her into an embrace, I turned away from the window.

Minutes later, the key scraped in the lock and the door opened with a draught of warm air. I was now sitting in the kitchen, a cup of tea in front of me, and I could picture him following his usual routine: briefcase under the side table; keys clattering into the bowl; jacket shrugged off and thrown over the banister. I'd watched him do this nearly every day for the last thirteen years, most of that time from the hallway where I would stand ready to greet him with affection, but things had changed.

He tugged on his tie as he came to find me.

'Hey, you.'

'Hi.'

He planted a brief kiss on my cheek, his hand hovering unsure over my head. 'How are you? How was your day?'

I shrugged. 'Okay, you? How was the hospital?' I tried to sound less weary than I felt.

He shrugged and lowered his eyes. 'No change.'

I watched him as he went through the post, pausing at the letter from the lawyer, but not opening it. Instead, he waved it at me.

'I spoke to them today. They have a date for the court case. It's soon – end of October.'

My silence spoke volumes.

He sighed. 'Why don't I make us some dinner? Then I have some work to catch up on, some phone calls to make.'

'Sure, thanks.'

'Go and relax in the lounge. I'll bring it through for you on a tray.'

This had quickly become our new evening routine.

The next morning, after Tom left for work, I forced myself to get dressed. Felicity was right, Grace would need new school shoes. I moved on autopilot, not caring what I was wearing, but at the same time hoping I wouldn't see anyone I knew.

I went to grab my car keys from the bowl, then thought twice about it. Grabbing my handbag, I reached for the door handle and pulled it open, squinting in the bright sunshine. It was a simple task to put one foot in front of the other and leave the house, but I felt like an invisible hand was holding me back. *School shoes... school shoes...* played on repeat in my head.

By the time I reached the shoe shop on the high street, my hands were gripping my handbag so tightly that the straps were cutting into my fingers. The shop was full of vibrant children and harassed mothers. I stared steadfastly in front of me, cut through the noise and approached an assistant who was wandering around with a clipboard.

'I need to buy school shoes.'

'Yes, of course. Please take a ticket from the dispenser and we will get to you when they call your number. We'll measure your child's feet first, then see what style suits best.' She turned away, but I seized her arm a little too aggressively.

'I don't need her feet measured.'

The woman frowned at me, then smiled tightly. 'In order to get the best fit possible, we advise measuring your child's feet. Have them take a seat and I'll get you a number.'

'She's not here.' I was still gripping her arm.

'We really need her here to fit the shoes correctly. It's against our policy to sell you shoes without a proper fitting. Perhaps you can come back when she is with you?'

'You don't understand. I need to get the shoes today. I know her size – she's a 13G. That's what she was the last time anyway and her feet haven't grown—'. My voice caught in my throat.

The sales assistant took a step away from me, then gently removed my hand from her arm. 'Perhaps you should come back when it is quieter. It's very noisy and overwhelming in here today, isn't it?' She spoke slowly, enunciating every word.

'I have to get them today. I can't...' My voice was too loud in contrast. I looked around. Faces were staring, eyebrows raised. 'Sorry,' I mumbled and backed away.

My eyes wouldn't focus. I rushed for the exit and collided with a bony shoulder. My handbag fell from my stiff fingers.

'Oh! Veronica!'

Felicity. Perfect.

'Are you okay?' Zara too. This just gets better.

I ducked to the ground, scrabbling to gather the detritus that had fallen from my bag.

Felicity knelt down to help me, her fingers stuffing used tissues and a stray pen into the pockets. 'Hey, slow down! Let me do that.'

Zara shuffled awkwardly behind her.

I stumbled to my feet. 'I... I... I have to go.' I grabbed the bag from Felicity's outstretched arm.

'Wait!' Zara called.

I ran, head down, the handbag clutched to my chest.

Felicity

Seeing her like that was a bit of a shock. Her dark hair was lank and scraped back in a messy ponytail – not the charmingly messy kind; rather, the kind that looks like you slept in it. The circles under her eyes made her look haunted and her skin had the grey tone of someone who has been indoors too long.

Not so perfect now, are we?

'She looks awful, doesn't she?' Zara said, a concerned frown wrinkling her forehead.

'I know, right? Didn't I say to you last week how worried I was that she was pretty much in hiding? And now look at her. Frankly, she should've stayed at home.'

'Yes, but can you blame her after what she's been through?'

Felicity immediately checked herself and quashed the warm glow of pleasure she had felt at seeing Veronica in such a wretched state. 'Oh, no, of course not. I'm not being critical, just really worried.'

Felicity had watched her bolt from the shop like

a spooked horse, all jittery and white knuckles. She could hear the shop assistant speculating wildly to her colleague in low tones. 'I don't know what was up with her, but there was something not quite right. What if she's done something, like… I dunno… kidnapped a kid or something and that's why she couldn't bring her in?'

'Maybe she's just had enough of shopping. Don't be so dramatic,' her colleague replied, bored already.

'We should be doing something to help,' Zara was saying.

'I've tried. There's no getting through to her just now. Anyway, are we done here? That's rather killed the mood now, so I'm going to rush off.'

'Yes, yes, you go. I've got some more errands to run.'

Felicity turned to leave, immediately pulling her phone from her bag as she went. She scrolled to the recent calls list and dialled the number listed at the top.

His voicemail.

Injecting concern into her voice, she said, 'Tom, it's me. Call me, please – I've just seen Veronica in the shoe shop. She didn't look good. We should talk.'

Veronica

I stood in the lounge in the calm after the storm that is the school run, staring out of the window and contemplating the emptiness of the day before me, a cup of steaming tea in my hands. The sky was dank and grey, with a steady, soaking drizzle falling. Hello September.

Children had been safely escorted into class a week into the new term and the street was now quiet again, with just the occasional car splashing through the puddles.

In a blaze of colour, a woman wandered into my line of sight. Completely alone in the miserable street, she was wearing a bright red raincoat, with black wellies covered in multi-coloured butterflies, and I found myself thinking, *Grace would love those wellies*. I followed her with my eyes as she stepped off the pavement and into the road. She was smiling to herself and splashing in the puddles like a carefree toddler. Then she lifted her face to the sky and flung her arms out wide. With complete abandon, she began to spin in the rain with her face turned up to the steadily falling drops, like a scene from a feel-good TV commercial. I was captivated. My stomach ached with envy at how trouble-free she seemed. Then she stopped spinning, shook her wet hair so that droplets of water sprinkled in every direction, and looked directly at me with a wide smile. My grip on the hot tea nearly slipped. I looked behind me, although I knew I was alone. All I saw was my perfectly tidy, perfectly orderly lounge. When I turned back, she was gone.

Days passed before I saw her again. I can't say what I was doing with my time in between; hours blurred into each other.

I don't know why I had chosen today to do it, but I had braved the great outdoors again after the disastrous shoe shopping debacle a few weeks earlier and was standing in the supermarket with an empty trolley, contemplating the cereals aisle and trying to decide which brand would suit Grace's fussy tastes. Should I give in, knowing she would prefer something chocolatey or could I convince her into porridge? Perhaps a chocolate-flavoured porridge?

Out of the corner of my eye I noticed a flash of emerald green and turned to see the woman standing next to me, studying the back of a packet of muesli.

For a second, I struggled to place her, but knew I had seen her before. Then it came to me: the woman in the wellies. I was taken aback at the coincidence.

She glanced over at me and smiled; I looked away.

'I hate raisins. Any dried fruit really, but especially raisins. Why do they have to put raisins in everything?' she said with a roll of her eyes.

I looked back at her and smiled with polite reservation.

'I mean, I get that it's good for you, but not in everything,' she continued, warming to her topic. 'It's like coriander – why do they have to put it in everything these days? Are you a fan?' Her piercing gaze made me uncomfortable.

I blinked at her, momentarily thrown by the question. 'Of raisins or coriander?' I asked in little more than a whisper.

'Both, I guess. On the whole, I don't think I'm a fussy eater, although my mother would probably say otherwise, but the things I don't like seem to be in everything and very much in fashion at the moment. Fennel, for instance!'

'I quite like fennel,' I said. 'Not a lover of raisins though.'

She leaned in and touched me feather-soft on the elbow. 'Well, we're going to get along famously then,' she said with satisfaction, as though I had just pledged allegiance to Raisin Haters Anonymous.

That brief physical contact from such a confident, beautiful woman startled me and I flinched, my arm warm from her fingers.

'I've just moved into the area and need to stock up on all sorts of things for my bare cupboards,' she continued, apparently oblivious to my reaction.

I glanced into her basket and saw a bottle of wine, a slab of milk chocolate, a cucumber and a jar of Thai green curry paste.

'You've got the basics covered,' I offered, nodding at the basket. I could feel a blush creeping up my neck at my uncharacteristic attempt at humour.

She laughed. 'Too right!'

'Well, I...' I paused and turned back to the shelf in front of me.

'Yes, must get on...' she said with an easy air of distraction. 'Nice to meet you.' She turned to walk away. 'I'm Scarlet, by the way.'

I looked back at her to see a small smile tickling the corner of her lips.

'Veronica,' I replied.

She waved, then floated down the aisle towards the crisps section.

I watched her go, thrown by our brief encounter. I looked down into my trolley and found I couldn't quite remember what it was I needed from the shop and why I was there at all. I thought back to my kitchen cupboards and all the food stacked on the shelves patiently waiting for Grace to decide whether to try it this week, and thought better of it.

I left the trolley where it was in the middle of the aisle, turned on my heel and walked out.

Two days later, I found myself taking fortifying breaths outside a coffee shop as I worked up enough energy to put on my happy face. I had been relieved to notice that the impromptu visits, pestering calls and texts feigning concern had dwindled away, but Tom was worried enough to persuade me to meet up with my old friends after Zara Newton had called him and suggested it. Apparently, according to Tom anyway, Felicity agreed with Zara and thought it would do me good, help me to move on, but I had the irrational feeling that she wanted to parade me like a freak.

Look what can happen if we don't take care, ladies. Watch and learn.

I wished I had stood my ground and held them off a bit longer. As I concocted exit strategies in my head, a woman pulled open the door from inside the café, then struggled to push an oversized pushchair, complete with a red-faced, screaming toddler, through the gap. Her hair was dishevelled and her face was flushed – from exertion or frustration, I couldn't tell. Sympathising with her anxiety, I stepped forward into the café and offered to hold the door open for her.

She smiled wearily and hurried through, and I found myself in the lion's den.

It was mid-morning on a Thursday and the café was buzzing with artificial energy. I looked around, hoping none of the others had turned up. The air was thick with steam and the heady aroma of coffee beans. A group of mums sat at a large table just inside the doorway, their pushchairs and nappy bags blocking my way as they talked over each other while jiggling small babies with one hand and sipping frothy skinny lattes with the other. I could feel the gossip hanging heavy in the air as I stepped over the obstacles and headed to the counter to order. Their voices followed me, loudly bemoaning their lack of sleep, useless husbands and below-par lives.

I cast another surreptitious glance around the room, then noticed Zara in the far corner sitting with the others, her hand raised in greeting and lips pulled back to show impossibly white teeth. I raised a hand in return, managed a rictus smile, and turned back to the counter with a sigh.

While the woman ahead of me, dressed head to toe in Boden, placed her order with the young barista, I opened my bag and rummaged for my purse. My fingers brushed past an empty, snack-sized raisin box and my mind flicked briefly to the woman I now knew as Scarlet. I remembered the vivid green of her dress, bright against the harsh strip lighting of the supermarket and the predominantly beige hue of my own outfit that day. Then my fingers closed around a familiar but incongruous object in the bottom of my bag and my breath caught. I pulled my fist out and forced apart my ossified fingers to see Grace's old dummy in my palm, the teat yellowed and stiffened. How the hell had it got in my bag? Grace hadn't used it for over seven years.

'Ma'am? Ma'am?'

A deep voice broke through my haze and I looked up to see the barista leaning over the counter impatiently.

'Your drinks order?'

'Oh, sorry, I...' I stuttered through my clenched jaw. Taking a breath, I tried again. 'Tea please, to drink in.'

'Size?'

So many inane decisions to make. My brain was on a go-slow.

'Um, regular.'

Keeping the dummy clamped in my fist, I pulled out my purse. My eye caught on a woman at a table to my left. She was looking at me and waving enthusiastically, her elbow threatening to knock over the mug of coffee in front of her. She was alone, but had an enormous chocolate muffin to keep her company. It was Scarlet. I smiled, this time genuinely, and waved back.

The barista placed a pot of tea on a tray in front of me and turned away to fill a miniature milk jug that was better suited to Grace's tea parties for her dolls. Tempted by the sight of Scarlet's muffin, I called after him and ordered the same in a moment of unexpected self-indulgence. Then I noticed Scarlet stand, gather her things and head for the door. My heart fell as I watched her go. Bizarrely, the idea of having tea with her was more appealing at that moment than seeing my old friends. I followed her with my eyes and, as she reached the door, she turned and smiled at me again before disappearing into the street traffic.

Tray in hand and moderately more in control of myself, I wound my way past the table where Scarlet had been sitting towards the group of four women in the far corner. Three expectant faces turned towards me as I manoeuvred into an empty chair; the fourth stubbornly kept her eyes averted, her thin lips pulled down in an astonishing likeness to the grumpy toddler at the next table.

'Hi there,' the three chorused in unison. I returned the greetings with less enthusiasm. After meeting in an antenatal class, I had considered these people my support network when my young baby was the centre of my universe. We had much in common then and had spent many hours chatting while our children played, fought and cried at our feet, but without the kids, I doubt any of us would have made natural friends. Except for Felicity of course.

'You made it!' Zara announced.

I put the tray down carefully and took the spare seat. Directly opposite me was Penny Rhodes. She seemed pleased to see me, but then she was the kind of woman that saw the glass as permanently half-full. To her right was Virginia Paynes, her mass of curly hair bouncing as she leaned over the table to give me a hug. I returned it awkwardly, keeping as much distance between us as good manners would allow, my shoulders stiff. She almost managed to hide her dissatisfaction at my response as she returned to her seat, but I noticed the look that passed between her and Zara, seated to her right, who contemplated me like she was examining an endangered species exhibit in a museum. Despite her initial enthusiasm at getting us all together, Zara seemed to exude an overwhelming sense of fatigue as she sat slumped in her chair, but this wasn't surprising considering her vast number of children. I'd stopped counting at four, but there could be more by now. She watched me warily, as though afraid I would bite if she came too close, the incident in the shoe shop clearly still top of her mind.

Only once the others had greeted, gushed and settled did the smiling assassin that is Felicity Green acknowledge me with her characteristic brief, tight smile. My acidic next-door neighbour and the only one of the group whose friendship predated the children. In fact, I had known her longer than I had known my husband – only by a matter of weeks, but still.

Tall and upright in her chair, she radiated a quiet sense of authority over the other women. She had a reputation for being direct with her comments, no holds barred. It won her more enemies than friends, but that had never seemed to bother her. At times over the years, I had struggled with how unapologetic she was.

She was considering me across the table, her cheeks sucked in and her nostrils flaring as though I had dragged something fetid in on my shoe. Although to be fair, she always looked like that. Her resting bitch face was second to none.

Straight off, she said, 'I didn't think you'd come when Zara said she'd invited you. You've said no to me enough times lately. What's that in your hand?'

I looked down. The dummy peeped obscenely through my knuckles.

'Oh, er… nothing important.' I shoved it to the bottom of my bag.

'How've you been?' Zara asked.

I busied myself with pouring my tea, not making eye contact, hoping she wouldn't bring up my episode in the shoe shop.

'Okay, I guess, keeping myself busy. What about you all?'

'All good, thanks,' Virginia answered. 'It's been absolutely ages since we saw you last. You look… good.' I registered the pause.

'You do too – have you lost weight?' I countered.

Virginia beamed back at me. An early point to me for saying the right thing.

Felicity replied for her, saying, 'Virginia was just

telling us about the new diet she's trying. The Hawkins diet?'

'Oh?' I asked. 'What's that then?'

'You must've heard about it. Everyone's trying it,' Felicity's eyes fell to the muffin on my plate.

I didn't want to give her the satisfaction of knowing how out of touch I was with everyday superficialities. Besides, they were always pledging allegiance to the latest fad diet when their waistbands felt a millimetre too tight, a holiday was approaching or if the others in the group had lost a few pounds and they needed to keep up. Yet another eating plan was not what I considered newsworthy, but for this crowd it could be life or death. I turned to Virginia, pointedly cutting Felicity from my gaze. 'I've heard it's good, but tell me how you're finding it?' The lie dripped off my tongue.

'Well, you know me, never quite losing that baby weight—'

'Yes, and our girls are nine years old now!' Felicity interjected.

Virginia paled, but rushed on, her perfectly shaped eyebrows riding high on her forehead as she looked everywhere but at me. 'So I heard about this diet, where you eat only fat-free yoghurt and fruit for two days a week, under 800 calories on the three alternate days and normally on the weekend, and I thought that it didn't sound too bad. I tried it and I've lost four pounds in two weeks! I'm over the moon!' She clapped her hands together with glee.

How lovely it must be to only have your waistline to worry about.

As she spoke, her hands waved and gesticulated enthusiastically, threatening to sweep everything off the little table. She babbled away, as though she had overdosed on caffeine. She wasn't the kind of person who left you feeling revived in her presence; rather, there was a faint whiff of paranoid anxiety about her, reflected in the children's glittery hairclips restraining her untameable hair and the mismatched socks contradicting the muted beiges and navy blues that all four women had donned. Small nods to individuality saved them from morphing into each other – Virginia with her socks, Zara with her very short pixie hair, Penny with her neatly tucked in blouse and no-nonsense creases, and Felicity's perfected air of condescension. But then, I was just as bad. Knowing whom I was coming to see, I had resignedly pulled on my beige uniform, styled my hair and painted on a glossy smile. I guess you could say my nod to individuality was jagged nails and chewed, raw cuticles.

'And here I am parading a chocolate muffin in front of you,' I said, although my appetite had vanished.

'Oh, don't worry, I'm getting pretty good at controlling my urges,' she said cheerfully. 'I would never endure a place like this on a yoghurt day. I hide away.'

I knew a thing or two about that.

'Well, feel free to share. I'm not actually that hungry after all.'

'Oooh, lovely.' I could practically see the saliva dripping from her incisors as she reached across, grabbed the cake fork and pierced a large chunk. Crumbs rained down on the table as she shovelled it in like it was her last meal before execution.

'Yesterday was a yoghurt day, so I can forgive myself a smidge of cake today,' she spluttered at us. Felicity looked away in disgust.

Virginia then regaled us on the finer details of what constituted 800 calories and how to survive on minimal food, while inhaling muffin between words. The conversation grew more animated about whether celery was indeed a negative calorie food and the minutes ticked on.

Felicity kept steering the conversation onto the children. I fiddled with my teacup, now disliking the bitter aftertaste coating my tongue, but needing to keep my hands busy while they twittered on about the mundanities of their lives. Virginia had managed to eat the entire muffin on autopilot, while Zara was telling us about her daughter's latest gymnastics achievements at Felicity's insistence. I was finding it hard to focus on the details. I forced myself to zone in on Zara's face and watch her lips moving, but my eyes were drawn instead to a little girl at a table nearby, with a dummy in her mouth similar to the one I had found in my bag. She had ridiculously curly blonde hair that hung above her head like a cloud and was busying herself with tearing up a paper napkin while her mother chatted full force on her mobile phone. Miniature shreds of napkin fell like confetti around her and every time the door to the café opened, the breeze would lift the shreds, making them dance in her tiny hands. One fragment had landed in her curls and I found myself staring at it, enthralled.

'Veronica?' A hand on my arm dragged me back to the faces in front of me. Penny was leaning towards me. 'Okay?'

I looked at her, realising I had zoned out, then replied with an exaggerated smile, 'Sorry, daydreaming there for a minute.'

Zara looked worried and began a rambling apology, 'I'm so sorry, banging on. I wasn't...'

'Don't be silly,' I placated. 'Really.' I waved her off, not wanting to give Felicity the satisfaction of witnessing another public breakdown. I sat up straighter in the hard chair.

Hurriedly changing the subject, Virginia asked Felicity, 'So have you decided on your dress for the party yet?'

'Oh? What's the occasion?' I asked.

Again, the hesitation, the shifting in the seat. 'Um, it's, er...'

Felicity was quick to help Virginia out. 'It's Penny's

fortieth birthday party in a couple of weeks – a black-tie dinner dance with all the trimmings? It should be such fun. I phoned you about it last week, left a voicemail.' She sat back in her chair and crossed her arms under unnaturally large breasts that didn't fool anyone.

Penny looked as though she was sitting on a hotbed of angry ants. 'I did send you and Tom an invitation, but you never got back to me, so I assumed you couldn't make it,' she said, redness burning her cheeks.

'Oh, yes of course. So rude of me, but we are busy that weekend – a work thing for Tom that we can't get out of...' I trailed off in the hope of not having to make up too many fake details. 'But the party sounds lovely.' I tried to keep my voice light, but felt no disgruntlement whatsoever. In fact, I was relieved that I didn't have to spend hours discussing a dress for a party and how to find the perfect pair of shoes to match. These days I was lucky if my underwear matched. Freeing myself from the pressure to conform was strangely liberating.

Penny looked tortured and I could almost hear the cogs in her brain grinding as they worked overtime to find an escape route. She reverted to type. 'We've discussed the logistics, haven't we? I'll be at the venue at 4 p.m. to start decorating the room. Then once you've had your hair done, Zara, you can come and take over while I get mine done, then Felicity can step in. Now, on the actual night...' She pointed a perfectly manicured nail at each in turn as she outlined the plan of action.

Felicity looked taken aback at being ordered about, but Penny rattled on oblivious, organising her minions with military precision. Once they had received their detailed instructions, Penny sat back in her chair, sated, and Felicity took the opportunity to change the subject again.

'Virginia, what was the outcome of the tutor for Matthew?'

Virginia looked uncomfortable again and threw visual daggers at Felicity. She then offered me an explanation I didn't need in a quiet voice. 'We've decided to push Matthew for his 11+ exams in the hope of Kingston Grammar for secondary school. He seems excited by the idea, but getting a tutor at this stage is difficult.'

I listened to them analysing the pros and cons of the tutors she had interviewed as they dissected Matthew's strengths and weaknesses (great at verbal reasoning, but lacking focus when it comes to maths, apparently) and could feel what little life force I had left draining out of me. The tiger moms were in full voice. They talked over each other distractedly, the words clambering for space as though they were too intent on getting airplay for their own stories to listen to what the others were saying. My grip on the conversation weakened again.

As they continued to babble, Zara leaned in and checked her phone, which was lying with everyone else's amid the cake crumbs and milk drops on the table. I hadn't even bothered to take mine out of my bag, but I noticed the four in front of me kept checking theirs while they talked, even though none had rung or vibrated. They couldn't seem to pass five minutes without tapping the screen like a nervous tick. I wondered who they were hoping would call and what could be so important.

When I zoned back in, they had moved from tutors to the cost of extracurricular activities and I wanted to run screaming for the door. Remembering my manners instead, I said, during a pause for breath, 'So what have you all got planned for the summer? Cornwall again?'

Silence greeted my question. Virginia shuffled uncomfortably in her chair, while Zara rummaged in her bag, suddenly in need of a tissue, and Penny busied herself with stirring her empty coffee cup. However, Felicity was more than happy to share the group's plans.

'We've all booked for our usual two weeks in Cornwall, yes. We didn't think you would want to come this year, especially after the accident.'

I locked eyes with her. The others had the good grace to look at Felicity in mortification, who for once looked suitably uncomfortable, as if realising she had thrown a dart too close to the bull's eye this time.

Every summer since our children were babies, the group had travelled to Cornwall for two weeks in August. It was like an epic, middle-class pilgrimage. Days were spent on the beach with the kids running wild surrounded by the picnic debris of empty hummus pots and breadstick crumbs; evenings were spent sharing food and laughing over gin and tonics while exhausted children fell asleep in front of an endless stream of Disney heroes and villains. Penny was particularly in her element and given free rein to let her organisational skills run wild with meal plans and activity rosters. Last year was the first year Tom and I hadn't joined in, choosing instead to chase some sunshine as a family; this year was the first time we hadn't been invited.

The awkwardness stretched on. Felicity tried to cover her callousness by discussing arrangements and chatting animatedly about the new friends who had apparently filled our spot on the holiday. I felt hollow and knew that coming today had been a mistake. What Felicity didn't realise was that I actually didn't care about any of it: the holidays, the parties, the diets. But I did mind being the subject of her amusement, indicated by her occasional sideways smirks that she thought I hadn't noticed. It was taking all of my strength not to grab hold of my cake fork and stab her in the back of the hand. I bet that would crease her unlined, Botoxed brow. My fingers twitched and flexed as I pictured the metal prongs jabbing into the thin flesh, temptingly within reach. The depth of anger that washed over me was somewhat surprising.

I focused on the dark sludge left in my teacup. I could feel Zara's eyes on me and knew she wanted me to look up, but I wouldn't. I didn't want to see the pity.

Her voice reached me nervously, like she was sending out tentacles to test the water. 'How are things going with the trial? That must be coming up soon? October, I think Tom said? If it helps to clear your head, I'm looking to start running again – we could go together like we used to?'

'Sure, because popping on a pair of trainers will make everything better, right?' I snapped.

Zara recoiled. 'No! I... er... it just might ... give you some headspace....' Her voice trailed off and she looked away.

I had to get out of there. The air was stifling. The noise of children started to hammer at my eardrums. The anger had dissipated as quickly as it had come, replaced by panic inching up my throat, tenuously attached to a scream by an invisible thread of anxiety. I looked towards the door, my mind trying to find a plausible excuse for my retreat. Outside the windows, people hastened about their business, striding with purpose, places to go and people to see. My eyes fell on one person in particular, who moved slower than the others at more of a saunter than a stride. Auburn hair, loud coat – it was Scarlet again. Or was I just hoping I had seen her? Either way, there was my excuse, not that I owed anyone an explanation. I had earned the right to just get up and leave.

I stood up abruptly, almost toppling my chair.

'Ladies, this has been great,' I said, my voice brittle.

'But I must be off – I promised a friend I would go shopping with her this afternoon.' I couldn't help myself, still offering explanations and platitudes. 'You all look great, haven't changed a bit.' I surprised myself at how much sarcasm I managed to inject into that last comment. 'Let's not leave it so long next time.' I ducked down to grab my handbag, then paused, looked directly at each of them in turn and said, 'Have fun in Cornwall.'

Felicity's eyes narrowed. Zara got to her feet and started to say something, but I didn't hang around to hear any more.

It took every ounce of strength I had to stop my legs from collapsing under me as I reached the door, pushed it open and took in some deep gulps of fresh air.

The house was quiet. I closed the door on the world and leant against it, letting my cocoon of safety fold around me. Eyes closed, I ran through my encounter with Zara, Virginia, Penny and Felicity, and wanted to feel tears prick my eyes, but there was nothing. Life goes on around you with its villains and superheroes.

I heard a muffled tinkling sound. My mobile was ringing from the depths of my Tardis of a handbag. I dug in and began to rummage, but my hand fell on the dummy again. I pulled it out and threw it across the hallway as hard as I could, as though it had stung me. My eyes followed it as it landed, spinning on the beige carpet and coming to rest under the table, the yellowing teat eyeing me from the shadows. I gulped air, could feel the panic rising again, once more surprising myself at the sudden surge of emotion. Through it all, the phone kept ringing. I slumped to the floor, my bag falling open as it dropped to my feet. My mobile fell out and landed screen up.

One missed call from Tom. Who else would it be?

The cold air on my face felt good. My lungs ached as my feet pounded the trail, my ears full of a loud bass beat, a song I didn't recognise but needed to keep me focused. I had set off for a run as soon as I heard Tom leave for work. He had mentioned before heading out that he was meeting with the legal team later in the day and had wanted to discuss technicalities with me, but I shut him down, told him to take care of it. Then a tide of rebellion swept over me and I suddenly had the urge to run, no destination in mind, the idea planted by Zara a few days earlier. I wouldn't make good company though, so had headed out alone, my running cap pulled low over my eyes.

An hour later and I was still in my stride, oblivious to everything except the burning in my chest as I ran at too fast a pace, waves of heat suffocating my head inside my cap, the exertion keeping all other thoughts at bay. Zara was right, I'd missed this.

The park was full of sturdy women in boots walking muddy, overexcited dogs and men on bicycles, ties and trousers tucked in as they weaved their way through the pedestrian traffic on their way to work.

I could feel my energy ebbing as I approached the ten-kilometre mark, so headed back to the park gate and the route through the streets that would take me home. As soon as I left the park, I realised that I had inadvertently timed my return home to coincide with the Monday morning school run and now found myself dodging pushchairs, young children on scooters and ranting mothers. I kept my head ducked, pulled my cap lower over my eyes and concentrated on the music in my ears as I accelerated.

Rounding a corner a few streets from home, I collided with a young girl who tore into me on a scooter. I looked down into an angelic but startled face as she fell and felt my heart contract.

I pulled my earphones out and crouched down to help her up off the pavement. She wasn't hurt or crying and, after looking at me for a few seconds, burst into a wide smile, just as her mother rushed up to us.

'You're Grace's mum!'

I froze. The girl was still grinning at me. Her mum looked at me and paled as recognition dawned on her too.

'Tilly, are you okay? I'm so sorry,' the woman babbled without looking at me again. 'She was going far too fast. I do hope you're not hurt. These scooters are treacherous things. Come along, Tilly, or you'll be late.' She shuffled the girl along just as the tiny voice began to say to me, 'How is Grace? When will she…?'

'Come, come, let the nice lady finish her run!'

As she was shepherded away, I heard Tilly say, 'But that's Grace's mum! I wanted to ask her…'

I didn't wait to hear any more. I stuck my earphones back in, turned the volume up as loud as it would go and headed back down the road, desperate to get home and close the door on everyone again.

Just as I pushed on around the next corner, I collided again, this time with an adult. I almost shouted out in frustration but raised my eyes to find Scarlet in front of me, rubbing her arm where I had elbowed her.

I removed my earphones again, this time saying in mortification, 'I am so sorry. Are you okay?' I didn't expect her to recognise me in return, but she did.

'Veronica, right?' She smiled.

'Yes, hi.'

'Well, this looks very energetic and exhausting,' she said, indicating my running gear. 'Better than me anyway.' She held up a bag from the bakery up the road and I caught a whiff of freshly baked croissants.

'Your idea smells better than mine,' I replied. I was surprised at how pleased I was to see her again.

'Do you live near here?' she asked.

'Yes, just two streets over on Hawthorne Road. You?'

'Yes, a little up this way.'

I felt very aware of my sweaty face and red cheeks. 'Well, it was great to bump into you. Enjoy your breakfast.'

'Thanks,' she replied and turned to walk past me, then paused. 'You know, I've just moved into the area and don't know many people around here just yet. Perhaps we could meet for a coffee or something one day?'

'Um,' I was momentarily stunned and slightly panicked. 'I, er...'

'Besides, we keep bumping into each other – literally as the case may be!' She chuckled. 'Anyway, I'm sure I'll see you again.' She began to walk away.

'I, er... Coffee would be great,' I heard myself say, much to my surprise, especially after the other day.

She stopped and turned back. 'Great, are you free tomorrow?'

I had countless empty days ahead of me. 'Tomorrow would work.'

'How about that coffee shop we were both in the other day? That was you, wasn't it? Say 10 a.m.? The perfect time for tea and cake in my opinion.' Her smile was so natural that I felt some of my anxiety subside.

'Sure.'

'Tell you what, what's your mobile number? I could call you quickly so that you have my number in case something comes up?'

'Um, okay.' Part of me wondered at the ease at which I was prepared to hand over my number to a stranger, but I did it anyway. The phone attached to the running holder on my arm vibrated as her call connected.

'Great, done! Hope to see you tomorrow then.' With a small wave, she wandered off, trailing the aroma of croissants.

I stood watching her for a moment, then smiled to myself and ran at a less frenetic pace back home.

For the second time in a week, I found myself walking up to the door of the coffee shop, but this time I was looking forward to it. It was as busy as it had been the week before and the women inside looked as if they'd never left. Doubtless, the conversations would be the same too.

I scanned the room, part of me not expecting Scarlet to be there, but she was sitting in the far corner, facing the room and waving at me. I waved back, then went to place my order with no hesitation this time: a cup of tea and a slice of red velvet cake that I fully intended to eat myself.

When my order was paid for, I grabbed my tray and weaved through the chatter. As I approached her table, Scarlet beamed up at me.

'I felt sure you wouldn't come in case I'd scared you off the other day! I can be a bit full on sometimes. So pleased you did though,' she said, spraying crumbs across the table as she waved a chunk of muffin at me. 'Sit, sit!'

I did as I was told, my back to the room. As I poured my tea, I sneaked casual glances at my new acquaintance. She had a youthful liveliness to her face that was in stark contrast to my sallow, grey complexion. Although I guessed we were of a similar age, in our early forties, compared to me, her eyes sparkled under a subtle layer of expertly applied but girlish make-up, and there was not a grey hair in sight amongst her beautifully silky auburn hair. Her full lips seemed to be set in a permanent smile and her fingernails were manicured and impeccably painted. Unlike my friends the other day, she was colourful, from her vivid green dress that brought out her eyes to her sunshine yellow nails and candy pink lip-gloss. She was chattering away, but I had been so intent on studying her that I hadn't heard a word.

'I'm sorry, pardon?' I replied.

'I was just saying how much I love this area. So many lovely little treasure troves. Have you lived here long?'

I thought back to Tom and I buying our house when Grace was a baby and how excited we were to move to the suburbs after years in a tiny London flat.

'We're nearing nine years now.' I looked down into my cup, surprised at how much time had actually

passed. So much can happen. The shadows can form
and the dust can settle quickly in a decade.

Scarlet reached over and put her hand on mine. 'Are
you okay?' she asked.

I've never been a tactile person and normally such
physical demonstrations would make me feel prickly,
but this was strangely comforting, helped by the faint
scent of her perfume, which was familiar, but I couldn't
pinpoint why.

'I'm fine – low blood sugar maybe. Some cake will
help.' I took hold of my fork, pierced a generous chunk
and filled my mouth before she could comment further.
The cake was soft, warm and utterly delicious. A second
and third forkful followed very quickly after the first.
It felt like ages since I had had anything close to an
appetite for food.

'Where did you say you live?' she asked.

'We're on Hawthorne.'

'Oh, it's a lovely road. Some beautiful gardens,' she
replied. I pictured Felicity's immaculate roses in her
front garden next door and agreed with her. I used to
have one of those beautiful gardens, but now it was
unkempt, overgrown, with roses that needed deadheading and bushes in need of a bit of TLC. While
Felicity's flowers bloomed and flourished, mine were
patchy and diseased.

'So, husband? Children? Job?'

'One husband, one child – Grace, who's nearly ten,' I answered without hesitation. 'No job right now.'

'You mean you have the hardest job of all as a mother! I haven't had the courage to follow that path myself.'

'Do you work?'

'I do whatever takes my fancy when I wake up. I've been known to write, paint, work in an art gallery, serve chips – you name it, I will likely have done it,' she replied. 'Of course, I'm lucky in that I don't have to work – an inheritance…' She left the sentence hanging, but I didn't want to pry. 'What about your other half? Tell me about him,' she continued.

I didn't want to be the focus of the conversation, but found myself telling her all about Tom, with his handsome smile, neat suits and sensible hair. 'Tom and I have been married almost thirteen years now. We met at university about twenty years ago. He came here from Australia to study and never went back. He's a doctor.'

'How romantic – the British girl who stole his heart!'

I laughed a little bristly. 'I don't know about that. There's definitely history, I guess. All of his family are still in Australia, which is hard for him sometimes, but we've never thought of living anywhere else.'

'Well, I'm sure he's perfectly lovely.'

That was it in a nutshell: perfectly lovely, always polite, never saying what should be said, always doing what was best for everyone.

Scarlet was now chattering away, trying to name Australian actors. I struggled to refocus.

'Of course, there's nothing too strange about a fascination with Russell Crowe, but everyone has a sneaky weird crush, don't they? Mine's particularly British – Tony Blair.' I had no idea what she was on about, but she didn't seem to have noticed that I wasn't quite following her. She thundered on, going through a list of who I assumed were young male celebrities and whether they were worthy of her attention, as if it was quite feasible that one of them would knock on her door. I listened to her ramble, feeling myself relax as she steered the conversation, happy to nod and smile in the right places. Before I knew it, half an hour had passed over trivial chit-chat, a few laughs, a large chunk of cake and little else of consequence.

There was a pause as Scarlet suggested another cup. Then, before I could agree, she changed tack altogether.

'Actually, no, that's dull. Let's go and do something. Maybe a bout of retail therapy...' She trailed off as she took in my outfit of knee-length denim skirt, beige pullover and opaque tights.

My lack of enthusiasm must've shown on my face.

'Oh come on, it'll be fun. Besides, do you have anything else you should be doing while Grace is at school?'

I didn't correct her, but thought back to my empty house, which I had half-heartedly cleaned from top to bottom yesterday to fill the day, but after a morning of listening to Scarlet's chatter, I couldn't face the silence at home. I thought about my dated wardrobe that hung on my thin frame now and how, for the first time in ages, I was enjoying someone else's company without feeling anxious, ridden with remorse and on edge – or worse, numb. Today, she was keeping my demons at bay, her chattered words forming a shield against boredom and the dangerous thoughts that accompanied it.

'Okay, why not?' I heard myself say. 'We could hop on the bus and head into Kingston for a bit.'

'Yay!' Scarlet clapped her hands in glee. 'Besides, what's the worst that can happen?'

She drained her cup, then looked at me, her forehead creasing. 'Veronica – it's quite a formal name, isn't it? I shall call you Ron,' she declared.

'My husband used to call me that. A long time ago.'

The mall was quiet, dotted with mothers pushing subdued toddlers in buggies. I remember the days, it felt like aeons ago, when I was one of them, squeezing an hour of shopping into the small window of time between naps. Everything was overlit and perfectly acclimatised, with neon signs and garish marketing assaulting my senses as we entered the massive space. A tinny acoustic soundtrack played through unseen speakers, the tune unrecognisable but inoffensive.

Scarlet and I wandered aimlessly, her still chatting about this and that as I followed like a sheep in and out of shops. She would pause in front of a top or skirt, hold it up to me, make suggestions on what she thought would suit me. I would nod politely or comment without commitment. Everything she chose was brighter and more daring than anything I would've picked out, but I was happy to shadow her. She looked so completely at ease in an environment that had become alien to me that I was swept along.

I noticed some of the shop assistants watching us from time to time and wondered whether they were sizing Scarlet up or me. We looked an unlikely pair with my taupe tightness and her neon vivacity.

As we passed a small, exclusive shoe boutique, a pair of expensive-looking, knee-high boots in the window caught my eye. I paused to consider them, then continued on, but I could almost hear them calling my name.

Scarlet had stopped as well and was pointing straight at them. 'Look at those stunning boots!'

I loped back to the shop window. 'Oh, they are lovely,' I replied as nonchalantly as I could, but was relieved that she had endorsed my taste.

I drew closer, taking stock of the soft, dark brown leather, high heel and pointed toe. They were unlike anything I already owned, but reminded me of a pair I used to wear in my uni days when shoes weren't meant to be functional.

'You have to try them on.' She was looking at me with big eyes, like a pleading puppy.

I looked back at the window, then shrugged. 'Okay,' I said and strode into the shop.

The room was small and lined with precarious glass shelves displaying ridiculously impractical footwear. In the centre of the room was a circle of leather cubes, presumably for customers to perch on Cinderella-style.

A young, painted assistant approached, subtly looking me up and down in judgement. 'Good afternoon, can I help?'

'Yes please, the brown boots in the window – can I try them in a size 4 please?'

'Let me check if we have them in stock,' she answered and teetered off, her own boots clicking against the shiny floor.

I looked around at the display. Every imaginable colour and style was represented apart from flat shoes. Even the sports shoes on show had a wedge heel. I pointed this out to Scarlet under my breath. The look on her face showed that she was completely in her element and I could imagine her wardrobe piled high with shelves of inappropriate footwear in every conceivable hue.

After five minutes, the assistant returned with a long box in her hands. I had caught some of Scarlet's enthusiasm and was momentarily overjoyed until the assistant said, 'We only have a size 3 or a 5. I've brought the 3s out for you to try though?' Something about the way she looked me up and down made me think she thought it preposterous that I would wear such boots, so I flung her a haughty, 'Fine.'

She crouched down, opened the box and began to unwrap a thin layer of tissue paper. A faint hint of new leather teased my nose. They looked so soft and beautiful, lying snuggly in the close-fitting box. It had been ages since I'd felt a ripple of delight at the idea of buying something new.

Perching precariously on the cube, I removed my old pair of worn Converses and picked up the boots, enjoying the feel of the cool, silky smooth leather under my fingertips. I slipped my toes in and began to ease the zip up over my calf, aware of Scarlet and the assistant watching me closely. The zip on the right boot slowed and for a moment I thought I would have to face the embarrassment of having a calf too big, but to my relief it glided up to the top.

My hands were damp – from excitement or from being in the spotlight, I wasn't sure. I looked up at Scarlet and she licked her lips like a predator. I noticed I was leaving fingerprints on the cool leather as I grabbed hold of the zip on the left boot. Things were going well – the zip was moving freely and I had a moment of exhilaration in thinking they would fit after all until it caught on my opaque stocking and stopped. I wormed my fingers in between the zip and the stocking, and could feel that the material had snagged on the metal teeth. I tried to unhook it, but it was imprisoned.

'Damn,' I whispered.

'Everything okay? Do they not fit then?' the assistant gloated.

I gave a hard pull on the zip, which dislodged after a moment of hesitation so that I could force it up to the top.

I smiled in satisfaction and relief. 'Nope, see? All perfect.'

I looked down at my feet and took a short stroll over to the floor-length mirror, where I turned and flexed to see the boots from every angle. They were beautiful and made my legs look slim and long, but the pointy toes were nipping like pincers. A size 4 would've been perfect, but maybe the 3 would stretch with wear, I reasoned silently. A small part of me actually liked the sharp pain accompanying every step. I could imagine that after half an hour of wear, my feet would feel like they were in a vice that would tighten deliciously with every step.

My decision already made, I preened in front of the mirror, enjoying the moment but not letting myself focus on how long it had been since I'd looked at my reflection properly like this. Behind me, Scarlet gurned in delight and urged me to buy them. The assistant sighed. After stringing it out even longer just to annoy her, I casually asked how much they cost.

'Two hundred and ninety-nine pounds.' My eyebrows shot up. 'Well, they are such good quality and made from very expensive Italian leather,' she simpered.

'You have to buy them, they look amazing,' Scarlet gushed.

'Um, I don't know, they're really expensive,' I replied hesitantly.

Under a mirage of devil horns, Scarlet's eyes gleamed. 'Go on, treat yourself.'

I paused, not for long, then surrendered. 'I'll take them.'

Sitting down again, I unzipped the right boot with relative ease and handed it to the suddenly very friendly assistant. She fussed and fawned with the tissue paper, ready to slip the boots back into their cardboard coffin that would likely end up in the mausoleum of my wardrobe and hardly ever come out again. I then took hold of the left zip and tugged. It slid down an inch, then stopped. I frowned, re-zipped it to the top, then tried again. This time it stopped after a few centimetres and refused to go any further. I felt sweat trickle down my spine as I gave it a third go. It went no further than before.

'Everything okay?' the assistant asked brightly, holding out a clawed hand for the other boot.

'Yes, yes, just caught on my stockings I think. Um, let me have another go.'

Scarlet was watching with a look of mild amusement.

I continued to struggle, but the zip refused to move a millimetre and I could feel panic building.

'Let me have a go – maybe your hands are a bit damp or something,' the assistant said in a nervous tone, all fake friendliness now gone.

She tugged and pulled, but nothing happened, save for the zip now not going up or down. The assistant's drawn-on eyebrows, previously sitting like commas on her perfectly made-up face, now formed a tight, straight line. As she wrestled with my leg, I could feel humiliation warming through me. I looked over at Scarlet, who seemed calm and unfazed. She was gesticulating rudely behind the assistant's head, which was practically in my lap as she crouched in front of me. I looked down and noticed glaring flecks of dandruff showing along her ruler-straight hair parting. As I contemplated the scales of dead skin clinging to the dark strands of hair, I suddenly felt quite serene and removed from the absurdity of the situation.

'I'll have to get the manager, I think,' she said and hurried away.

My fingers were red and tingling from pulling and tugging, and I held them up in front of my eyes, turning them this way and that.

Scarlet crouched down and looked at my feet. 'Well, this is a thing.'

'I think it's caught on my tights,' I answered matter-of-factly. 'Karma's a bitch.'

'Well, it is clearly a poor-quality product then. Not your fault at all.' Scarlet's voice was even, but loud with defiance.

A young man, victimised head to toe by the latest trends, minced out of the back room with the assistant, looking worried. I could feel sweat sticking the stockings to my calves as my body reacted, even if my mind was in denial about the severity of the situation.

'I understand there's a problem with getting the boot off, ma'am?'

'Yes. It went on fine, but I think I must have got my stocking caught in the zip.'

'Perhaps you shouldn't have forced it on in the first place, fat legs and all that,' the assistant muttered, just loud enough to be heard.

Scarlet's reaction was immediate and volatile. 'What kind of a shop is this? And at this price, I would at least expect the zip to work properly. Thank goodness this didn't happen after she bought them,' Scarlet exploded.

I added in a quieter voice, 'I didn't force it on at all. It went on perfectly fine,' knowing that wasn't exactly true, but not wanting to surrender so easily in front of Scarlet.

'Perhaps we can pull it off without undoing the zip. It may dislodge whatever is trapped. If I lift your leg and pull from the bottom, it may work,' the manager said. There was no way it would work, considering how skin-tight the boots were, but I allowed him to lift my leg, the feeling of detachment growing until mentally I was standing next to Scarlet and watching it all happen to a stranger. I concentrated on the manager for a moment, noticing the razor-sharp creases in his trousers and witch-like point of his patent shoes as he pulled and tugged on my leg.

The handful of customers in the shop had begun to stare and two teenage girls were sniggering into their hands. I had an overwhelming urge to laugh with them and had to swallow hard to dislodge a manic giggle that took residence in my throat.

As both the assistant and the manager gripped onto the boot while my leg in my denim skirt lifted higher and higher, the bubble of mirth popped and I guffawed loudly just as the tights gave up the fight with an amplified ripping sound. The boot remained resolutely in place. The manager dropped my leg abruptly and crossed his arms in anger while I concentrated on stifling any more explosive laughter.

Scarlet could still be heard ranting behind them about the quality of the boots and customer service, even raising the possibility of suing the shop, for what I wasn't sure.

'We're going to have to cut them off,' the manager said melodramatically. 'But I hope you realise that if we cut the boots, then you will have to buy them in their damaged state.'

'But the boot must be defective if the zip got stuck so

easily,' I reasoned. 'Surely you can't expect me to still buy them?'

'You are not paying for those boots, Ron,' Scarlet said indignantly. Turning to the manager, she added, 'I'm a fashion journalist. One poor recommendation on Twitter from me and this store is ruined. Remember that.' This had to be a blatant lie, but at that moment I didn't care.

'There is nothing defective about these boots. More to the point, I think next time you should be more aware of the dimensions of your legs before trying on such a high-quality and expensive item.' He turned to the assistant. 'Bring me the scissors.'

'Do not cut those boots until you agree that she will not be charged,' Scarlet shouted in outrage.

'I'm not paying for these boots.' The low menace in my voice surprised even me.

The group of spectators had turned into quite a throng and an audible gasp rippled through the onlookers at the prospect of a fight breaking out between the manager, now armed with a pair of lethal, glinting sheers, and me, with nothing but my principles.

We glared at each other, neither willing to back down.

Eventually, he nodded his head and reluctantly said, 'Okay, no charge, but in return please refrain from any negative social media comments.' Little did he know that I had long ago abandoned advertising my pathetic life on Facebook, Twitter and the like.

'Agreed. Cut away,' Scarlet said.

'Agreed,' I concurred.

The steel blade of the sheers glinted as they bore down on the beautiful leather and sliced through like a scalpel. After a moment, I felt cool air against my skin as the boot fell away and exposed my shredded stockings.

The manager looked mournful as he turned on his heels and stormed off to the counter, clutching the ruined boots.

I squared my shoulders and looked down at the ruined tights and my pale, sweaty skin beneath, marked in red where the boots had dug in. Without a second thought, I reached under my skirt and found the top of my stockings, wriggled them down to my knees and pulled them off unceremoniously, before balling up what was left in tight fists and plonking them on the counter in front of the manager's horrified glare. Then I pushed my feet into my old Converse, grabbed my handbag and stalked defiantly through the faces staring at me, some in sympathy but most in glee.

Reality flooded over me and it took all of my strength not to burst into sobs, but I refused to let my head drop. As we got to the door, I turned to see the assistant looking smug.

'Oh, and you should do something about that dandruff. Most unattractive,' I said as a parting shot, then glided out with Scarlet at my heels giggling.

'Oh my God, that was funny!' Scarlet exclaimed when we were finally free of the stares.

I groaned. 'I can't believe that happened – or that I said that.'

'Don't be silly! I have the fattest calves in the world and get boots stuck all the time. I think we need a drink to steady our nerves.'

'It's the middle of the day!'

'Perfect! All the more reason,' Scarlet replied, looping her arm in mine.

'You're a very bad influence on me, Scarlet,' I teased.

As we walked, I could feel my heart hammering in my chest in indignation. Scarlet was humming under her breath, her pace ambling and casual. She then pulled up short and I turned to see what had caught her attention. A small girl was standing to our right, alone, her thumb in her mouth. She looked to be little more than four years old. Someone had tried to plait her hair in an intricate French braid, but most of it had unravelled and escaped the pretty butterfly clips so that wisps reached out in every direction, making her look untidy.

'I think she's lost,' Scarlet said and started walking towards her.

I looked around and couldn't see an adult nearby that she may belong to. I closed the gap between Scarlet and I, my heart still racing, but now accompanied by a dull thud deep in my head that kept time with my pulse.

As we approached, I took in her miniature denim dress with a dark red juice stain down the front, frilly white ankle socks smudged with dirt, one rolled up and the other down, and the pint-sized Nike running shoes on her impossibly tiny feet, scuffed at the toes.

'Yes, definitely lost,' Scarlet was saying in a faraway voice.

I stretched an arm out to the child, then drew it back quickly, not wanting to startle her. Instead, I said, 'Hello' and crouched down at her eye level.

She stared at me with wide brown eyes, tears dripping silently from her long lashes.

'What's your name?'

'Mummy says not to talk to strangers.' Her voice was little above a whisper.

'That's very true, but if you're scared, I think perhaps we can try and help you. Where is mummy?'

She looked around, her eyes sweeping the faces walking past.

My knees, bent at an awkward angle, were beginning to complain loudly. I reached to the floor and steadied myself with a shaky hand.

Scarlet was close behind me. 'Maybe we could go and find an information booth or something.' She was also scanning the vast space around us.

I studied the wretched face before me – the innocent eyes, flushed cheeks and quivering lip – and I felt angry. What mother could leave this beautiful creature alone like this? She looked unkempt and uncared for, and my heart choked at her helplessness. She was so unlike Grace at that age, and yet something about the expression on her face and the startled eyes made me think of her.

An image started to take shape of me scooping the little wretch up and carrying her out of the mall, taking her home, brushing her hair, caring for her…

As if echoing my thoughts, Scarlet said, 'You know, we could so easily walk out of here with her. No one would notice. Everyone is completely ignoring her.' She looked over at me. 'Of course, we wouldn't, but you know…'

Of course I wouldn't. Would I?

I took her hand in mine gently and stood again, my knees creaking, then started walking.

'Mummy!' The child lurched from my grasp and ran towards a young blonde woman who had appeared from an accessories shop to our right.

'Jade! There you are.' She grabbed hold of the girl in a smothering bear hug and, when she held the girls at arm's length again, I could see panic etched in the lines of her forehead.

'Oh my God. I thought I'd lost you.'

Noticing me standing there, she came over, saying in a rush, 'Thank you so much. I was beside myself when I realised she wasn't next to me. I only turned away for a second.'

I looked at Jade and this time I didn't see an unkempt, uncared for child, but a regular girl whose mum had tried in vain to tame her wild hair into an intricate braid, complete with girly bows and sparkly clips; who had probably started the day looking beautiful in her new denim dress, only to spill juice on it by lunchtime; and wearing shoes that had spent a lot of time running, jumping and exploring. I didn't see an uncaring, distracted mother, but a woman who had just had a taste of her worst nightmare when she realised her daughter wasn't holding her hand any more.

'Really, I can't thank you enough. I hate to think what could've happened,' the woman was still rambling in relief.

'It's no problem at all. I was looking for an information booth or something,' I said by way of explanation, but the words were thin.

'Right, I think we've earned an ice cream, don't you, Jade? And you and I need to talk about you wandering off like that, don't we?' They walked away, the woman holding onto Jade with both hands. As they turned towards the ice cream shop, Jade looked back at me and waved.

I felt sick.

Scarlet was oblivious to my distress.

'Right, where were we? For a moment there, I thought we would have to postpone our drink.'

She started walking again, then stopped abruptly a second time. This time she was staring, with a snide half-smile playing around her lips. I followed her eyes into one of the large department stores towards the mall entrance. Like the shoe shop, it was full of glamorously painted, pointy shop assistants selling their wares to impressionable women who wanted to look younger, live longer and find skin-deep happiness.

'You know...' Scarlet said. 'That woman in the shop thought she was so special, treating us like clapped-out housewives. Well, I'm tired of it.' Her voice was low and menacing, so unlike her usual tone. I certainly didn't want to interrupt her to point out that I was a washed-out housewife.

My hands were still shaking and I was struggling to detach from what had just happened.

'I can imagine that they in there' – she gesticulated at the department store – 'would be just as bad.' She had a steely look in her eyes. 'Let's get our own back, shall we?'

I almost expected her to burst into a maniacal laugh, the way she was speaking. A stone of dread weighed down in my stomach and I felt exhausted.

'Really, Scarlet, I'm over it now. No need for further action. I gave as good as I got anyway. Let's just go and get that drink. I'm done in.'

'Oh, come on,' she said with an eye roll, dragging me by the arm towards the store.

I followed, eyes down, trying to make myself as small as possible.

Scarlet wandered past a few counters, gesticulating and commenting, before approaching the mirrored shelves of the more expensive make-up labels. She casually picked up eyeliners and mascara tubes, as if considering her options, then zoned in with sniper precision on a lipstick in a shiny gold case. It was top-end stuff, the kind of thing I would never consider normally, but probably the type of brand Felicity would wear just to pop to school, only so that someone would comment and she would have to explain how expensive it was.

'You know, this looks just like another one I have in my bag, but that one's a much cheaper brand,' Scarlet said cheekily.

'I know, I think I know which one you mean. My Maybelline looks very similar but was a quarter of the price of this one.'

'How much better can a lipstick be for twice the price, you may well wonder?' Her voice was light and conversational, but her eyes were hard.

I still wasn't sure what she was getting at. She twisted open the lipstick and examined the colour, frowning as she did so, turning it this way and that, then put the cap back on and returned it to its case.

'Nah, not my colour. Too boring.' It was a pinkish shade of brown and definitely something I would wear.

Under her breath, she muttered, 'Act normal, keep quiet. Just two ladies considering lipsticks...'

What the hell was she thinking of doing now? I could feel sweat tickle my upper lip as I raced through various scenarios in my head.

'Red – that's more like it!' she said a little louder. She picked up another version of the lipstick in what was subtly called 'Crimson Pout' and opened it for a closer look, rubbing some on the back of her hand to test the shade. It was bright, garish and in your face – perfect for her and not my usual taste at all.

She handed it over to me, saying, 'Try that. I think it could suit you.'

I took it from her and opened it, testing it on my hand as she had done, a red slash of colour against my pale skin.

Scarlet reached into my cavernous handbag, scrabbled around for a few seconds, and brought out a lipstick that was almost identical from the outside, but in a battered, dull and scratched gold case. The pattern around the edge of the case was slightly different, but that was the only discernible difference, apart from its used state.

Then she said, 'No, you're right, not your colour at all,' and casually slipped the old, used lipstick onto the display where the new one had sat, while simultaneously tossing the brand new version into my bag without flinching. My mouth dropped open, to which she commented, 'You're catching flies, Ron,' with a wink. I snapped my mouth shut.

Then she turned on her heel and began to meander between the counters towards the door. I followed her, shocked at her brazen act of retribution. At any moment, I expected a store security guard to drag me away for questioning and a strip search.

Once we were clear of the store, Scarlet veered away from the shops and headed for the outside world.

'There, they took your dignity, so I took something from them! You can thank me later.' She giggled excitedly.

I pulled the lipstick from my bag. The gold case rested cold against my palm like a bullet. I wasn't sure what to say. It wasn't like I had been physically assaulted or anything; I had merely had an argument with a manager about trying to squeeze too-small boots onto my legs. Then I started to giggle as the absurdity of it all – the boots, Jade, shoplifting – hit home and I realised I was strangely thrilled. The frisson of danger and drama had woken me up. My earlier exhaustion had dissipated and now I was buzzing like a tuning fork.

'I think I should be buying you a drink, don't you?' I said, my fingers closing tightly over the lipstick.

It went completely against the grain for me to walk into a bar on a weekday afternoon and I was expecting lecherous stares from an all-male congregation, but in fact, of the smattering of men sitting like giants at tiny tables or propping up the long bar counter, no one gave me a second glance. They were all too intent on staring into their own drinks. There was no laughter or frivolity in the air, just the stale smell of beer and quiet resignation.

Although the bar looked out over the river, Scarlet pointed out a table towards the back corner.

'There's a table over there. Make mine a double gin and tonic,' she said and walked away. I was taken aback somewhat, then remembered that I had said I was buying. Her candour was something I would have to get used to if we were to be friends – and I realised that I wanted that very much. I had experienced more excitement and drama in one morning than I had in the last year – but the good kind of drama, not the kind that leaves you trembling and weeping on the bathroom floor in the middle of the night when the nightmares get too much. And I found myself enjoying not being alone.

The barman was watching me carefully. 'All right?' he said as I approached.

'Um, yeah, can I have two large gin and tonics please?'

I looked away as he turned to pour the drinks, feeling self-conscious, and started fiddling with a cardboard drinks mat, bending it this way and that.

'Ice and a slice?'

'Er, yes please?'

'Twelve pounds forty then please,' he said, placing the drinks in front of me.

I produced a twenty-pound note from my purse and handed it over. 'Thanks, keep the change.'

The barman raised an eyebrow, thanked me with a smile, and returned to wiping glasses.

'Did I see you tipping the barman there? And rather generously, I might add,' Scarlet teased as I returned with the drinks.

'No, I, well...' I could feel myself blushing. 'I was worried about what he must think of us in here at this time of the day.'

'Who gives a shit what he thinks?' Scarlet replied, taking a huge swig of her drink. 'Ah, nice.' She placed the glass down on a coaster and, with one of her flourishes, said, 'I think you're going to be my pet project.'

'Pet project? Why?' I didn't like the idea of being someone's pet. It all sounded so subservient. But then, the former rebellious, defiant self of my youth had been tortured into submission of late, so that was pretty much what I had become. I still clutched the beer mat in my hand and took to bending and flexing it again.

'Look at you! You're a beautiful woman – I would kill for your hair' – she reached out a hand and lightly stroked a curl near my ear – 'and yet you act like a little mouse, hiding away behind your brown clothes, peering at people from beneath that long fringe. I think if we scratched the surface, it wouldn't take long to expose your inner wild child. Everyone has one – and yours is crying out to be liberated.' Her eyes flashed.

I ran my finger through the condensation on the glass, before taking a sip of the drink. The gin was bitter on my tongue, but cold and refreshing, so I followed it with another, bigger sip.

'I don't know. I used to be more like you, I guess – independent, opinionated, up for a laugh – but that was a long time ago. Before kids. Now I'm just... well, I don't know what purpose I serve anymore. Besides, we've already established today that I have fat calves and, to be honest, no one wants to see a middle-aged woman acting like she's all that in her pointy boots when she isn't. Did you see the way the barman looked at me when we walked in?'

'Yes, with a glint of interest in his eye!'

I pushed her playfully on the arm. 'Er, no, it was more a *you should be at home and does your husband know you're here?* look.'

'Rubbish! He fancied you – and why not? You are beautiful, fat calves or not,' she teased, 'and I think a few weeks with me and you will be way more Ron and a lot less Veronica.'

My drink was going down very smoothly now.

I giggled. 'What on earth would Tom say if he saw me in a bar drinking gin in the middle of the day?' I said conspiratorially, although I'd be surprised if he noticed.

'Who cares? That's half your problem – you need to

think more about yourself and less about other people's opinions of you. There's more to life than playing it safe to keep the neighbours happy.' Scarlet necked some more of her own drink.

'Sometimes I do feel like something is missing,' I said, then stopped myself from continuing. I didn't want to go there. I physically shook the thought away. 'I'm not convinced I can be anything other than what you see: beige. I think you may be disappointed with what you find. I may be incorruptible.'

'No one is incorruptible. Now get some more drinks in.' Scarlet clinked her almost empty glass to mine.

'I can't – I have to think about Grace later. See? Incorruptible.'

'One more won't hurt...'

'Oh all right.'

Felicity

Sitting primly on her soft leather couch, she half-heartedly scrolled through her Facebook account on the iPad, catching up on the day's social media activity. She had that familiar bilious feeling looking at all of her apparent 'friends' with their smug posts about their beautiful child geniuses and amazing days out with their families. Most of it was a crock of shit and they were likely sitting on their arses doing nothing except arguing, but on Facebook nothing is as it seems. She knew that as much as anyone.

With a shake of her head, she threw down the iPad in frustration. Through the bay window, the sun was starting to set, the haze of dusk illuminating the dust settling on the windowsill. She hopped up and went into the kitchen to grab her duster. Returning to the lounge, she vigorously attacked the thin layer of dust, her pointy face a mask of determination. The artificial glare of car headlights through the window suddenly lit up her face and she hoped in vain that Ian had made it home before dark for a change and could go and pick Tabitha up from her dance class.

It wasn't Ian. Felicity could see Veronica trying to clamber out of a car she didn't recognise and, considering that you could count on one hand how many times she left the house these days, Felicity's curiosity was piqued. She leaned further into the window to get a better look.

Veronica was taking a while to get out of the car. Eventually, the driver's door opened and a man came around to help her out. Felicity frowned. Veronica was actually smiling to herself. She was also swaying slightly and Felicity felt a frisson of pleasure as she deduced that Veronica was drunk and trying to pull herself together before going into her house. The man got back into the car and drove off.

Veronica fumbled with her keys, considering each one, holding them in front of her eyes one after the other, all the while smiling in the carefree manner of the intoxicated. After dropping the bunch, only to nearly fall over in the process of picking them up, she finally held up the right key, did a little victory dance and staggered to the door. She spent a few more moments trying to fit the key into the lock, before disappearing inside, tripping over the door frame in the process.

Felicity grinned rapturously and knew the school run tomorrow would be that bit more interesting now. But more importantly, what would Tom make of all of this? His car was already in the driveway and Felicity wished she had front row seats to the confrontation that was about to play out next door. He hadn't responded to her voicemail from the other day, but she knew he was spending most of his time at the hospital lately and it had probably just slipped his mind. She'd call him again tomorrow.

Tom

The sun was fading into evening when Veronica eventually stumbled into the kitchen and found Tom sitting at the table, worry etched into his eyes.

'V,' he said, getting to his feet. 'I was getting worried. Are you okay? Where've you been?'

'Yes, I'm fine. I just met a friend and we went out,' she replied nonchalantly. 'Why? It's not late, is it?' He heard the uncharacteristic challenge in her voice.

'A friend?' His suspicion was immediately palpable.

A giggle escaped from her lips.

'Are you drunk?' he said, stepping closer and sniffing the air near her like a disgruntled headmaster. He detected perfume and a tang of something, maybe gin? That was fitting – 'mother's ruin'.

'I dare say I am,' she replied and giggled again, quickly followed by a small hiccup. Tom felt cold as he watched her reach a hand out to steady herself on the kitchen counter. 'It's been an absurd day – lost children; stuck boots; shoplifting; and now pissed on a school day.'

'What are you on about?' He stared at her with a tight frown, not sharing her amusement. 'Bloody hell, V! I've been sitting here worrying about you, especially since you never leave the house these days, and you're swigging wine and having a laugh. What do you mean about shoplifting anyway?' His voice raised an octave in incredulity.

'It was gin actually – and nothing... just something we saw...' Her voice petered out.

He shook his head and looked away.

'Oh, come on Tom,' she challenged. 'Like you haven't let your hair down before? I made a new friend the other day and we got chatting, and I like her. She cheered me up, so we had a couple of drinks. Look at me, I'm smiling for a change!' She held out her arms in celebration.

Tom had a sudden mental flash of Grace as a teenager and sunk, defeated, into a chair.

V seemed to completely misread his sadness in her gin-sozzled state.

'You know, you look damn sexy sitting there with your sensible tie and your salt and pepper hair. Still handsome after all these years.' She sidled over to him.

He could see she was trying to be seductive, but her

face was loose, like she was melting under her thin mask of make-up.

'You know, since I'm already drunk, you could take advantage of me, right now, here on the table,' she said in her most alluring voice, interspersed with hiccups. She grabbed his tie in a none too gentle tug and attempted to loosen it with unsteady hands.

He reached up and moved her hands away. 'Now you're embarrassing yourself,' he said.

'Come on, you used to like spontaneity.' Giving up on the tie, she let her fingers trip over the tiny buttons on his pin-striped shirt.

Tom pushed her fumbling hands aside with enough force to make her stagger backwards. 'Veronica, enough! Why would I ever find you attractive in this kind of state? Go and sober yourself up.'

She bit her lip like a naughty schoolgirl.

'Thank god you didn't drive. How did you get home anyway?'

'Uber.'

'Well, that's something I suppose.'

She sneered at him. 'I wouldn't make that mistake, would I?'

Right now he didn't recognise the woman in front of him. He moved away to lean on the sink, his head bowed and his shoulders sagging. The silence was absolute.

She turned and left the room.

*

The altercation with V had unsettled him. In all the years they had known each other, she was not one for overt displays of affection, let alone literally throwing herself at him as she had just done, not to mention getting that drunk. He busied himself with preparing a simple pasta arrabbiata in the hope that something carb-heavy would soak up the booze and sober her up a bit.

Pausing in the process of chopping onions, he tried to remember how long ago it had been since he had seen V with a drink in her hand and laughing. Maybe the neighbourhood Christmas Eve drinks last year? No, before that, because they hadn't attended last year after everything that had happened. That dinner party just before their holiday last year? Either way, it was way too long ago and he felt a twinge at ruining her mood this evening.

Maybe he had been too hard on her. How many times had he wished to have her back, like she was before? And the first day she shows some signs of life and he jumps all over her for it. But, he reminded himself, it wasn't the drinking as much as the way she had looked. She seemed different... on edge. What had Felicity said in one of her voicemails? Something about seeing her in a shoe shop in a state?

He pushed the thought from his mind, picked up the knife and carried on chopping, concentrating hard on the blade and not on the chill in his blood.

Veronica

A week passed and I saw nothing of Scarlet, but I wore a cloak of shame and self-recriminations for days, paranoid as I was over my drunken behaviour. My fragile ego got a lot of mileage out of it. Tom was hardly around that week. We had eaten in silence that evening in front of the television blaring a news programme full of sadness and destruction, then I had retreated nauseously to bed while he pretended there was more he wanted to watch. Although he had acted as normal the next morning, even stopping to tease me about my hangover while on his way out the door to work, he had a busy week and spent more time than ever at the hospital, which suited me fine as I couldn't look him in the eye after my embarrassing seduction routine had failed. I felt a wave of queasiness every time I thought about it.

I could feel myself retreating again. My brief brush with friendship had been a welcome change to the norm and I had really enjoyed spending time with Scarlet, someone who couldn't compare me to who I was before, but she would probably not want anything to do with me after the other day. I can't remember her being as drunk as me. God knows what she must've thought.

Then Friday rolled around with a lack of purpose. I had no idea what I would do with myself, apart from clean away more imaginary dust and lie on the couch watching reality TV stars embarrass themselves in the name of entertainment.

That morning, I got up as usual, dressed for a run and kissed Tom goodbye like a dutiful wife as he headed out. I opened the door, then returned to the kitchen to grab a bottle of water and some headphones. Behind me, I heard Felicity call my name.

'Hey stranger.'

I fought the urge to close the door in her face.

'Hi.'

'You going for a run? I'm heading out too – we could go together.' She was already stretching her arms above her head. The whole idea filled me with dread and made me want to crawl back to bed, especially since our last few meetings had been awkward to say the least.

'I... er... I promised a friend I would go to the gym with her,' I answered vaguely.

'Really? Which friend?'

'Just someone I met last week. She thinks more exercise would do me good, so I'm going to try a class with her.'

'She's right, of course. Didn't I tell you that? Well, she sounds interesting – we should meet up some time.'

'Sure, yeah.'

An uncomfortable silence fell between us as Felicity began to stretch her hamstrings in her brightly coloured leggings, never once taking her eyes off me.

'Right, well, I... er... I better get my stuff together,' I said, starting to back into the house.

'Fine, another time then,' she said, her voice now tense.

I closed the door on her and leant against it with my eyes closed. Pulling off my running shoes, I left them lying in the middle of the carpet before heading into the lounge. The curtains were open and blades of sunlight carved up the walls, but all I focused on was the soft couch, the comfortable-looking cushions and the beige quietness of the room. I lay down with my face in a cushion, steadying my breathing and shutting the world out.

Minutes passed, but I lay where I was, not moving, struggling to pull in breaths through the fabric of the cushion, but perversely enjoying the suffocation.

All at once, I had the overwhelming feeling that someone was in the room with me. My skin prickled as though eyes were tiptoeing over my skin. It took me a minute to react, scared of who I would see, but close behind the fear was hope that I would see her.

I slowly lifted my head and looked towards the lounge doorway, but it was empty, the room quiet, the air unmoved. I wanted to weep at the flood of disappointment that washed over me and I went to bury my face again, but heard a subtle noise in the hallway, the scuff of a door or a shoe perhaps.

This time it was pure fear that prickled through me. Was there someone in the house? Had I closed the front door properly behind me? Was the back door locked?

I lay still and quiet, my ears reaching above the sound of my pulse. But there was nothing to hear. The feeling of being watched dissipated, replaced by doubt at whether I had heard anything at all.

She is lying face down on the couch, as unmoving as the dead. I am so close to her I could reach out and push her face further into the pillow if I wanted to, hold her down, put her out of her misery once and for all.

That's what friends are for, surely? To help in times of need? To clear a way forward when you cannot see it? She may not know it, but my eyes are wide open and she needs a nudge in the right direction. Liberation.

My hands reach out and hover above her scalp, suspended in indecision. I can imagine her thrashing as my arms strain to hold her down, my breathing quickening as hers slows.

No, not yet. Patience. It's too easy. My hands pull back and I retreat soundlessly from the room. Focus on the matter at hand.

Her running shoes are lying in the middle of the carpet, abandoned. I pick them up and put them neatly to the side. Behind me is a door to a small cupboard under the stairs, full of winter coats and the pungent aroma of well-worn shoes. I pull the photograph from my back pocket and ease open the door, my eyes searching. I recognise the bag I'm looking for pushed towards the back behind dusty yoga mats and tennis rackets. Teasing back the zip, I push the photograph into the bag, then pull the door closed behind me.

Satisfied for now, I pause again in the lounge doorway. She has not moved and I have to again fight the urge to suffocate her. Slowly, slowly, catchy monkey.

I notice her stiffen, so I retreat and head towards the open back door.

I sat up and rubbed my hands over my face. The room grew sombre as clouds sauntered in front of the sun. My earlier urge to run was now a distant memory, but part of me wanted to get out of the house, away from the ghosts hiding in the corners and the walls closing in.

I dragged myself to my feet and headed back into the hall. As I reached for my shoes, I froze. I was sure I had left them where they had dropped, but now they were set neatly to the side. I cast a quick glance down the hallway towards the back door. It was closed, as was the front door. I shook the paranoia away. I must've tidied them without noticing.

Outside the front door, a fine drizzle had started to fall and my enthusiasm ebbed again. My mood was swinging like a pendulum. I cast my eyes around in case Felicity was still lurking nearby and I caught a flash of neon up the street. I went to duck back inside but saw, as she drew nearer, that it wasn't Felicity after all, but Scarlet. I hesitated, my recent drunken behaviour still playing on my mind. She ran over enthusiastically.

'Hey!'

'Hi, how are you?' I replied tentatively.

'Good, thanks. What about you? It's been ages.'

'Um, I'm fine, I guess. What are you doing here?' I sounded accusatory, probably due to the chill of paranoia lingering in my blood.

'I was walking to the bus stop at the end of your road, heading to the gym, if you can believe that.'

'Oh, right. Listen, I'm so sorry about my behaviour last week. So wrong of me to get that drunk on a weekday afternoon. It's not normal behaviour for me, promise,' I rushed at her.

'Don't be daft! I had an absolute ball. You are so

funny.' She smiled honestly at me. 'Where are you off to then?'

'I was going for a run, but this weather isn't motivating me much now.'

'Hey, come with me to the gym! It'll be more of a laugh than running. You can use one of my free passes if you're not a member.'

I laughed at the coincidence.

'What? Is the idea of me in a gym funny?'

'No, not at all! It's just – it's silly.'

'What?'

'I saw my neighbour this morning who wanted me to run with her and I just couldn't face it. Anyway, I made up an excuse that I was heading to the gym with someone else. It's just a bizarre coincidence, that's all.'

'Well, I prefer to think of it more as a sign, so grab your stuff and let's go.'

I was already a member of the gym she was referring to – we signed up to a family membership when Grace was younger and did swimming lessons there. I hadn't been in years, but Tom still went regularly. From what I remember, it would be a hive of familiar faces after the school run, but if Scarlet was with me, she could be my armour.

'Okay, let's go, but I'll drive – no need for the bus. I have a gym bag somewhere inside, let me just grab it.'

I hurried back into the house and quickly gathered up a change of clothes from upstairs. I had last seen my gym bag in the cupboard under the stairs – our 'Harry Potter cupboard' as Grace called it. Retrieving it, I noticed the zip was open. Strange, since it had been a long time since I had needed anything in it. I checked to make sure there was a towel and toiletries for afterwards, then shoved my clothes in and zipped it back up before heading out with Scarlet.

The gym car park was indeed full of spotlessly clean 4x4s as predicted. We walked through the café, me keeping my eyes averted, Scarlet striding with purpose. Outside the studios, a noticeboard listed the various forms of torture on offer.

'What about Zumba?' Scarlet suggested.

It was an immediate no for me; I needed torment, not celebration.

'Okay, spinning or Body Combat then,' she suggested next.

A voice called out my name over my shoulder and I turned to see Penny, clad head to toe in perfectly accessorised mauve Lycra. Just the kind of person I had hoped to avoid.

'Veronica, what a nice surprise! You doing a class? It's a great stress-buster, I must say. I'm sure it will do you the world of good.' Did everyone have to tell me that? 'Which class are you doing? I'm off to spinning.'

I took one look at Scarlet and said, 'Body Combat I think.'

'Oh, well, enjoy. Must dash, I like to get a bike near the front.' She waved her fingers vaguely at me as she sauntered up to the studios, but couldn't help a backwards glance at the top of the stairs, probably to check if I was backing out and going home, before reporting her findings to the playground police.

'Body Combat it is!' Scarlet led the way.

As we walked through the door into the studio, I headed to the back, but Scarlet had other ideas.

'I'll never see back there. Come on, there's room up front. Let's show these ladies – and one man' – she stared pointedly at a middle-aged man in very tight football shorts with socks pulled up to his mid-calves – 'what we can do, eh?'

'I dunno,' I replied. 'I'm not that co-ordinated and really don't want to stick out.'

'Nonsense – let's go.' She pulled me into position right in front of the muscled, blonde instructor who was bent over an elaborate sound system, her pert neon bottom providing great advertising for her class.

Hi-tech microphone headset and fake smile of encouragement in place, the instructor hit play and loud club music began to belt out of the speakers, vibrating the floorboards beneath our feet. The instructor shouted above the beat, inquiring about injuries and abilities, and pretending to be interested in each of us. Then she started the warm-up.

I looked over at Scarlet as I started to move and

knew straight away that this was not going to end well. Scarlet took high energy to a whole new level and was so uncoordinated that I felt positively graceful next to her. She wasn't fazed one bit though. She bounced, punched and kicked her way through the hour-long class without a care in the world, with the odd whoop of joy that left me cringing, but laughing too. Everyone else in the class was too politely caught up in their own movements to care, but it had been ages since I had enjoyed exercise as much. Her enthusiasm pushed me to let go, and by the end of the class I was high-kicking and whooping along with her. She even threw in some inappropriate jazz hands for good measure, which made me keel over with mirth.

Afterwards, as we filed out of the studio, dripping in sweat and guzzling water, she turned to me with a huge grin, saying that she had had the best fun ever, and I felt huge affection for her at that moment.

Scarlet noticed one woman and her friend who were particularly interested in us, throwing looks and whispering as they walked past.

'Seems we were a hit with some people,' she said to me under her breath. 'And I don't mean in a good way.'

'Why? What's she saying?' I could feel the edges of my good mood dissipating.

'Let's just say it's not complimentary. I have a good mind to trip her up on the stairs.' Scarlet's voice was low and edgy.

'That's a bit harsh,' I replied, cold goose bumps creeping over my warm skin.

'I can't be doing with snide, under-breath comments, just because they don't have the guts to say anything to our faces! We weren't that bad. There's no point in doing something if it's not going to be fun, so we made it fun.'

'Just ignore them. Come on, let's go,' I said, corralling her towards the stairs.

As we passed them, Scarlet suddenly grabbed hold of the water bottle in my hand and squeezed it so that a jet of cold water shot out and hit one of the women on the naked shoulder.

She shrieked and turned to glare even more at us. I hurriedly said, 'So sorry, didn't realise it was open,' before hurrying Scarlet down the stairs and out of harm's way. 'Scarlet!'

'What? Just cooling her down,' she said innocently, but with the same steely look in her eye as she had had that day in the department store. Then in a flash it was gone and she was saying, 'Right, quick coffee before we go?' as we headed into the changing room.

The changing room seemed to be full of shouting mothers and screaming kids. I could feel my blood pressure rising with every niggling, pocket-sized voice.

I wriggled out of my sweaty Lycra and straight

under my towel. Scarlet threw everything off, grabbed her towel in one hand and strode proudly towards the showers in all her naked glory while chatting away over her shoulder. She was completely at ease with herself and I envied her lack of inhibitions.

I stood under the hot shower spray, listening to her singing in the cubicle next door, and for a split second I hated her. Her blithe carelessness and refusal to consider the consequences of her impulsive behaviour showed a woman who had never had to face up to reality, had never had a real problem creep up and tap her on the shoulder to see if she could handle it. Then I hated myself for thinking that way and for being jealous. Why would I wish this on someone who had been nothing but nice to me so far? The hand she had been dealt in life may well have been luckier than mine, but that was the nature of the beast. Besides, how much did I really know about her history?

I felt worse about myself, at how quickly I had wished ill on such a seemingly kind person. I could hear a child laughing beyond the steamed glass and all I wanted to do was crouch down on the tiled floor and stay there until the water ran cold. Instead, I turned my face up to the spray and cranked the water temperature up a notch until it was scalding. The bullets of stinging water helped to bring some clarity back. Once the child had left, I forced myself to turn off the taps and emerged from the safety of the cubicle.

Wrapped securely in my towel, I returned to where we had left our bags. Scarlet was also out of the shower, but still standing completely naked and unaware.

'You took a while,' she said with a frown.

I shrugged non-committedly and turned away from her. There were only a few other women near us, but her nakedness was making me feel uncomfortable and exposed.

While I struggled into my jeans, I heard an unfamiliar buzzing noise and turned to see Scarlet with an epilator in her hand. I watched in shock as she propped her leg up on the bench and began to epilate, still completely naked. She chatted away as though this was the most natural thing in the world to be doing in front of strangers and was oblivious to the stunned look on my face.

Legs akimbo, she carried on until both were smooth. I was considering objecting if she started on her bikini line, but she turned it off, ran a hand down her leg to check for patches, and began to slather body cream generously over her skin, all the while chatting exuberantly about everything from celebrity scandals to her latest purchase of a pair of leather-look jeans.

My shock abated and I found myself considering her in a new light, my earlier flash of jealousy forgotten. This was what I should aspire to be. So life had thrown me some bad hands, but I needed to shrug them off and show that I wouldn't be beaten. I needed to start asking myself: *What would Scarlet do?*

'You're not listening to a word I'm saying, are you?' I heard her say then, annoyance clouding her face.

Still in the throes of my revelation, I felt an overwhelming surge of love for this wanton creature and I grabbed her to me in a tight bear hug in all her naked glory.

'Steady on there,' she said in surprise. 'What's that for?'

I shrugged. 'Because you've made me realise something – and I'm very grateful.'

'What's that then?'

'That I need to let my hair down a bit more,' I said with a smile.

Scarlet raised her eyebrows, 'Sounds like trouble – but I like it!'

That afternoon when I returned home, I felt good walking through the door. I made a cup of tea, turned on the radio and found myself humming along to the song that was playing as I pottered in the kitchen. I was surprised to see my reflection smiling when I looked out of the window into my overgrown garden.

It was now a cold, damp day, with autumn beginning to whisper through the trees, but that wasn't going to burst my bubble. I realised then how much I craved the company of a good, honest friend and, although Scarlet and I hadn't known each other for long, I felt a connection with her. When I was with her, I didn't want to be the guilty shadow dancer any more. But experience had also taught me to slow down and tread carefully. A momentary flash of rebellion can end in a lifetime of regret and hurt.

I could hear my mobile phone chime in the hallway as a text message came through. I wandered through to where I had tossed my gym bag. Fishing around inside it, my hand fell on a piece of paper stuffed towards the bottom and I drew it out curiously.

It was a photograph taken against a bright blue sky. Tom, Grace and myself were smiling happily into the camera, seemingly without a care in the world. It was from our holiday last year when we decided not to go to Cornwall with everyone else. Well, Tom decided. He wanted a holiday just the three of us. Who knew it would be our last family holiday. I wasn't sure how the photo had found its way into my gym bag, but there was a mark across Grace's face where the wet towel had damaged the paper. I stared at the rippling damp patch, feeling my throat tighten and a hand of panic close around my neck.

All at once, the memories were tangible: sickly-sweet strawberry ice-cream drips that dotted our path as we walked along the beachfront; coconut suntan cream spread in stripes across a button nose; salty sea air mingling with the aromas of garlic and lemon from open restaurant doorways.

I suddenly dropped the photo, as though it had scalded me. It floated gently onto the carpet and lay face down, but I couldn't erase the imprint behind my eyes. The three of us were so unaware of what was to come.

I had tucked this photograph away in my bedside drawer afterwards when looking at it became too much, so how had it got here?

My ears filled with her childish giggles and seagulls shrieking, before morphing into the insistent message tone on my phone. I thrust my hand back into the bag as though I was reaching into a sack of scorpions.

I had two messages. One was from Tom, saying he'd be late home from his conference. There'd been a few more conferences and evening meetings than usual of late, but I refused to consider the implications. The other text was from Scarlet. It was short and to the point:

Drinks round yours – what number are you again?

followed by a demonic smiley face emoji. The pendulum swinging wildly again, I suddenly felt giddy in the face of another coincidence where Scarlet was coming to my rescue, which was almost immediately replaced with self-recriminations when I realised how pathetic it was to be so thrilled by a mundane text message.

The self-pity then dissolved into panic as I realised this would be the first time Scarlet had come inside the house. Was it clean and tidy? Did I even have a drink to offer her? God, I was a mess.

Stepping over the photo on the carpet, I strode into the kitchen and swept my eyes over the room. Everything was neat, tidy, orderly. I knew I was being ridiculous. The ironing was done and packed away; the counters were clean; the oven sparkled; the dishwasher was loaded. There were no toys on the floor or Lego underfoot in the play area at the far end of the room. Even the felt-tip pens were capped and arranged in colour order in their cases, Disney DVDs were alphabetised, books were stacked and waiting for small hands to open and enjoy them. Of course it was; it was all I spent my time doing now.

The radio was still playing away to itself, a cacophony of sales pitches and adverts rather than music, and I wondered whether I should turn it off. Then my mind flitted to what we would drink. I walked over to the fridge and opened it in a futile search for a bottle of wine. Nothing but healthy salad, fruit and vegetables – very dull. I would have to tap into Tom's wine collection. It was the expensive stuff, but he probably wouldn't notice. Or maybe there was something in the booze cabinet that would suffice.

Only once I was happy with my surroundings did I text Scarlet back:

Great idea.

I agonised about following it up with a smiley face or a kiss, and settled on

Ron x

at the end instead.

In what felt like a lifetime, which I spent staring pathetically out of the window watching for her, but was actually only ten minutes, Scarlet turned up in a cloud of flowery perfume and smiles.

'I had hoped to bring something, but my booze cabinet is alarmingly empty,' she said unapologetically as I opened the door. 'Then I thought to myself that a woman like you must have an interesting booze cabinet yourself, so I'm sure we can rustle up a cocktail or two.'

She had changed into a bright floral tunic over purple leggings with knee-high boots, and looked as fabulous as ever. I was still wearing the jeans I had left the gym in, teamed with a pale cream blouse under a beige cardigan, and I felt drab and colourless next to her.

I closed the front door and went to show her through to the kitchen, but her confidence made it seem as though she knew exactly where she was going, her eyes sweeping every room as she went. She ignored the photo still lying on the carpet, stepping over it just as I had done.

'This is lovely – very open and light,' she said as we moved through to the back of the house.

'Thanks, I love this room in particular for that very reason. There are no shadows or dark corners,' I replied, taking in the open-plan kitchen and dining area, with its crisp white walls and dark wood floor. At the end of the room by the play area, folding glass doors let in maximum light from the garden and picked up the teal accessories dotted along the countertops.

Scarlet pointed with one long manicured finger at the tall glasses on show in a cabinet and walked straight over to pull two out. I took a seat on one of the white leather bar stools tucked under the breakfast bar.

She busied herself with the ice machine on the front of the fridge freezer, loading each glass with crushed ice, before scanning the room and locating the booze cabinet in the far corner of the dining room. I couldn't say for sure what she would find in there, since it hadn't been opened in a long time. She crouched down and took an inventory of the multi-coloured bottles, before pulling a few out and bringing them over to where I sat. She passed me a dusty bottle of champagne to open – 'You do the honours' – while she poured a measure of what looked like limoncello into each glass. I studied the label of the champagne and had a niggle of a thought that Tom and I had been saving it for something important – something to do with Grace – but I couldn't place the details. I tore open the foil strangling the neck of the bottle and attempted to free the cork from its metal cap. The cork resisted at first, then gave way with a small explosion. Scarlet took the fizzing bottle from me and topped up each glass.

Passing one over to me, she held hers up and toasted, 'Here's to new friends.'

I chinked glasses with her, smiling but hesitating.

'Tut, tut, Ron, you have to drink after a toast, otherwise it's bad luck,' she scolded.

'Maybe that's where I've been going wrong all this time,' I said sardonically before taking a healthy swig of the cocktail. The cool, lemony fizz on my tongue was reminiscent of childhood sherbet and I liked it immediately. I went in for another gulp.

'Oh, I love this song!' Scarlet suddenly erupted from her seat and went to turn up the radio. It was a new song by a band I had never heard of, but the chorus was catchy and I found myself shuffling in my chair to the beat as Scarlet twirled across the floor with her arms outstretched, the glass still clasped in her hand. I wanted to ask her to put the glass down as sprinkles of cocktail dripped onto my immaculate floors, but I didn't want to ruin the moment, so I rolled my head from side to side in an attempt to loosen the tightness in my neck and tried not to focus on the drops as they fell in front of my eyes like nervous ticks.

I took a few small breaths and another swig of the cocktail, put the glass securely on the breakfast bar and swung myself off my chair, determined to loosen up. Then I was swirling around with her and we were giggling like teenagers.

The song ended and, out of breath, I slumped back into my chair and drained my glass. The immortal sound of David Bowie then floated out of the speakers, reminding us to be heroes, and the atmosphere shifted again.

Scarlet immediately refilled my glass, followed by her own, her hands as quick as a gunslinger. My previous vows to lay off the booze were easily forgotten.

Sitting watching her, I realised that I still knew very little about her. Our conversations up until now had been superficial and frivolous.

'You know, I envy you,' Scarlet said.

'Why?' I replied, not sure if there was a punchline to follow.

'Well, all this...' She waved her glass around, indicating the room. 'All this domesticity.' She almost spat the word, like it was completely foreign to her. 'You're settled, seem to have it all. I'm more of a wild card, a bit of a floater, but one day I'd like all of this.'

And right there was the main difference between us: I was settled, domesticated, perfectly house-trained, like a family pet, while she was the stray who wandered free and only had herself to please. Before I met Tom, I would like to think I had been drifting down the same path, with life stretching out before me, full of promise and mystery, and I was determined to grab it with both hands, but then I chose the path that led to marriage, a home and a family and I had donned the clothes of the perfect housewife and mother. Looking back now, part of me wished I had played it less safe.

'It's all a façade,' I said. 'I feel like I'm just hanging onto it all by my fingernails these days. Most of the time I'm about ten seconds away from violence.'

The air grew heavy as my mind started to wander to the photograph still lying face down on the hall carpet, which I couldn't bring myself to touch. I could feel Scarlet's eyes boring into me.

'Right, top me up again!' I burst out and jumped up to turn the volume of the radio up another notch now that Bowie had finished serenading us. 'We'll have no more serious talk today.'

By the time Tom opened the front door late that evening, looking worn out and resigned, I was slumped in an armchair with the remnants of countless cocktails in a warm glass in front of me. I grinned drunkenly at him and looked around for Scarlet, hoping to introduce her.

'Hey!'

'Hi. You okay?' he said warily, eyeing the glass in my hand, no doubt thinking, *Here we go again*.

'I'm more than okay. My friend Scarlet is here and we've had such a laugh. You'll love her – I think she's gone to the loo, but I can't wait for you to meet her,' I said, looking around eagerly.

Tom frowned, then left the room to hang his tie over the hall banister.

I pushed up out of the chair, swaying on my feet, and followed him.

'Scarlet!' I called out. There was no answer. Then I noticed her bag and red coat were missing from the peg. 'Oh, she must've left already,' I said, confused.

'You didn't notice she'd left? How many have you had?' Tom asked, disapproval radiating from him.

'I... er...' I thought back: one minute I remember laughing and dancing; the next I was in the armchair. Clearly the cocktails had sneaked up on me. There was a black hole in my memory that had swallowed the last few hours.

'Jeez, V, is this becoming a habit? You were pissed the other day too. I don't mind you having a bit of fun now and again – God knows we both deserve that – but getting pissed all the time doesn't help,' he shot at me. He bent down and picked up the photo from where it still lay at our feet. 'What's this doing here?' His face was pale and tight.

'I found it in my gym bag. I don't know how it got there...' I replied, my buzz fully evaporated now.

He couldn't look at me, but retreated up the stairs, taking the photograph with him.

'And it's not all the time!' I shouted, then stumbled into the kitchen.

The debris from our impromptu session littered the countertop – empty crisp packets, chocolate wrappers (which I didn't remember eating), an empty bottle of Bacardi and various mixers, lids off. We had moved on from the champagne when the bottle was finished and had hit the harder tack apparently. There was also an empty Martini glass standing in a pool of melted ice, with a tell-tale ring of red lipstick on the rim. No wonder my memory was patchy.

I sat on the stool at the counter and picked up the glass, my thumb tracing the lipstick. Then I noticed the gold lipstick case hidden behind the Bacardi bottle and opened it: the red lipstick that Scarlet had lifted from the department store. I looked at my reflection in the oven door and saw traces of the colour on my lips. Come to think of it, I had a vague recollection of laughing about the whole episode.

Using the glass as a mirror, I reapplied the lipstick to my lips as carefully as my shaky hands would allow, then stood back to admire myself. The face looking back was distorted, unfocused and covered in shadows, but I felt dangerous and edgy, like how I imagined Scarlet felt when doing something outrageous.

I listened to the quiet in the house, the occasional thump from above as Tom readied himself for bed, and knew that I should be joining him, maybe reaching out to him in the dark, but my feet wouldn't move. I found myself dreading the walk up the stairs and chose to stay where I was for a while longer.

The overhead LED lights were suddenly too bright and I leapt up to turn them off. In the darkness I resumed my position on the stool and just listened, trying not to think or feel too much. But I couldn't help it. My head was spinning and images of life before flooded through my mind. A barrage of people and places. I thought about Scarlet and began to make up theories about her life – where she has been, who she has loved – since I didn't know much of the truth. I could picture us, years from now, growing old disgracefully, wearing inappropriately high heels and getting into trouble, and I loved the idea. I didn't want to play it safe anymore; I wanted to break out of the prison I had locked myself in all those months ago. I was tired of the whole charade of my life and of hiding in the past while the rest of the world moved on.

I heard the toilet upstairs flush.

Who was I kidding? In a few years, Scarlet would've grown tired of me and my baggage and I would still be sitting here, in this house, alone with my memories and culpability. By then, Tom would have moved on too – and Grace… My head bowed under the weight of my thoughts and the tidal wave of alcohol.

What felt like a lifetime passed. I could feel absent

tears on my cheeks. Eventually I stood up and headed towards the stairs, knowing full well that sleep would be hard to find tonight. As I passed the hall mirror, I caught a glimpse of myself with the garish lipstick still painted on my lips. The case itself was still clenched in my fist. I put it down on the hall table, then raised a hand and smeared the red lipstick across my mouth with my thumb. I considered myself for a moment, now more clown than starlet, before navigating the stairs to bed.

Scarlet and I started to see more of each other while Tom was at work. The days fell into a new routine. I would head out of the door and filter into the steady stream of hassled parents and dawdling children as we marched in line to the school gates over the road. The mums around me would be rushing and fussing, but I found the chaos calming. At the scene of the handover, as small children brushed off their mum's kisses or ran back for an extra hug, I would stand back and soak it all in, letting the unconditional love regenerate me for the day. Then I would take my time returning to a quiet, empty house, before doing an hour or so of unnecessary cleaning and tidying or going for a run, pushing my lungs to breaking point and enjoying the desperate breathlessness. At 10 a.m. I would make a cup of tea and open the lounge windows wide to let in the sounds of the children in the playground at the school, the laughing, shouting and frivolity acting like a soporific drug.

A knock at the door and Scarlet would be standing there, all smiles and bright colours, and the rest of the day would be spent swapping stories of our youth, discussing the trivialities of the celebrity world – always her topic of choice – and generally passing the time as superficially as possible.

I was careful to spread out the amount of alcohol I was drinking, so that Tom wouldn't have any more ammunition against me. That wasn't to say we didn't drink; we did, in copious amounts. The alcohol kept us loose and relaxed. I found myself consciously leaving enough time in the afternoon for it to work out of my system before Tom made his increasingly later trips home in the evening. Thank goodness he didn't see my Ocado delivery receipts; the clatter of wine bottles as the driver carried the bags in would be a giveaway of how much we were getting through, not to mention the weight of the recycling bin on rubbish collection day. I was getting clever at hiding the bottles out of sight.

Felicity remained tenacious in her attempts to get me out of the house, but I avoided her as much as possible, not answering her calls or the door, avoiding eye contact when I saw her in the street. I figured she'd get bored soon enough and move on to trying to fix someone else. I needed space from what had developed into a parasitic friendship. The more space I had, the less I wanted to see her.

In contrast, Scarlet was becoming the air I needed to breathe every day. Our conversations had covered careful ground until now and I was reluctant to be completely honest about my home life, but as the days built, I found I wanted to confide in her. Talking to her was easy. It wasn't a battle for attention that any exchanges with Felicity would evolve into, because we didn't try to outdo each other. There seemed to be no judgement or criticism, no playing games. It helped to think that no matter what I said, she would have said, thought or felt worse herself, and such freedom of speech was a rare feeling for me after years of tiptoeing on eggshells around Felicity.

Our conversations also helped me to feel more accepted and happier than I had for some time and a weight started to lift from my shoulders. As the days wore on, I began to confide in her more about Tom and my hidden relief that he was choosing to work late rather than subjecting us both to excruciatingly silent evenings. There were still things I didn't talk about, like where we were a year ago. That could wait.

The week after our cocktail binge, Scarlet arrived as usual and we opened our first bottle of prosecco at about 11 a.m. I would've been content to stay inside, but Scarlet pointed out that because the previous week had been so grey and lacklustre, it would be a shame to waste what was proving to be a bright day full of the contrived promise of autumn. She decided we would take our drinks into the garden and she was right: the sky was an endless cornflower blue, there was a hint of warmth in the air, but the trees were turning golden, ready to try and survive another winter.

As soon as we stepped outside, I looked around embarrassed. Once my pride and joy, lack of attention meant that the garden was now a shadow of its former self and sadly neglected. The grass was long, with bare, muddy patches from the blasts of sun and rain over the summer; weeds poked through whatever shrubs had leaves; and many plants needed deadheading and pruning. For the first time, I noticed all the colour had drained from the garden palette.

Surprisingly though, Scarlet said, 'Look at this amazing garden!' Part of me thought she was taking the piss, but the expression on her face was the opposite of sarcasm. 'So much space and potential here! I love getting my hands dirty. I could get stuck in and help you with this, if you want? It can't be easy staying on top of it.'

I tried looking at it from her viewpoint rather than through my own self-critical eyes. It was long and narrow, but the overgrowth gave it a woodland feel, the kind of haven where children could make dens and secret hideaways. Grace had often asked Tom to build a treehouse in the bottom corner against the fence, where the trees met overhead, but he hadn't followed through and it had been ages since anyone had been out to enjoy any of it.

'That would be great, thanks. I used to spend time gardening with Grace when she was younger, explaining to her where vegetables come from and planting wild flowers, but I've neglected it lately. Entirely your fault, of course,' I replied, smiling at her but feeling a shadow creep over me. 'I'm hoping the wild flowers will look after themselves so that there may be some colour showing through when spring comes around again.'

'This summer was punishing in many respects,' she replied. 'Well, we can start tomorrow – but today we drink!' She raised her glass in a flourish. 'To the promise of winter, and whatever lies ahead.'

'Hear, hear!' I replied, chinking my glass to hers.

She started to look around her more attentively, from the overgrown trees along the fence to the rosebushes running along the edge of the shaped and bordered lawn. To the right, set back from the lawn on a small stone patio, stood a large outdoor table covered in a tablecloth of dead leaves and dirt. Next to this was the trampoline, cloaked in spider webs. Grace would have a fit if she saw that and wouldn't go anywhere near it until they were all removed.

Refilling our glasses, Scarlet moved towards the outdoor furniture. 'Do you have a wet cloth? Let's wipe this down and take the weight off.'

I put my glass down and returned to the kitchen. Rummaging under the kitchen sink for a bucket and some old cloths, the smell of cleaning products mingled with the taste of prosecco in my mouth.

As I stood up, movement over the fence caught my eye. Felicity. My heart sank, just like it always did when I saw her these days. I had spent too many wasted minutes on what had always been a toxic relationship. Why had I stayed so loyal for so long? I had always had more in common with her husband, Ian, than with her. He was a kind-hearted, generous man who could never do right in his wife's eyes. It was as though he had never fulfilled what she perceived to be his potential and she made him pay for that on a daily basis with her constant air of discontent and resignation.

Ian and Felicity's daughter, Tabitha, was nothing like my sweet, gentle Grace, but Felicity was constantly comparing one to the other. Whether one child was doing better at school, did more sport, had more friends and was generally a higher achiever underlined many of Felicity's conversations. The two girls weren't natural playmates, but tolerated each other if we forced them into the same space.

The dynamics shifted following a dinner party we hosted last summer. After that, the distance between us began to grow until it reached unassailable proportions and I began to realise that our friendship was premised on habit rather than real affection. When the bottom fell out of my world, Felicity became less of a priority and more of an annoyance that buzzed around on the periphery of my life. I had reason enough to hate her, but I couldn't muster the energy. But I also knew I would have to address it eventually. Ignoring her did not mean it would all go away, but I was managing to for now, even though it was a challenge to avoid someone who lives right next door, especially someone so tall and pointy.

With her sharp nose and prominent chin, Felicity would never win any beauty pageants, but she did have a regal quality that came across as prim haughtiness, only adding to the permanent air of disapproval that clung to her. She was still taking too much interest in me for my liking, her eyes following me on the school run and peering from behind her curtains. On the days when we did physically pass each other in the street, we would greet each other, me half-heartedly, her with thinly veiled resentment. Part of me couldn't blame her. We've been friends a long time and I was now freezing her out, hoping she'd move on. Ironically, it's called 'ghosting' apparently. It was exhausting having to avoid her outside and Tom inside, and there were days when I wanted to crawl under the covers and sleep for a hundred years.

I kept my eyes on her through the window as I ran the cleaning cloth under the hot tap. She was straining her neck to see as far over the fence as she could. I could

see Scarlet inspecting the leaves of a bush at the far end
of the lawn, out of sight of Felicity.

As I walked back into the garden, Scarlet turned
and walked towards me and immediately noticed the
giraffe's neck as it retreated away from the fence. I could
see Scarlet's hackles rising as she said coolly, 'Well, we
have company. Who's that then? She looks familiar.'

Feeling confrontational, I muttered, 'That's Felicity –
my nosey pain in the arse neighbour and an old friend.'

'Old in age or in length of service?'

'I've known her since Tom and I were at university.
We've got a long and complicated history.' Then I heard
myself call out, 'Hello Felicity. Nice day, isn't it? Taking
a break, are you?'

The face appeared again and Felicity's eyes narrowed,
before she replied, 'Well, the cleaner's in, so I thought I
would come out here out of her way. The sun is shining
after all. And I heard voices. It's been ages since anyone's
been in your garden.' There it was, the first stinging dart,
as her eyes took in the dead flowers and rotting leaves.
Her pointy nose swung back at me like a dagger, the
lines in her neck sharp and straining.

'We're just having a drink actually while we plan
what we're going to do with the garden.' I cringed
inwardly as I indirectly made excuses for myself when
I knew I shouldn't care what she thought. Old habits
die hard. 'I would invite you over, but there's only
the one bottle. Nice to see you though,' I said in a

treacled voice, artificial sweetness dripping from every syllable.

'Oh? Who are you with?'

'No one you know,' I replied crisply.

She paused, then said, 'Do be careful, Veronica, you wouldn't want to overdo it in the middle of the day. What would Tom say?'

Inwardly berating myself for letting her get one last jibe in, I turned to Scarlet and, with a wink, said, 'I fancy a jump on the trampoline.'

Scarlet looked at me quizzically, then a grin spread over her face as she seized the opportunity to put on a show. Felicity was scowling even more when she realised I wasn't going to bite back.

'Race you there,' Scarlet said and took off like a rocket.

I dropped my empty glass in the long grass with a dull thud and raced after her, catching her on the arm as she reached the trampoline. After much argy-bargy and the odd elbow prod, we managed to muscle into the safety net around the trampoline at the same time. Then the urge to bounce took over.

Like two little kids, we jumped faster and higher, laughing louder with each elevation. My memory wanted to draw parallels with Grace and her friends as I used to watch them, itching to shout out warnings to be careful, but holding my tongue in the face of such liberating delight. I had an overwhelming feeling of being free and weightless as I jumped with an astounding newfound energy. We timed ourselves perfectly so that as one landed, the other launched into the air, but after a few minutes of intense bouncing, I timed my take-off wrong and we landed in a heap next to each other, laughing hysterically. The sound was unfamiliar in my ears.

I clutched my side as tears rolled down my face and my cheeks hurt. 'Oh dear, I think a little bit of wee came out on that last jump,' I said, before giving into peals of laughter again.

Wiping my eyes, I noticed Felicity staring wide-eyed at us. She saw me looking back and shook her head pointedly, before stalking away into her house.

'Well, that shut her up,' Scarlet said, watching my expression carefully as the giggles receded.

I knew our impromptu show would come back to haunt me and, just like that, the carefree feeling vanished, replaced by a chill in the pit of my stomach, like a dark cloud had passed over the sun.

'Oh never mind Mrs Pinchnez!' Scarlet said, pushing me over on the canvas, then lying down next to me. 'All she's going to do is spread it around the playground that she saw you laughing, drinking and jumping on a trampoline in the middle of the day. Where's the harm in that? It just shows she's an uptight bitch. Anyone else will be wishing they were here too,' Scarlet said, noticing my sudden silence.

'You're right, I know,' I replied. 'But she has a knack for killing my buzz.'

'Then fetch me the bottle and let's get you buzzing again. What's the real story between you two anyway?'

'That's a tale for another day,' I replied. 'Where's my glass?'

Felicity

Felicity fumed in the comfort of her immaculate kitchen. That woman knew how to wind her up.

She stomped around, adjusting a vase slightly to the left, running her finger across the windowsill to make sure the cleaner was doing a proper job, all the while seething. She could just see her from the window, sitting with her back to her, a full glass in her hand, laughing. Felicity frowned. Come to think of it, it had been ages since she had heard Veronica laugh. She almost seemed to be back to normal.

Felicity massaged her temples with her fingers as the beginning of a headache pulsed behind her eyes. Her eyes fell on the thin white scar on her finger. How long ago did that happen? Last summer maybe, just before all that trouble with Ian and his job, before everything changed.

'All I'm saying is rein it in a bit. Does she really need to

do four different kinds of dance classes? Is there much of a difference between them?'

'Ian, it's what she loves. She's no good at sport as such and she doesn't enjoy it, so where's the harm in letting her do the things she really enjoys?'

'Then why are we paying for swimming, netball and these other activities too if she doesn't like them?'

'Because her friends play and it's important for her to take part in a team sport. Seriously, we pay for your golf membership, but I don't see you turning into fucking Tiger Woods!'

Ian rolled his eyes and headed out the front door. 'If the accountant is worried, then we need to make a change, Felly.'

'Don't call me that. You know I hate it.' She tugged on her dress, noting to herself that Ian hadn't commented on her outfit at all. So much for making an effort.

'Can't you just consider finding something part-time? Tabitha is in school all day, so even a morning job would help, just until the pressure is off. I'm trying here, but you have to help me. You have to start cutting back.' His voice was weedy and grated on her nerves.

They had reached Veronica and Tom's door and she could see through the lounge window that the others had already arrived for the dinner party. Ian's timing was appalling as usual, choosing just as they were about to leave the house to raise the subject of her recent extravagant spending. Knowing him, it was probably calculated that way so that she didn't have time to argue back.

'Do you know what your problem is, Ian? You're still as tight now as you were when we were at uni.' She marched up to the front door, leaving him to scowl behind her. She thought she heard him say, 'If only you were,' under his breath, but couldn't challenge him further because Veronica was opening the door and welcoming them in. Tom stood behind her, ready to take their coats and immediately commented, 'Wow, you look great, Felicity.' Her cheeks warmed and she felt some of her annoyance dissipate.

Veronica looked annoyingly perfect as usual, with her auburn hair piled up in a knot, loose strands tickling her face, making it look like it was casually swept into place. A similar style would take Felicity ages and she would still look like she'd been dragged through something unspeakable. Veronica's enviable figure was draped in a simple yet stylish pale grey shift dress with beautiful grey suede Mary Jane heels adorned with deep red bows and understated jewellery. Everything screamed elegance.

Once inside, Felicity made the rounds to greet the other guests – Zara and Will, Virginia and Miles, and Penny and Hugh – who were politely sipping champagne cocktails in the lounge and nibbling on olives and spiced almonds.

Felicity had always resented the effortlessness of

Veronica's dinner parties. She never looked flustered or under pressure; never a bead of sweat on her unlined brow. She just rolled out course after course of delicious, home-cooked food and everyone felt completely at home. In comparison, Felicity secretly ordered in the food for her dinner parties because she found the whole idea of preparing everything far too stressful. Hosting ranked up there with a trip to the gynaecologist in terms of stress levels in her opinion, and was about as much fun.

Veronica's house looked as immaculate as ever, with its clean, minimalist lines and white walls. One would never think she had a young daughter as everything was so tidy and handprint-free. How the hell did she manage it? Tea lights flickered subtly on every surface while safe dinner party music – Adele, Ed Sheeran and the like – played in the background. Felicity felt like she'd crashed the wrong party.

Their friendship had changed substantially since their university days, not necessarily for the better in her opinion. It had grown into one of play dates with the girls, running in the park once a week, coffee before the afternoon school run – none of it thrilling. Felicity could probably live with that, but not with the mundanity of the people Veronica chose to surround herself with. Looking around at the other guests now, they all seemed like clones of each other, looking and thinking and speaking the same. Felicity felt marginalised among them, as though she wasn't quite sophisticated enough to be part of the true inner circle.

What surprised her the most though was how readily Veronica had allowed herself to morph into them too. She was the epitome of the perfect wife, mother and housewife, and Felicity wanted to scream at the tediousness of it all. It all seemed to come so easily to Veronica, whereas Felicity had to work incredibly hard and always fell slightly short of the mark, the décor always one shade of grey wrong, the food ten minutes too long in the oven, the dress one season out of style. Just once she would like to see a bead of stress sweat on Veronica's brow. It was the same when they were at uni. Exams, socialising, chatting to guys all came so easily to Veronica while Felicity ruminated and overanalysed every word.

Veronica seemed to have it all: a perfect husband with his chocolate-box good looks, secure career and charming ability to make you think he was hanging on your every word; a beautiful house that never seemed to suffer from blocked drains or cracks in the plaster; complete self-control in the face of food, drink, everything. She never seemed flustered, didn't raise her voice to her daughter in public and oozed contentment. If there was a crack in her veneer, Veronica was very good at hiding it.

Resentment began to creep over Felicity as she listened to Veronica's narrative of domestic bliss.

She found herself sneering at her behind her back, desperate to expose a fault line in the Pullman façade.

The others thought Veronica to be an open book, but she only let people see what she wanted them to see. You never really felt like you knew her because she was so diplomatic and careful. You never saw her with her guard down and that just wasn't natural. She didn't make you feel like she was judging or looking down on anyone, which was why so many liked her. Sure, they all made mistakes, acted inappropriately on occasion and openly exposed their faults at times, but Veronica would merely be there offering a shoulder to cry on or some sensible words of support. She had a quiet confidence that rubbed off on those nearest to her, so that you felt like she was always on your side. It was very annoying.

Even more grating was that if you asked Veronica how she did it all, she merely laughed and admitted that it took a lot of hard work and juggling, but that she happily accepted her lot in life, the hardship that it was. She knew her station was to be a mother and supportive wife, and she was fully prepared to fulfil that role to the best of her ability rather than trying to have it all like other women. She had put her career on hold so that she could immerse herself in motherhood – and had done so seemingly without resentment or a sense of injustice. Of course, it wasn't much of a career as such, just a bit of journalism, all those plans of hers at uni forgotten once she and Tom got married. She didn't tell people that though.

It was nauseating how self-deprecating Veronica was, but others found it endearing. Their friends would always be seeking out her opinion and advice, and Felicity often felt pushed aside.

In stark contrast, she felt like her life was descending into a constant battle of wills. Tabitha was turning into a demanding, overachieving drama queen. She was at loggerheads with Ian most of time, predominantly over money as his consultancy business struggled to maintain clients and his stress levels rose beyond what was healthy. She resented him every day for making her give up her career to be a housewife when Tabitha was born and now he wanted to move the goalposts again. He was supposed to be the breadwinner, but here he was suggesting she go back to work to bail him out.

The thought of returning to work after all this time left Felicity cold, particularly the idea of giving up her privileged freedom to do whatever she liked during school hours. It was ludicrous and would be considered a failure on her part. Besides, what would the others say on the school run? It would ruin her social standing.

Felicity accepted a champagne cocktail from the gracious host and hoped it would settle her down. When she was in this kind of mood, she knew she would end up sniping her way through dinner and not doing herself any favours with the In Crowd.

She also felt overdressed in the clinging black and red dress she had picked with teetering black heels that were pinching her toes. The dress had been a conscious choice to show off some of her recent weight loss (and to rub it in Virginia's nose as she was still sporting a few too many pounds around her middle), but looking around at the muted colours and classy attire, she realised she looked like she was trying too hard. She tugged at the waistband with her free hand, but Veronica had noticed across the room.

'You look amazing in that dress, Felicity. Wow, I need to get back to the gym – it's clearly paying off for you!' she announced.

The others murmured in agreement, but rather than feeling proud and complimented, the words sounded contrived and rehearsed to Felicity.

Patronising cow.

It took a matter of minutes for her to drain her first glass.

After the cocktails and general small talk, they all moved onto the patio outside where twinkling fairy lights lit up the landscaped garden and the outdoor table was set with jam jars of bright pink gerbera daisies and green chrysanthemums, adding colour to the immaculate white tablecloth. Her hackles still raised, Felicity had the inexplicable urge to knock her glass over and watch the stain spread.

The usual seating rules applied of mixing up

partners, which suited her to the ground as, still rankled by their argument, she couldn't face sitting next to Ian tonight. There was an awkward moment as everyone jostled for position around the table (with more than a few of the ladies trying to get on either side of Tom). Felicity managed to elbow her way past Zara and land the prime spot between Tom and Miles. She then accelerated onto cocktail number three and started to relax. Since she hadn't eaten all day in order to have the flattest silhouette possible, her tummy now gurgled with cocktail bubbles.

Course after course of delicious food followed: a spicy Asian prawn and avocado salad; slow-cooked lamb with dauphinoise potatoes; rich chocolate tart with thick vanilla cream, all punctuated with magically never-ending glasses of wine. The conversation around the table flowed as freely as the alcohol, although the other wives politely held their hands over their glasses while Felicity accepted the refills with gusto. She was acutely aware that most of the attention was directed at Veronica as she soaked up compliments on her décor, the food, her daughter's recent award at school for creative writing... the list was endless. The air was full of muted laughter, polite exclamations and politically correct observations. Felicity supressed a yawn.

Seated on Veronica's right and directly opposite Felicity, Ian was clearly in awe of his hostess as he laughed at her jokes, complimented her endlessly and helped her to clear the table. He never paid his own wife that much attention, let alone cleared a table at home, and Felicity could feel her blood boiling over. She also noticed how Tom was constantly checking on Veronica, winking at her across the table, touching her hand as she leant across him to remove dishes, filling her glass when it was empty – and yet Veronica seemed oblivious to his attention and in some instances annoyed by it. She hoped as much anyway. Veronica would occasionally toss him a quick smile, but was certainly not paying him back in kind, from what Felicity could tell.

Her temperature rose the further into the bottle of wine she fell. As they moved back indoors for coffee and homemade truffles – home-made for fuck sake! – Felicity felt unsteady on her heels, and her stomach now protruded with air and food as she tugged her dress down over her thighs. She noted the disapproving glare her husband tossed her as he followed Veronica like a puppy. Glancing around, none of the other wives looked as flushed and tipsy as Felicity felt, or as uncomfortable. She chose the armchair near the window in the lounge and flopped into it, still fighting with her dress.

The subject of secondary school choices came up over coffee. A number of opinions were offered on the benefits of private versus state schools and whether the expense was necessary in such a middle-class town as this. Felicity knew that they could afford to send Tabitha to a private school if she went back to work, but was also aware that it would require many hours with a private tutor to enable their daughter to pass the necessary entrance exams. Veronica didn't seem too concerned about this for Grace, who had always been a star student and model child, but no one else seemed to notice her smugness. Felicity glanced across at Tom as Veronica preached to the converted about the pros and cons of private schools, and noted the look of pride as he gazed up at her perched on the arm of his chair.

Suddenly she wanted to wipe all that pride and smugness away. She wanted to scream at him that no woman could be so perfect. She was more mannequin than human. Felicity wanted someone to look at her with that much pride rather than looking at her with indifference, as Ian seemed to do lately. She reached forward in the chair to grab her glass off the coffee table, the angle of the seat making her lurch.

'Careful honey, you'll put someone's eye out,' Ian joked loudly. Felicity looked down and noticed she was showing more of her cleavage than was socially acceptable, the lace of her push-up bra exposed above the tight fabric of the dress. The men chuckled; the woman averted their eyes.

'Nothing wrong with her, Ian. If I had a cleavage like that, I'd be showing it off too. I can't fill anything, so I'm envious. Do you remember that time at uni when we went to that women's rally and we had to wear your

bras over our clothes because mine weren't big enough?' Veronica replied with a chuckle.

Felicity wanted to crawl behind the chair and hide. Outwardly, she laughed it off along with everyone else, but as Tom gathered up the coffee cups and walked through to the kitchen, she saw her opportunity to escape and offered to help.

She staggered out of the deep armchair, feeling like a hippo wading through mud, and picked up the milk jug and sugar bowl, both exquisitely hand-painted by Veronica of course. Her hands were unsteady and milk sloshed over the edge of the jug, leaving an opaque pool on the coffee table in its wake.

In the kitchen, Tom was rinsing cups at the sink, his back to her, as she placed everything on the countertop.

'That was a lovely dinner, Tom, thank you,' she said, coming around the kitchen island towards him. 'Here, let me dry those for you.'

'Thanks, all V's work naturally. I just turn up,' he said, his hands busy in the water. He passed her a thin china mug to dry as she fumbled with the tea towel.

'But you're there to support her – she's very lucky to have someone like you after all these years,' Felicity replied. Even to her own ears, she sounded saccharine sweet.

Tom looked at her with a slight frown. 'Everything okay, Felly?' Her old nickname didn't sound so ridiculous coming out of his handsome mouth, especially when said with an Australian lilt, but then she'd always been able to forgive Tom anything.

'Yes, yes, just... you know...'

Tom passed her another cup and, as she reached for it, her fingers brushed across his and she felt a familiar ripple in her stomach, like butterflies taking flight. As her breath caught, her fingers slipped on the wet porcelain and she watched in slow motion as the cup tumbled and somersaulted before smashing onto the slate floor, just as a loud guffaw could be heard from Ian in the lounge, conveniently covering the sound of breaking china.

'Oh, I'm so sorry – I didn't get hold of it properly and it just slipped,' she rushed out, warmth flooding her cheeks as she bent to pick up the shards at her feet, her dress riding high on her thighs.

Tom knelt down next to her, saying, 'Don't be silly, just an accident.' He began to collect small pieces of the cup in his palm.

'I really hope this wasn't an heirloom or anything. Is it replaceable?'

'Really, it's nothing. I told V not to use her grandmother's china tonight, but as usual, she knows best.' He rested a hand on her arm for a moment. 'I'm kidding, of course. It's just a cup. Be careful, you don't want to cut yourself.'

Her face was centimetres from his as they bent over the floor, hidden from the lounge by the large kitchen island. Her heart was hammering loudly in her ears *as she watched his hands delicately picking up the fractured pieces. She'd imagined those hands doing all sorts of things over the years and she yearned to reach out and take them in hers.*

He stood up and turned away from her. A few of the bigger shards were still lying fractured on the tiles. She reached for one while watching Tom as he busied himself with tearing off pieces of kitchen towel to wrap the breakage in. She felt the sharp point of the china and, with her eyes still on Tom, slowly ran it along her finger.

At first, she felt nothing. Then a burning sting took hold and she looked with wonder as a bright red line of blood pooled along the cut.

'Oh!' she exclaimed.

'Are you okay?' Tom turned to see Felicity crouched and holding her bleeding finger up. 'Now see, you've gone and done that on purpose to test my medical skills,' he said gently, smiling into her eyes and taking hold of her hand so that he could inspect the cut.

'No, I… er…' she stammered.

'Kidding again.' He released her hand to reach up and grab some of the kitchen towel.

Felicity had dropped to her knees and was holding her finger out obediently like a child as he patted at the blood. She raised her eyes and, taking a deep, contented, infatuated breath, leaned in and none too gently pressed her mouth against his. She was slightly off target and it was more of a crush than a kiss, with her tongue pushing and searching more into the corner of his mouth than inside. She felt his hands grab her shoulders and push her firmly away from him and her head bumped lightly against the cupboard behind her.

'Whoa Felicity, what's that about?' he said, colour rising in his cheeks. His eyes immediately swivelled towards the lounge and he stood up abruptly.

'I... just thought...' Felicity answered, looking up at him in confusion.

He crouched down again and said low and firmly, 'No, Felicity, you didn't think. Look, we've been friends a long time, the four of us. This – us,' he gesticulated at her, 'is not an option.' He kept his voice low. 'If you're having problems with Ian, that's your concern, but I love Veronica and nothing will come between us.' Every word was a sting.

'But she doesn't appreciate you, Tom! Look at her, all smug, holding court over everyone in there – it's you that pays the bills, works hard, puts in the hours. Does she really make you happy?' she spat back, vitriol dripping from every word. Felicity pulled herself unsteadily to her feet and tugged her skirt down a centimetre.

His face was a mask as he stood up, but his eyes shifted towards the other room and this time she saw the tiniest hint of... what? Sadness? Defeat? Just as quickly, it was gone and he was steely-faced again, leaving Felicity to wonder if it had been there at all.

'Look, let's just pretend this never happened, okay? I'll go and get a plaster for your finger.' He turned on his heel, bypassed the lounge and headed upstairs.

Felicity stood for a moment as embarrassment began a slow-fingered crawl up her spine. Then she heard the quiet click of a door and noticed Zara emerge from the downstairs bathroom in the hallway. Their eyes connected for a second before Veronica appeared from the lounge doorway.

'Oh, is that blood? Did you cut yourself? Here, let me get you a plaster and clean up this mess before we have any more injuries. I think I only have Grace's Hello Kitty ones, I'm afraid, but it'll do the trick.'

Zara returned to the lounge without saying a word.

'Tom said he would get one from upstairs,' Felicity replied quietly.

'I don't know why, he knows there are loads here,' Veronica replied, reaching into one of the kitchen cupboards.

Tom returned to the lounge ten minutes later and you would never have thought anything had happened. The shards of porcelain had been swept away along with the whole mortifying encounter, consigned to the dustbin. He immediately took up his place next to Veronica and was as polite and charming as before. Felicity felt physically sick to her stomach watching him

– clearly a side effect of Veronica's rich dinner more than anything else – and motioned to Ian that it was time to go. She felt relief as the cold air hit her face on the walk home, leaving behind Tom's unreadable expression as he closed the door on them. She barely heard Ian waxing lyrical about Veronica's hosting skills and cooking prowess; all she felt was a slow, steady ember of hatred smouldering in the pit of her stomach.

And look where we are now, Felicity thought as she wiped down her perfectly clean kitchen counters, all the while keeping an eye on the activity over the fence. Never would she have thought that a little over a year later, the fortunes of their two families would have changed so much.

She picked up her mobile and dialled a number near the top of her recent calls. It rang a few times and she worried he wouldn't pick up again. Just before she disconnected, she heard his deep voice and her heart skipped a beat like it always did when it came to him.

'Hi Felicity. What's up?'

He's obviously busy, but he answered my call, she reasoned with herself. 'Hi Tom, are you busy? Can you talk a minute?'

'I've literally got a minute.'

'It's just… I'm worried. About Veronica.'

'Why? Has something happened? Is she okay?'

She chose to ignore the concern in his voice.

'Nothing has happened as such. It's just that she's acting strange, well stranger than normal anyway.'

She heard him sigh. 'Look, Felicity, I really am busy. I'm sure she's okay. She's made a new friend who she's been spending time with and I think it's doing her good.'

'Well, between you and me, I've just seen her in the back garden bouncing on the trampoline and drinking prosecco.'

There was a moment of silence on the line, then she was surprised to hear him laugh.

'I wish I was there – sounds like great fun!'

'Seriously Tom, it's not her usual behaviour, is it? I'm worried.'

'I know you are and you're a good friend to her, but I think we need to give her some space to work through this herself.'

That was not what she wanted to hear. She had been hoping for a distraught Tom to come rushing over to discuss what was happening, after which she could soothe him and offer him support, not for him to be amused by the news.

'I think she knows about us,' she blurted.

'What? Did you say something to her?' His panic was audible.

'No, of course not, but it's the way she's looking at me lately. I can't explain it. And I've told you before she's avoiding me.'

'You're panicking about nothing. She's just trying to come to terms with the accident, the trial is coming up, Grace's birthday, this new friend distracting her. She can't know anything. Surely she would've said if she did. Look, don't let it worry you. Just keep an eye on her and she'll slowly come back to both of us eventually. I really have to go now.'

He disconnected the call.

Felicity clenched her jaw in annoyance, biting back a scream of frustration as her headache leapt up a notch.

Veronica

'We should go out one night – margaritas and dancing or something,' Scarlet announced a week later as we sipped a particularly cheeky mojito in the cool mid-afternoon. The sun was weak but shining, we were reclining in brightly coloured deckchairs, there was a faint breath of lavender in the air from the neatly pruned flowerbeds, and the clink of ice and tang of lime was certainly lifting my spirits.

Going out. Apart from the odd daytime trip to the pub with Scarlet, I couldn't remember the last time I had been 'out', even just for dinner with Tom. These days I was asleep by the time he came home from the hospital – or pretending to be. It was the way we both liked it.

'Yeah, we could go out,' I replied without conviction.

'I've heard good things about the wine bar in town. There's a dance floor – we could just let loose for a bit. Let's try it – tonight!'

'Um, I'd have to check with Tom first.'

She looked at me unconvinced. 'Okay.'

We settled into companionable silence. Tom still hadn't met Scarlet. I was careful to keep them apart, not wanting the reality of my domestic life to intrude on our friendship. Besides, Tom was hardly around these days. He was married to his job and we had become relative strangers, miles away from the people we were when we first met. In those days, I was studying a degree in social anthropology and had had grand dreams of travelling to exotic locations to live with forgotten tribes, with Tom by my side. As it turned out, he hadn't necessarily shared my dreams of a life of adventure. We had settled down into married life soon after graduation and I abandoned my dreams of exploring the road less travelled to write lifestyle and general interest articles for a local magazine, while playing the role of the supportive doctor's wife. Then along came Grace and our fate was sealed.

Sometimes I would find myself contemplating how things could've been if I had given in to my wanderlust, packed a bag and embarked on a voyage of discovery to uncover an unknown civilisation somewhere. Just how different would I be? I would probably be more like Scarlet and the last year wouldn't have threatened to pull me under. Perhaps I would've been better equipped to deal with it all; perhaps not. You don't know how you'll handle tragedy until it rears up in front of you.

I turned my attention back to Scarlet as she lazily swirled the ice around her glass.

'What's your house like?' I asked her out of the blue.

She looked over at me thoughtfully. 'What do you think it looks like?'

The picture in my head was of a house full of bright colours and strange ornaments collected on her travels. Unlike mine, her youth seemed to have been lived in a variety of cities around the world as she travelled to unusual destinations, often on a whim and following whichever man was in favour at the time. She could talk for hours about the places and people she had seen along the way and I loved to hear her stories, whether they were true or not. There did seem to be an element of the fantastical about it – as though she was recounting what she thought I wanted to hear, but I didn't mind. Her stories helped me to remember that there is a life out there to be lived – and perhaps one day I would start to live it again once I could remember how to breathe in and out.

When I asked her once why she didn't travel any more, she said that she had started to crave a place of her own where she could lay down some roots. The main difference between us, apart from me having familial and emotional baggage, was that she had given in to her youthful dreams, while I had turned my back on them and chosen the safe option. I envied her international knowledge and experience, real or otherwise, but at the same time realised that we had both made sacrifices for our choices. She had given up the possibility of a husband and children, the clichéd place to call home, and the safety that comes with knowing you are not alone. Of course, that was ironic in itself since, although I was not alone, loneliness had become my invisibility cloak. I could safely say Tom and I weren't friends anymore; just two people who shared a space. And Felicity... well... Scarlet was my friend now.

'I imagine your home to be bright, cheerful, full of clutter and chaos, but where everything has a place. Loads of artefacts and souvenirs from around the world, and tons of books piled high. Oh, and an untouched kitchen,' I added cheekily. That was another one of our differences: I used to love to cook for the family, but rarely had the energy these days; Scarlet abhorred anything to do with a kitchen that didn't involve a corkscrew.

Truth be told, there were plenty of differences between us; she was the antithesis of everything I had believed to be true about myself. But I think our connection and friendship stemmed from the realisation that I could've been Scarlet had I made different choices once upon a time. Now I could only live the life I had missed out on by seeing it through her eyes, all the while wrestling and writing with the life I had been given.

'You're not far wrong,' she replied. 'There is indeed an enormous amount of clutter, but then I've never been a domestic goddess. I'm allergic to housework. I have overflowing bookshelves everywhere and at least three books on the go at a time. But it's my space and that's what I love about it. The bookshelves may be skew because I put them up myself and the paint colours may be a bit out there, but it's all mine. I chose them; I live in it; and I don't have to answer to anyone else about it.'

I sighed as I thought about my immaculate living space, all clean lines and white walls. Granted, I had insufficient enthusiasm to do anything other than clean and tidy, but part of me knew that Tom was proud of our home and its orderly, clinical arrangements. Yet another part of me yearned for a life less ordinary, where I could disappear and pretend none of it mattered, where I could feel the blood circulating through my veins again.

My daydreaming wasn't lost on Scarlet. 'Of course, I'm not knocking this place. I wish I didn't keep walking into things and stubbing my toe on the clutter. And sometimes a whizz around with a duster wouldn't go amiss.' She paused, then smiled at me. 'You know what we are?'

'What?' I said, staring into my glass at the melting ice and suspended lime segments.

'We are two halves of a whole, you and me. We complement each other, and I'm glad I stumbled across you.' She grabbed hold of my hand and patted it maternally. 'You complete me,' she said gravely, dropped my hand, and held her fingers up in the shape of a heart, with a yearning expression on her face worthy of a lovesick teenager. For a second, I felt extreme sadness at that: Tom should be my other half, the man I chose to have a family with, not this ditsy woman I had only met a few weeks ago. Then the earnest look on her face made me laugh and I knocked her hands away playfully.

'Oh, stop,' I laughed. She had also inadvertently pointed out that life on someone else's side of the fence isn't always better. She may have had the adventures and the thrills while I played happy families, but I had memories too: my beautifully clichéd wedding straight out of a magazine feature; a stunning honeymoon in Mauritius; Grace as a baby and chubby toddler; her first anxious day at school...

'You're right, let's go out tonight,' I said suddenly.

You would've thought I had given her the moon wrapped in Christmas paper.

*

We stood in front of my wardrobe, contemplating the layers of colour. My initial choice of dark blue blouse and black trousers had immediately been dismissed by Scarlet.

'How long has it been since you went out, for God's sake? You're forty, not ninety!'

'So what would you suggest?'

'Okay, let's have a look.' She started to rummage through the dresses, skirts and trousers hanging abandoned in the wardrobe. The further along the rail she went, the older and less worn the garments became, some of them hanging like museum artefacts. I could count on one hand the outfits I still wore. Scarlet looked like she was trying to find the door to Narnia, head and shoulders buried deep in the textured fabric. I perched on the bed waiting, pulling the edges of my robe close, my hair, still wet from the shower, dripping down my back. Eventually, she pulled out a skater-style blue dress that I don't think I had ever worn. 'This one.'

'Really? Okay...'

'Yes, try it on, let's see.'

I hesitated, then shrugged the gown from my shoulders and took the dress from her, goosebumps leaving a Braille trail across my skin. I pulled the dress over my head. The light fabric fell to just above my knees and I turned, arms outstretched, presenting myself for appraisal.

She turned her head this way and that, then pronounced, 'Perfect.'

I looked at my reflection in the mirror, then I diverted my gaze. 'I'll need a cardigan. It's getting chilly in the evenings.'

She rolled her eyes at me. 'There you go again, granny. Right, hair next.' Scarlet took hold of my shoulders and directed me to the stool in front of my dressing table, the top of which was covered in potions, perfumes and all manner of witchcraft to fool the eyes into believing I was more than the mask.

We were unusually silent as she fussed, dried, straightened and sprayed my hair into obedience. I watched submissively as her hands worked, then closed my eyes and allowed her to apply a layer of make-up.

When I opened my eyes, I looked like a younger, brighter version of myself, but inside I knew the shadow still lurked behind the fakery.

'There, what do you think?' Scarlet stood back proudly.

'I like it. Very... subtle.'

'You sound surprised. There's no point painting you like a Barbie doll if it means you'll feel uncomfortable all night. I wanna have fun, not watch you squirm. Let's go.'

Scarlet didn't need to change her outfit. She

always wore clothes that traversed boundaries and occasions.

All I had to do now was grab some appropriate shoes and… Then I realised I hadn't told Tom about going out.

'What should I tell Tom?'

'That you're going out! He'll probably be pleased to hear it. Give him a ring and tell him you've been invited for a drink with a friend. That's all you need to say. He doesn't need details.'

'True.' I looked down at my hands, suddenly nervous.

Scarlet was rummaging in my cupboard again and emerged with a pair of grey suede heels with cute little red bows that I hadn't worn in well over a year.

'Put these on.'

I did what I was told, then stumbled out of the room to navigate the stairs.

On the landing, I stood for a moment trying to find the words to say to my husband. I pressed his number in my favourites list and listened to it ring. Hearing his voice, I was about to speak when I realised it was his voicemail message. I was relieved. I left him a rambling message about meeting a friend for a drink and not to worry as I may be home late.

That chore tackled, I descended the stairs on wobbly, out-of-practice feet, grabbed my handbag, then changed my mind and rummaged in the wicker basket by the door that housed any number of hats, scarves, gloves and random accessories that may be needed for excursions. My hand closed on a bright red glove with a Hello Kitty motif. I prickled, then tossed it back into the mix before grabbing a small, blue clutch bag that was hiding in the corner of the basket. I tossed a few necessities into it and followed Scarlet out of the door before I could change my mind.

It turned out to be more fun than I had anticipated. After some alcoholically induced persuasion, we hit the dance floor, and my initial self-consciousness when I wasn't sure what to do with my hands and was convinced everyone was watching me soon dissolved as I followed Scarlet's lead. She immediately unleashed herself, thrusting her hips and rolling her arms around her head like she was shadow-boxing. I couldn't help but laugh at her uninhibited movements and felt myself loosen up as I copied her less frenetically.

I twirled and twisted across the floor, feeling myself getting lighter with every song. The wine flowed steadily until the dancing became more expressionist and I remember angering a few of the others on the dance floor as I got more animated in my moves. My self-alarm started ringing when I staggered and fell during a particular move that resembled the 'running man' and ended flat on my back on the floor. Someone helped me up, I'm not sure who, and I had the good grace to be embarrassed enough to tell Scarlet that it was time to go.

My memory dips in and out after the cold air hit our faces, but I do remember us deciding to walk home rather than getting a cab, and me removing my shoes and walking barefoot as they were pinching after all the activity on the dance floor.

My first thought the next morning was how hot my cheeks felt. Without opening my eyes, I lifted my head to turn my pillow over and felt the heavy weight of my brain as it throbbed inside my skull. The cold pillow against my cheek brought welcome relief. I opened my eyes to slits, letting my pupils adjust to the dim light.

Pulling myself upright, I swung my legs out from under the duvet and sat for a moment, feeling my head lurch and sway as the cheap wine from last night made itself known. I looked across at the alarm clock and saw it was still early. I propelled myself to my feet and grabbed my gown from the floor next to the bed. Shrugging it on, I headed downstairs. It wasn't the worst hangover I'd ever had. I could cope.

I noticed one of my shoes lying under the hall

table and that brought back memories of the frenetic dancing. I shook my head at myself, which only served to heighten the banging against my skull.

Tom was sitting in the kitchen, a newspaper in hand and a cup of coffee at his elbow. His tie was draped around his neck, unknotted as yet, and his feet, clad only in socks, gave him an air of vulnerability. He looked up as I came in.

'Morning. Good night?'

I avoided his gaze and headed to the cupboard to find a mug. 'Yes, thanks. Just out with my friend, Scarlet.' I busied myself with putting a teabag in the cup, flicking the switch on the kettle, listening to the water roil and bubble.

'I'm glad – that you're getting out again, meeting people...' His voice trailed off. 'Maybe... you and I should go out sometime, have dinner together like we used to?'

The click of the kettle punctuated the silence that greeted his request.

'Right, well...' His chair scraped back as he got to his feet, folded the newspaper and carried his mug over to the dishwasher. 'I better be off. Oh, I'm seeing Gerald Osbourne later.' I knew I was supposed to recognise the name, but it eluded me in my morning-after fog. 'He used to be so lovely to Grace,' Tom continued, not noticing. 'Remember when she had that imaginary friend for a while and he used to talk to her as though it was all real? What did Grace call her, Ruby or something...?' He smiled sadly. 'Anyway, I'll tell him you were asking after him?'

I could feel his eyes on my neck. 'Um, yes please.'

He walked past me into the hall to find his shoes and I let out a breath that I didn't realise I was holding.

Tom came back into the kitchen as I was pulling the milk bottle from the fridge, my mind still preoccupied with the elusive Gerald Osbourne. I didn't notice he was right behind me until I had closed the fridge door and turned around.

'I'll see you later?' He leant towards me to give me a kiss.

I instinctively recoiled and stiffened. My grip faltered on the bottle of milk. It thudded to the tiles and milk started to seep through the cracked plastic. I looked down at it, then back at Tom, who had stepped back and was looking at me achingly.

'You frightened me, sorry,' I mumbled, then crouched down to salvage what milk was left in the bottle.

'Bye.' This time he didn't try for the kiss but left without another glance, his eyes saddened.

I wiped up the spill and decanted the leftover milk into a jug. As I crouched on the floor, my attention consumed with the order of cleaning, it came to me who Gerald Osbourne was: the elderly gentleman who had lived at the far end of our road. Well into his eighties, we used to say hello to him when he was out and about running errands. He would always stop to talk to Grace.

I sat on the cold tiles, my back against the fridge, feeling numb as I remembered one such encounter when he had bought Grace an extra gingerbread man for her 'friend', Ruby, when he saw us in the bakery one day. She had been delighted.

'Who are you talking to, Princess?'

'Ruby.'

I peered around her bedroom door and watched her laying out the cups and saucers on the brightly coloured rug, all the while chatting quietly to someone I couldn't see.

'Can I join the tea party?'

'Of course you can. Ruby doesn't mind.'

I left the pile of clean laundry on her bed and sat cross-legged on the rug in front of the place settings. Ruby was a new fixture in our lives. Grace had gone to play at Tabitha's the week before when I had to go to a PTA function and had come back in tears because Tabitha had pinched her hard on the arm for telling Felicity she was happy with pasta for dinner; Tabitha had wanted pizza. That evening, Ruby had made her first appearance, sharing Grace's bath.

I decided to go along with it and hope that she would grow out of it. I also chose not to mention Tabitha's bullying to Felicity, knowing full well that she would defend her daughter unquestionably and find a way to blame Grace for what had happened. Things were tense between her and Ian again and I didn't want to aggravate her mood. Besides, these things usually worked themselves out.

'Did Ruby like her gingerbread man? It was very kind of Gerald to buy it for her.'

'Yes, she thought it was delicious, thank you.' She busied herself with the tiny cups.

'Does Ruby like Tabitha?'

Grace looked up cheekily. 'Why don't you ask her?'

I turned slightly to my right, feeling a little ridiculous. 'Ruby, what do you think of Grace's friend Tabitha? Do you like her?'

Grace giggled behind her hand and my heart puffed with joy.

'Mummy, she's on your left, silly.'

'Oh, pardon me, I didn't put my special Ruby glasses on this morning.' I turned to my left and repeated the question.

Grace paused for a moment, her young brow lined in concern, then said, 'Ruby doesn't like Tabitha at all. She says she's mean and always trying to hurt me, but only when she knows no one will see.'

She handed me a tiny china cup, which I accepted

with a nod and drank from with an elevated little finger, as though the Queen of Hearts was sharing the table with me.

I lowered the cup. 'Do you think I should speak to Tabitha's mummy about it?'

Again, her brow furrowed. 'Maybe not. Tabitha will just get crosser.' She paused, thoughtful. 'This tea party is missing something... I know! More of Gerald's gingerbread men.'

I laughed. 'Perhaps we should go and get some then.'

I never did mention the bullying to Felicity. Too late now.

Felicity

Felicity rushed from the house, keys in hand, phone thrust into her back pocket. They were late as usual. Tabitha had insisted on a special hairstyle for school that ended up taking much longer than necessary until she was happy with the way it looked. Her teenage years were going to be hell.

As Felicity rushed down the road, cajoling Tabitha the whole way, she spotted Zara, who looked like she was having a similar morning, if not worse. She debated acknowledging her, then raised her hand in a slight wave.

Zara waved back. She was surrounded by her masses of children and it looked like all four had been giving it large all morning. As they approached Felicity, she could hear the youngest, Jacob, singing the Peppa Pig theme tune from his seat in a battered, well-used Maclaren buggy while five-year-old Lucy dragged her feet and sloped along sulkily, wailing as she went, 'Why, Mummy? It's not fair!'

'Because you aren't allowed toys at school. I've explained to you that Mrs Watson doesn't allow it. Besides, what about some of the children in your class who can't afford to have toys like that? Surely it will just make them feel sad?' Felicity heard Zara reason in a tight voice.

'Why is "no" never a suitable answer any more?' Zara complained as she drew alongside Felicity and Tabitha. 'Hi Tabitha.'

Tabitha ignored her. She was intent on staring at the screen of her new smartphone, something she had pestered Felicity for until she gave in.

'But I would let them play with it,' Lucy pushed.

'Kids, look, it's Aunty Felicity. Say hello.'

'Hi Aunty Felicity,' came the sing-song reply.

Felicity shuddered internally.

Zara's two older boys, twins Cyrus and Lucas, who were in the same school year as Tabitha, shot off ahead on their scooters, having started an impromptu race. Ahead of them Felicity noticed the taillights of a car appear from a driveway. She considered this for a moment, then heard Zara screech, 'STOP!' Felicity couldn't help but be impressed as both boys stopped abruptly and turned to look back at her, feigned innocence on their faces.

Zara grabbed hold of Lucy's hand and marched her none too gently towards the boys. The car backed out of the driveway and drove off, taking the danger with it, and she could hear Zara berating the boys for their lack of care.

'What have I told you about racing on those things? Neither of you saw that car, did you?' Two sets of identical eyes gazed up at her, before they scooted off again at a slightly slower pace.

Zara sighed and rolled her eyes as Felicity caught up to her, with Tabitha still trailing behind.

'God, I sound like a screeching fishwife today.'

Jacob continued to sing tunelessly and Felicity desperately wanted to tell him to shut the fuck up.

'Thank goodness they'll all be in someone else's care in a few minutes,' Zara continued. 'Then maybe I can have some peace and quiet. I'm shattered as it is – both Jacob and Lucy kept me awake last night. It was like Chinese torture, the two of them playing tag team as they came in and out complaining of nightmares, tummy aches, spiders, you name it. Of course, bloody Will was blissfully unaware and slept right through. Okay, so he does have an important meeting today, but still…'

Felicity was only half listening.

As they neared the school gates, the bell rang. Zara headed off to the scooter racks to hurry the twins up, calling over her shoulder for Felicity to keep an eye on Lucy and Jacob. Ever the reluctant babysitter, Felicity hoped she wouldn't be long. Meanwhile, Tabitha had sloped off without even a goodbye, her eyes still glued to the phone.

'Bye darling!' she called, but Tabitha didn't acknowledge her. She turned to see that Lucy was trying to free Jacob from his pushchair. Felicity looked back at Zara who was wrestling with the lock on one of the scooters. If Jacob was allowed to escape, she knew he would be off like lightning.

'Lucy...' But before she could say anything more, Zara was back.

'Bloody scooters. I hope the damn things get stolen,' she muttered under her breath. 'Lucy, what are you doing?'

'Jake-Jake wanted to get out,' Lucy replied with big, innocent eyes.

'I'll say when he can and can't get out, thank you very much.'

'Now, now, now,' chanted Jacob, fiddling with the harness.

'Come on, you're late.' Zara steered Lucy towards the main gate.

Felicity was pleased to see that the twins had sauntered in without a second glance back at Zara either.

'Cyrus, Lucas, no goodbye today?' Zara called after them. Kids were streaming in around them, shouting, laughing, pushing, but Zara stood firm, one hand holding Jacob steadfastly in his seat, and waited for her two oldest to lope back, hands in pockets. She gave each of them a quick kiss and a hair ruffle, got a smile back before they were swallowed into the foot traffic.

Lucy still stood next to Zara, waiting patiently, needing more than a quick kiss. 'Bye, Lucy-Lou, have a good day.' She gave her a hug and a gentle shove away from her and watched her walk slowly towards the classrooms. Lucy turned and waved another three times before she was out of sight. Felicity envied her the closeness with her children to some degree; she would love it if Tabitha would just to look up from her phone now and again and acknowledge her.

Zara sighed in relief and turned the pushchair around. 'Right, one more to go, then I'll walk back with you.'

Felicity resisted swearing under her breath.

They headed towards the separate nursery entrance where Jacob would spend the morning. Felicity suddenly felt exhaustion nipping at her Converses and she desperately needed a cup of tea to revive her from what had seemed like a constant battle of wills over breakfast this morning. She loved Tabitha, but she could suck the energy from her like a leech. Seeing Zara hadn't helped – she managed to raise four kids a lot more effectively than Felicity could manage one, it would seem.

Zara stopped abruptly and grabbed Felicity's arm. 'She's there again.'

Felicity followed her eyes across the road to where a woman was standing completely still among the throng of activity, seemingly oblivious to the people streaming around her. It was Veronica. She wore a look of vacant calm on her ghostly pale face that was unnerving and completely at odds with the cacophony of the children. As the masses of children thinned out, leaving a few latecomers to rush past, Veronica then turned and headed back in the direction of her house.

Zara looked down at Jacob in his pushchair, then squatted down next to him and gave him a sloppy kiss.

'God, I feel so sorry for her,' she said, straightening up.

This wasn't the first time Felicity had seen Veronica on the school run, standing like a spectre, soaking it all up, as though breathing in the life and energy around her. The mums and dads had got used to seeing her and politely looked the other way now, but Zara obviously still felt some kind of empathy for her.

'It's getting a bit creepy though,' Felicity replied.

The first time she had noticed her was just after the accident and Felicity had approached her in the hope of escorting her back home, suggesting that she should take herself away from the prying eyes and whispered comments, but happy for the other mums to witness her fulfil her role as supportive best friend. Veronica had completely ignored her, turning to leave only once the last child had filtered into class. These days Veronica appeared two or three times a week, always in a soporific state, like a junky needing a fix.

'Come on, that's not fair.'

'What? She must know what people say about her.'

'I think most people get it,' Zara replied pointedly.

'She's lost more than I can comprehend and is clearly struggling to come to terms with it and I don't know how to help her.'

'Zara, I've tried to help. As her oldest friend, it is my duty to help her, but she's having none of it. She has completely withdrawn from me, Tom, everyone. I've tried cajoling; I've tried sympathy; I even thought a bit of tough love would break through, telling her straight that she needs to snap out of it, but she's getting worse. It is completely exhausting and I'm worn out.'

'I know you are. You've been a brilliant friend to her, better than I have anyway. I just feel so inadequate around her, like I'm flaunting my kids in her face or saying the wrong thing all the time, but it's not about you or me.'

'I'm so worried about her, I can't tell you.' Felicity lowered her voice conspiratorially as they carried on walking. 'Between you and me, I think she's losing the plot, you know, up here.' She tapped her temple. 'I think she's getting to the point where she needs professional help, if you know what I mean.'

'Really? Why?'

'Look, it's not for me to say as such, but we are her friends.' They had reached the nursery gate. 'We've all tried in our own way to support her, talk to her, lend her a shoulder to cry on, especially in the early days. Poor Tom is at his wit's end. He spends most of his time at the hospital now. You know, it's as though she doesn't know what she needs herself, so whatever help you offer isn't going to make any difference. She's unreachable, cut off, and only a true old friend like myself can possibly get through to her because I know her so well.'

'But why do you say she needs professional help? What has she been doing? She's not hurting anyone.'

'Yet.'

Jacob was starting to struggle in his seat again, trying to free himself. 'I need to get him into nursery. He's getting niggly.'

'You get on and take Jakey in. I have to get back anyway. But we'll have a coffee soon and I'll tell you more. You won't believe some of the stuff…'

'Sure, okay.' Zara looked rattled. 'I will tell you one thing: I won't be shouting at my kids later. They can be moaning little brats, but they're my brats,' she said as she steered Jacob through the gate.

'True,' Felicity replied, sagely nodding her head.

She walked away from Zara, humming to herself, the stress of the morning forgotten.

Veronica

I closed the front door on the noise of the morning streets and retreated back into the quiet mausoleum of my house. Almost immediately I felt a weight descend on my chest. Through the kitchen doorway, I could see the milk-soaked towel lying abandoned where I had tossed it earlier before I headed out on the school run. Without taking another step, I texted Scarlet and asked her if she could come over.

She was there within five minutes. She didn't knock to announce herself, but merely lifted the letter box flap and peered through the door to see me sitting on the stairs. The letter box clattered back into place and I dragged myself to the door to let her in.

'Am I talking you down from a hangover or something worse?'

'I just need a bit of company. One of those days.'

'Worse then... right, let's get the kettle on – or do you need a shot of brandy?'

I didn't answer and she walked ahead of me into the kitchen and started opening cupboards.

After five minutes of unusual quiet while she pottered and I tried to shake the numbing chill hanging over me, she placed a hot mug of tea and a shot glass of brandy in front of me. She laid the same out in front of herself.

Cautiously she said, 'You've never really told me what happened last year – and I suspect that what you're feeling now has something to do with that? But I'm not going to ask because you will tell me if and when you're ready. Besides, I'm not here to be your therapist; I think of myself more as a form of active rehabilitation, if you will.'

I felt a ghost of a smile on my lips at this thought.

She took a sip of her brandy, then nudged mine towards my closed fist. 'So your first step of rehabilitation is to knock that back.'

I followed her lead, relishing the heat as it filtered down my throat and immediately steadied me. No wonder they served brandy to people in shock.

'Hey, anyway, did you bring my shoe?' I asked.

'What shoe?'

'Last night? You carried one of my shoes when I walked home barefoot.'

'Did I? I don't remember to be honest. I don't have it now though.'

'Funny, I can't find the other one anywhere and I remember us each carrying one.'

I heard the doorbell ring, but didn't rush to get it. It immediately rang again.

'You going to get that?' Scarlet asked with raised eyebrows.

I shuffled off my seat and approached the door ominously.

Felicity stood on the doorstep, looking particularly smug, albeit with flushed cheeks and a sweaty brow. She lifted her hand and I flinched involuntarily. From her extended finger dangled my missing shoe, which looked far worse now than it had when I had worn it the night before.

'Morning Veronica.' She skipped straight past the pleasantries. 'I found this when I was out on my run this morning. It's yours, isn't it?'

She didn't wait for a reply.

'I recognise it from the night you hosted that dinner party last year? You were wearing a pair just like them and I admired them at the time because they were so unusual and elegant. Not so pretty now, are they?' She rotated the shoe in front of my eyes, just in case I couldn't see it closely enough. The heel was broken and the leather torn with what looked like bite marks on the toe. It had clearly been mauled by a creature in the night. I looked over my shoulder to see Scarlet hovering in the kitchen doorway, listening to every word.

'So I was running down the alley that leads to the park and I saw it lying in the dirt, looking very pitiful, and I didn't want you to wonder where it was, so I cut short my run and thought I would bring it over.'

I wanted to slap the self-righteous amusement off her face. My hands clenched at my sides. I could imagine her sprinting over here as fast as her bony legs could carry her, knowing she had one over on me. She had well and truly won this round. Now I had to decide how to handle it. Slamming the door in her face (and hopefully catching her with the door knocker) was looking like a good option so far.

'Can I come in? I haven't seen you in ages?' She moved to push past me, but I pulled the door towards me to block her.

'Er, no, it's not a good time. I have a friend here.'

Her eyes narrowed. She was straining her neck to see beyond me. 'I saw you earlier. I was walking with Zara.'

'Oh?'

'You need to stop doing this, Veronica. People are gossiping.'

'Let them.' I started to close the door on her, but she was still talking.

'So when did you lose this then? Sounds like there's a story there. You must've noticed you weren't wearing it? They are beautiful shoes – well, were beautiful...' Her thin eyebrows threatened to disappear into her hairline.

I stole another glance over my shoulder, expecting Scarlet to wade in and give Felicity a piece of her volatile mind, but she was giggling into her hand so much that she couldn't speak. That set me off and the anger evaporated into bubbling laughs. I took the shoe that she was still dangling in front of me and turned it this way and that, inspecting the damage and hooting even louder.

'Must've been a fashion-conscious fox!' I heard Scarlet chortle behind me.

'I must say, Felicity,' I managed to choke out, 'the fox that nicked it has fabulous taste in shoes.'

Her face was a picture of bewilderment. She had clearly hoped to leave me rattled with her discovery and her face dissolved into anger at my reaction.

My cheeks were starting to ache.

'You should head home to the shower, Felicity. I'm not sure if it's you I can smell or if the fox pissed in my shoe, but there's definitely a whiff of something.'

With that, I closed the door on her astonished face.

Our laughter was uncontrollable then, to the point where my sides groaned to stop. It had been a very long time since I had felt that kind of liberated, happy ache from laughing too much.

When we had managed to gulp some air back, we flung ourselves down on the couch in the lounge, completely sated.

It didn't take long for the mirth to be swallowed by my paranoia. 'Oh my god, did I really say that to her?'

'You did and I am immensely proud.'

'She's going to ruin me at the school gates this afternoon.'

'So what? Do you really give a shit?' She grabbed hold of my hand. 'And look at you. You are so different from that meek, timid mouse I saw in the supermarket that day. I remember how horrified you were that I had dared to speak to you.' She sat forward and looked at me earnestly. 'This is the Ron I like – the one who is starting to realise that she doesn't have to be the victim any more. The one who stands up for herself and is getting some of her fight back.'

I knew she was right, but I was also scaring myself. I didn't feel like I was moving forward as such; more like I was lurching from side to side. Every day I woke up thinking today would be different, I would start to feel better and less like I needed to remind myself to breathe, walk, eat. I had gone from numb inactivity to bouts of recklessness and I felt more unstable than ever. What kind of woman ventures out, gets drunk and loses a shoe to a fox on a school night?

But then I had to acknowledge the fact that my sides were aching and my cheeks were stretched, that I had laughed until I had cried on a few occasions in the last few weeks, that last night I had danced as though no one was watching. Six months ago I was comatose in comparison and barely able to pull myself out of bed.

'You're right. Fuck 'em.'

'Attagirl,' she said as she flung her arm around my shoulders. 'What's the story with you two anyway?'

'Who? Me and Felicity?'

'Yeah. I can't figure you out. You say you've been friends a long time, but you wouldn't think it to look at you. You're like cats circling each other.'

'It's a complicated relationship.'

'I'd say.'

'We met on the first day of uni. We were allocated as roommates and at the time neither of us knew anyone else, so we stuck together. Then we met Tom and Ian, her husband, and the four of us have been together ever since. When we were younger, I didn't question the dynamic between us. I guess it was easy to be friends with her and to fill the role I was supposed to play. But things change, people change and now the friendship has run out of steam.'

'She doesn't seem your sort at all. I can't imagine having a laugh and a drink with her.'

'We've certainly had a laugh together, sure, especially when we were younger and didn't have kids, but our conversations have never been casual as such. If I was drinking, she'd be counting how many glasses I'd had and pointing out the calories in the bag of chips I'd scoff on the way home. She's not one to do things for the hell of it. It's like we are opposing magnets pushing and pulling against each other. She's bloody competitive and she almost sees me as a rival rather than a friend, but I've tried not to indulge her. I'd rather back off than take her on, not because I think she could outdo me, but because I don't want the fuss really. We would have our battles at uni when I didn't back off and some of them were really nasty, but we always seemed to gravitate back to each other.'

'Why though? Why let her try and get one over on you?'

'Because I figured that was the way she was and sometimes it made me feel like the bigger person, you know? Does that sound awful? And sometimes you stay with someone out of habit more than anything else. I know, that sounds even worse.'

'No, I get what you're saying.'

'Lately, I don't have the energy for all the head-butting and I couldn't care less about being the better person any more. When we had the girls, the differences between us seemed to magnify and I realised that just because I knew she was dominating me, that didn't make it acceptable. I noticed that when we were out with other friends, she would talk over me in conversations or contradict what I was saying just to be argumentative, because she needed to be right and needed me to be wrong in order to boost her own confidence. My other friends would tolerate her because of me, which made me feel guilty. It's like she's used me to make herself feel better. Other stuff too – moving in next door, how that came about... It can be suffocating, but you can't just throw away a friendship that has lasted as long as ours. Tom and Ian are still best friends, which complicates things. That and the fact that I've always been a little bit scared of her.'

'Well, you don't need to be boosting anyone else's ego except your own. She can find another victim to bully, because now I've got your back.'

Strange, but I felt only tenuously comforted by this.

Later that afternoon after Scarlet had left, I sat thinking about what she had said about how much I had changed since meeting her as I sobered up over a cup of tea and a biscuit. I was starting to get snatches of my former life back and I knew I had some way to go to fix what was ailing Tom and I, but that seemed a good starting point. I had seen his hurt expression when he had left that morning, but sometimes I couldn't stop myself from pushing him away. I missed him though.

With that in mind, I decided to get back into the kitchen, make Tom a nice dinner, we could chat about whatever had been going on at his work and I could tell him some more about Scarlet – maybe. He may even find the fox story amusing.

I found some steaks buried deep in the freezer, put some jacket potatoes in to bake, and whipped up a mushroom and cream sauce – all Tom's favourites. Although I had knocked back a couple of brandies with

Scarlet, I popped a bottle of white wine in the fridge and made sure there were some beers chilling.

As the evening wore on and the preparations distracted me, I found I was actually looking forward to dinner. It had been ages since we had spent any sort of quality time together and I knew that was mostly my fault. But then he hadn't exactly reached out to pull me back as I drew away. Even so, one of us had to make the first move, so with Scarlet's voice in my head, I went upstairs to change into something moderately less bland, making sure I crept past Grace's bedroom door as quietly as I could.

Tom

He sat in his car in the dark, looking up at the house looming in front of him. Supposedly his castle, lately it had begun to feel more like a prison. The windows were dark, the curtains drawn. He sighed and ran a hand over his face, then loosened the claustrophobic tie at his neck. He knew there were problems that they needed to face up to, but he just couldn't bring himself to confront it or V. He wasn't afraid of her anger, but rather of opening up a wound that he knew he wouldn't be able to heal. Sometimes sadness clawed at him, but he pushed on, not giving in to it, knowing one of them had to be strong. He reached towards the ignition key and hesitated, before starting the engine of the car again. He had no destination in mind, but knew he couldn't bring himself to go inside just yet.

He looked across at Felicity's house, illuminated and bright in comparison. Ian's car wasn't parked in the road yet. He could...

No. Lately, all she wanted to talk about was V. She had phoned him again that afternoon, ranting about how rude V had been to her – something about a shoe that she'd found. Tom had actually laughed when she told him what V had said because it had sounded so ludicrous and unlike V these days. He'd been a little bit proud too. Sometimes Felicity could do with being put in her place, although he'd never say that to her face. He was under no illusions; he knew she could be poisonous. He could smell the venom coming off her in waves whenever she saw V these days.

A light flicked on in the main bedroom above him and he looked back towards his own house. He could make out V's shadow as she moved about, which was unusual. Normally he would get home and she would either be in bed with her back to him, asleep or pretending to be, or she would be sitting in a tight ball tucked in the corner of the couch watching mindless TV programmes, her face an empty canvas. She would say she had eaten already (although her skinny frame suggested otherwise) and he would sit alone with his ready meal in the kitchen and *Newsnight* on the small flat screen on the wall.

Tonight something seemed different. With a last glance over to Felicity's door, he reached around the steering wheel and cut the engine again. V was still moving around in the bedroom, from what he could tell. His eyes dropped to the lounge windows that had appeared dark and unwelcoming when he had pulled up, but now he could make out a faint flickering behind the curtains, as though candles had been lit.

He took a fortifying breath, climbed out of the car and opened the passenger door to grab his jacket and briefcase. As he pushed the door closed, he noticed movement at the Greens' window and caught a brief glimpse of Felicity as she ducked out of sight. For a split second he faltered. He felt ashamed at how he had distanced himself from Ian of late, but he was worried that one beer too many in the pub and he would blurt everything out. Besides, the shame was just another facet of the guilt he was harbouring.

Their affair had started slowly. It certainly wasn't something he had gone looking for. After the dinner party, they had acted like polite acquaintances, but it was clear she was interested. Little glances when they were out, subtle touches of her hand – it was obvious. V was so distracted then. The only thing that seemed to matter to her was how she was perceived by the mothers at the school gate, whether she was wearing the right shade of grey, was she involved enough with school events, and any spare attention was lavished on Grace. He came far down her list of priorities. He had needed more than that and Felicity was offering it on a plate.

He pushed through the front door, his legs heavy with exhaustion. He could hear the tinny sound of the television from the lounge. As he rounded the door, he smiled to see Grace curled up in V's lap, wearing warm pyjamas and ridiculous pink unicorn slippers.

'Hey you two.'

They both acknowledged him with a small, 'Hi.'

He came over to where they sat snuggled together and Grace offered up her tired face for a kiss. V mirrored her, then they turned their attention back to the CBeebies bedtime story on the television.

'I'm starving – what time do you want to eat?'

V raised weary eyes to him and replied, 'Sorry, I ate with Grace earlier. There's some leftovers in the fridge though.'

His heart sank. He'd eaten on his own nearly every night this week.

'Right.' He left the room and went upstairs to change. When he returned, they were in exactly the same position.

All of a sudden he felt angry at both of them. They weren't exactly overjoyed to see him. They probably wouldn't have noticed if he hadn't come home at all. He needed a beer.

Fed up, but also aware he sounded like a kid, he said

in a huff, 'I'm going next door to borrow Ian's leaf-blower. Might stay for a beer.'

He got a half-hearted 'okay' in return.

He knocked on the door, expecting to see Ian, but it was Felicity who opened it.

'Er, hey, I was hoping Ian was home? He said I could borrow the leaf-blower.'

'Oh, sorry, he dropped Tabby at her dance class, then went to the golf club. But come in, I'm sure he won't mind if you have a look for it.'

'Oh, it can wait.'

'It's fine, really. Come in.'

Tom hesitated, looked back towards his own front door, then stepped over the threshold, feeling awkward after the last time they were alone together.

'Are you okay?' she asked with what seemed like genuine concern.

'Yeah... no... it's nothing.'

'No, tell me. Come on, we're friends, aren't we?'

'I'm fine, really...'

'Come through, I'll put the kettle on.'

He perched at her kitchen counter, sipping hot tea out of a geometric-patterned blue mug and found himself telling her all about how overlooked he felt, even though he sounded childish to his own ears. She was surprisingly easy to talk to. He had never noticed that side to her. She had always been one part of the foursome, Ian's wife, V's friend.

'*One thing we both know about V is how much she loves Grace, but she's never been a tactile person and never will. But she showers Grace with affection – look at her: she's bright, happy, well-mannered, never misbehaves. V can't be doing too much wrong there,*' Felicity reasoned.

'*I know. And I know I sound like a spoilt child. It would just be nice to have V to myself sometimes.*'

'*She has a lot on. She is a bit bogged down in the social politics of the school, the PTA and stuff, but that's because she doesn't have anything else except school and Grace to keep her busy. You just need to talk to her, tell her you're feeling left out.*' She smiled sympathetically, her eyes shining. '*Here, let me take that mug from you.*'

Her fingers brushed his much like they had the evening of the dinner party, lingering ever so slightly.

That was how they had ended up half-naked on the cold kitchen tiles in an undignified and messy tangle. Ashamed at himself, he had made it clear that there would be no repeat performance, but he couldn't get her out of his mind after that. He took to popping in on his way to work once Ian had left for the day, sometimes texting her to meet him in between appointments. Then the initial excitement of the first few weeks had inevitably cooled and they met less frequently, but that irked Felicity and she had started putting pressure on him to decide on what their future would be. She started to take more risks, sneaking her knickers into his pocket for him to find later in the day, texting in the evening when she knew he was at home with V, as though she wanted V to find out, even relished the idea of it, and he started to regret the whole thing.

Then the unthinkable happened and he was awarded a 'get out of jail free' card. Not the way he would've liked to end things, but there it was.

He knew without a shadow of a doubt before the accident that he didn't love Felicity. She was too high-maintenance, too needy. But she was a physical distraction that he had needed right then and he had enjoyed the attention she poured on him, how she made him feel like he was the only important person in the room when they were together. She had stroked his ego. He'd become a walking, middle-aged cliché. Felicity had become like a drug to him and it had taken a catastrophic event to make him go cold turkey.

He didn't want to acknowledge the damage that would be inflicted if V ever found out about them and he hated himself for what he had done.

With heavy footsteps and contrition gnawing at him, he approached his own front door, took another deep breath and put the key in the lock. The hallway was illuminated and he could hear music playing softly from the kitchen. Ironically, it was the same tune that had been playing when Felicity had accosted him at the dinner party. Ed Sheeran – irrationally, Tom suddenly hated him.

He set his briefcase down gently, hung his jacket on the banister, and dropped his keys into the bowl on the table. The clatter reverberated in the still air. He paused as the smell of baking potatoes hit his nose.

'Hi V,' he called out, not expecting a response. None was forthcoming, so he wandered through into the kitchen. He took in the steak waiting on the counter, the table set for two. He noticed the glasses and cups standing in the sink, red lipstick kissing the rims. Picking one up, he sniffed at the glass but couldn't discern whether it had held a soft or hard drink. With no sign of V as yet, he wandered over to the recycling bin and pulled out an empty brandy bottle. There was his answer then.

He sighed. A voice in his head suggested he leave this battle for another night, especially since she was clearly making an effort and he didn't want to ruin their first chance in ages of enjoying a relatively normal evening like a regular couple, like before. He knew this new friend of hers had something to do with the excessive drinking, but also suspected she may have had something to do with the light that had started to flicker behind V's dead eyes. She had mentioned this friend on and off recently – Susan or Sherry, something like that? Perhaps she was starting to come back to him, although it seemed to be on the back of alcoholic fumes, which, considering V had always been a careful drinker, was a worry in itself. But in light of his own behaviour, if having a few drinks was the worst of her sins, he could ignore it for now.

He replaced the empty bottle in the bin and headed to the fridge to try and catch up with a beer. Taking a few long swigs, he headed upstairs, amplifying his footsteps as best he could.

'V?' he called again.

He found her standing in the bedroom, her back to him, as though she was ready to dart into the cupboard and hide. One of her hands was frozen on her blouse buttons, mid-way through fastening them. At first, she said nothing and the air between them crackled. Then she finished fastening the buttons, smoothed her skirt and turned towards him with a strange, plastic smile plastered to her face.

'Hi. Good day?'

She had applied a little make-up, but it didn't disguise the purple shadows under her eyes. If anything, the rather garish red lipstick on her lips amplified her pallor.

'Yeah, not bad. Yours?'

'I made dinner.'

'I see that. Great, thanks.'

They watched each other awkwardly.

'I, er... I'll see you downstairs then,' he said and turned to go.

Back downstairs, he changed the music straight away to the radio, preferring the normality of traffic reports and football results. Loosening his tie, he picked up his beer and drained it before opening another.

'You changed the music.'

He looked up. 'Yeah, sorry. I've gone off Ed.' He paused. 'You look nice.'

'Thanks – this old thing?' she chuckled, which surprised him.

'I made dinner,' she repeated, as though looking for kudos. 'Steak okay?'

'Absolutely, I'm famished.'

An uncomfortable silence followed. He stared at the pool of condensation forming on the counter around his beer bottle. His fingers itched to pick up his phone and check his emails or catch up on Twitter – anything to break the awkwardness.

Eventually, they both went to speak at once, him saying, 'How was your day?' and her 'Good day then?'

When had things become so awkward between them?

Veronica wandered over to the fridge and pulled out a bottle of wine, but he darted from his seat and took the bottle from her. She flinched, but all he said was, 'Here, let me do that,' and went to fetch a glass from the cupboard.

'So, what did you get up to today then?' he said as the wine glugged into the glass.

'Oh, you know, the usual: a bit of housework, ran some errands. Oh, and Scarlet came over this morning.' Her hand was already reaching for the glass before he had screwed the lid back on. He pretended not to notice the tremor in her fingers.

'You've been seeing a lot of her lately. You should have her over for dinner some time. I'd like to meet her.'

Part of him didn't want to meet this woman who had managed to breathe life back into his wife when he couldn't. He had a sudden strong feeling that he wouldn't like her very much.

Veronica chewed on the inside of her lip – something she used to do when she was nervous or uncomfortable.

'Mmmm, maybe,' she replied, then quickly veered off in a different direction to ask questions about his work. It was as though she had made a mental list of questions to ask him, but they sounded hollow. Each was preceded by a gulp of wine and a chew of her lip.

He found himself rambling on and cringed inwardly at how uptight he sounded. She didn't seem to notice, just made vague comments at appropriate moments while she prepared the steaks.

At one point, just as she placed the frying pan on the hob, she froze, as though she had completely forgotten why she was there. There was a faraway look on her face. She took another gulp of wine, then carried on with the task at hand, but Tom could see her lips moving slightly, as though she was reciting the cooking process like a mantra to keep herself focused. Tom felt dread tighten like a belt around his chest, but kept chattering away.

She passed a comment without realising that he had already changed the subject, as though the synapses in her brain were failing to ignite quickly enough, so the conversation lurched backwards and forwards, but, pleased to be at home and spending an evening with her, Tom kept up a steady stream of commentary. She concentrated on the dull slabs of meat changing colour in the pan, still chewing on her lip, so much so that he noticed she was drawing blood.

'V, your lip…'

'What?' She raised her hand tentatively, then inspected the blood on her finger with apparent fascination.

He came around and grabbed a tissue from the counter, before holding it up to the bead of blood. He caught a flash of impatience in her eyes and noticed how she baulked as he approached her and a familiar feeling of resignation settled on his shoulders, as though he had let her down again, but without knowing how. He backed off.

'Sorry,' she said. He assumed she was apologising for pulling away, but she said instead, 'I couldn't hear you over the steaks frying. What were you saying? I think

these came from the new butcher – really nice in there.'
Now she was babbling.

Tom took another drink of his beer. 'I was just saying
that Zara and Will are starting their new extension
soon. The architects have come up with a very clever
design. It won't be cheap though.'

'Oh, yes? I should phone Zara and organise another
coffee, look at the design. She's been planning it for so
long, she must be thrilled.'

He knew she wouldn't do any of these things.

'You should – Will was asking after you when I spoke
to him yesterday. Little Phoebe is apparently the star
striker for the girls' football team.'

She turned the steak, the sound of sizzling and spitting
fat punctuating the conversation with a full stop.

Neither said anything for a moment.

'V.' He tore at the label on his beer bottle, shredding it
into tiny bits of damp paper.

She drained her glass.

'I just wanted...' he continued and moved towards
her, wanting to reach through the mist surrounding her.

'Right, dinner's ready, I think,' she interrupted and
lifted the steaks onto a board to rest, the steam obscuring
her expression. 'Oh, I nearly forgot to warm the sauce.'
With her back to him, she busied herself with pouring
a mushroom sauce into the steak pan. As it began to
bubble, she reached into the cupboard for plates, then
held them out to him.

His fingers brushed hers as he took the plates from her, but she didn't react.

While he set the plates out, she opened the oven, lifted the steaming baked potatoes out and carried them over to the table.

Tom said, 'I'll bring the steaks and salad over, you sit,' but even he could hear the flatness in his voice.

She went to the fridge and refreshed her glass. Now it was his turn to bite his tongue.

As she sat down, he reached across the table and gently took hold of her hand. She recoiled again, but he persevered in trying to catch her eye, daring her to look at him. 'Thanks V, this looks great – and means a lot.' Their eyes met for a second, relief showing in his; he couldn't read hers.

'That's okay,' she said with forced joviality. 'Nice to get back into the kitchen.'

Tom handed her the salad bowl and began to cut into his steak. 'Will was saying it's Penny's fortieth next weekend? Did we get an invite to that?'

She avoided the question. 'I had a very strange – well, funny really – run-in with Felicity today.'

His hand paused in mid-air, the steak dripping blood onto the white plate.

'Oh?'

He lowered his fork without eating.

She frowned. 'Is your steak okay?' Was that feigned innocence on her face? He couldn't tell. Just his paranoia? Is this why she had made dinner? To confront him? Felicity's claim that Veronica knew about them echoed in his ears.

'Yes, yes, perfect,' he replied, his voice sounding strangled. He busied himself with the mushroom sauce.

'Anyway, so last night you know I was out with Scarlet. We went to the new place on the high street, which was great. We should try it sometime. I admit we had far too much wine and my shoes were killing me by the time we left. You know, those grey ones with the red bows that I haven't worn for ages?'

Tom was staring at her intently now, his steak forgotten. This was the most she'd said in months.

'So I walked home barefoot and I must've dropped my shoe at some point, because Felicity found it in the park this morning when she was on her run. But the funny part was that it had been mauled by a fox! Scarlet and I were laughing about it earlier, saying how there are some very well-dressed foxes in this neighbourhood.' She chuckled again.

He tried to rearrange the choked expression he knew he was wearing. Irrationally, part of him was still expecting some sort of accusation, perhaps that Felicity had finally confessed their affair after what she's said on the phone the other day about suspecting that Veronica knew. His heart was hammering in his chest and the belt had tightened another notch.

'What did Felicity say?'

'Oh, she was loving the whole episode, as you can imagine. Lording over me the fact that she had made such a discovery. Anyway, I put her in her place.' He watched her closely, looking for any clue as to whether she knew. She looked up at him, then said, 'It's a real shame about the shoe, but I guess you had to be there to see the funny side.'

Tom smiled tightly. 'I guess so.' He couldn't read her. 'What did you say to her then?'

'Oh, it's not important.'

He let out the breath he didn't realise he was holding as she changed the subject.

The rest of the meal passed in a series of pleasantries and polite small talk. Veronica asked Tom about Gerald and he said that he had passed on her best wishes. They then turned to current affairs, touched on the economy, discussed strategies for the Middle East – she seemed surprised to hear that various wars were unfolding around the world and said, 'I hadn't noticed above the sound of the gunfire in my own head.'

Her honesty jolted him. He reached across the table to take her hand. 'You know, the counsellor I've been seeing has really helped me to begin working through—'

She pulled out of his reach abruptly and stood to clear the table, signalling the end of the dinner and the conversation. He sighed, then went to help her, the chores completed in silence. It was becoming apparent that they had both pledged silent allegiance to not talk about what he clearly wanted to and she clearly did not.

Later, as they lay in bed, Tom hesitantly reached for her for the first time in months and he wanted to think that it was affection and honesty that propelled her to respond this time, but part of him recognised that it was more likely the wine warming her into it – and a sense of duty. He tried not to let his mind draw comparisons with Felicity, hating himself all over again for his betrayal.

The house is in darkness and I have complete freedom of movement. I've done this before, quietly moving between the rooms as they sleep, her plush, fancy carpets cushioning my footsteps. The moonlight illuminates the framed photographs above the fireplace in the lounge and I pick one up. My thumb fits perfectly over her face in the photo, blocking her from view. I replace the photo, leaving remnants of a thumbprint behind to smudge her features.

I move soundlessly into the kitchen and note the evidence of a shared meal: two empty wine glasses; a jug with the drips of a creamy sauce on the lip; two plates stacked and waiting for the dishwasher to finish its cycle, with blood from the dinner now cold and congealed. I don't really feel anything as I take inventory of it all.

I have learnt on my previous expeditions that it is best to creep along the edge of the stairs, close to the wall, to avoid creaks and floorboard groans. The main bedroom door is ajar. It yields to my touch and I glide through the ghostly light filtering through a gap in the curtains to peer down on them.

She is turned away from him, perched on the edge of the mattress with the covers pulled up to her chin, stiff and unmoving like a corpse. He is spread out, lying on his back with his mouth open, his breathing coming deep and raspy, as though his nose is blocked. I consider them for a moment, then take in the room around me.

It is as bland as I imagine their relationship to be, made even more so by the grey shadows of night-time, with no splashes of colour to suggest any hint of passion or frivolity lying beneath the surface.

The bathroom door is standing ajar and I can hear the overhead fan whirring gently, the sound masking my movements. I head towards the shower with my arm outstretched. My finger squeaks lightly as it traces shapes into the faint soap scum marks. I stand back to admire my work as a ghost of a smile plays on my lips, then I retreat.

I take a moment to sit in the chair next to the bed, perfectly still, watching over them again, marvelling at the depth of cold detestation that floods through *me, coupled with the hedonism of knowing that they do not suspect a thing. Nothing would thrill me more than to... No, a better idea comes to me and I return to the bathroom, knowing exactly what I will find in the bathroom cabinet.*

I retrace my steps and leave as soundlessly as I entered.

Veronica

In the first few seconds of consciousness, everything is as it should be. The sun is shining outside the window, the day is full of promise, Tom is making tea downstairs, and Grace is happily playing outside my bedroom door, her bird-like voice talking animatedly to her teddy as they scale the mountain that is the bannister. For one brief moment, I believe everything is normal. For ten delicious seconds, I am happily disoriented, not entirely sure what day it is. Then glaring reality swallows me whole, quickly followed by the sense that I had failed again last night.

Okay, so I had certainly made more of an effort with my husband than I had in months, but I was expecting to feel a small sense of achievement at least; instead, I felt just as empty as before.

Sure, we had eaten together, slept together, for all intents and purposes acted like any normal, happily married couple would, but for most of the evening I had felt like I was holding in a scream.

Last night, as I lay in the dark listening to his breathing slow and feeling his arm thrown casually over me, I wanted to feel warm, loved and safe, but instead I felt like the weight of his arm was crushing me, trapping me in this bed, marriage, reality. I had lifted his arm gently and turned on my side, curling into a tight ball and shifting my body as far over to the edge of the mattress as I could until there was an expanse of white sheet rapidly cooling between us. That had felt better and I finally fell asleep.

Tom had left early as usual, but not before he had brought me a cup of tea and a biscuit in bed and gave me a light, but lingering kiss on my brow. Little gestures I remember from before.

I took longer than usual to get up, slowly sipping the tea and chewing the biscuit, which tasted like cardboard in my mouth. Eventually I forced myself into the shower and stood under the hot spray.

Then I saw it. Cold goosebumps sprung up over my skin. I turned the water even hotter until it was unbearable, in the hope that it wasn't real, but I couldn't get warm and the billows of hot steam fogging every glass surface served only to accentuate the ghostly message low down on the glass shower screen in front of me. Childish letters spelling out 'Grace' had appeared with a smiley, almost lunatic face drawn underneath. I couldn't believe Tom hadn't noticed it when he had showered earlier. Unless he had written it? No, surely not. I smeared my hand through the spectral image before shutting off the torrent of water, keeping my eyes down in case there was more to see – or nothing to see at all.

I felt sick to my stomach. Lethargy wanted to propel me back into bed, but I resisted, knowing that if I gave in to the feeling, I wouldn't get up again. Instead, I stood in front of the rows of bright colours and fabrics in my wardrobe, before finally settling on my usual dull attire. I had good days and bad, never knowing what to expect from one to the next; the signs were that today would be a particularly bad one.

Every footstep down the stairs felt wooden and heavy, but I forced one foot in front of the other. Then I realised that I would be late for the school run if I didn't give myself a shake, which kick-started a flurry of activity: shoes, coat, brushing hair, putting a presentable face on for the world. I emerged into the weak sunshine and the familiar scene of rushing mums, dawdling children and busy traffic, and paused on the front step to take it all in. I could hear the school bell ring from my house. That bell had brought Grace and I running into the street on many previous mornings.

I stepped into the throng of rushing mums and followed their path to school, reached the gates, watched the children stream in, most without a backward glance to the parents they were leaving behind, then took a slow walk back home.

As I approached the house, I could see Felicity leaving her door in a storm of activity, well after the bell had rung, coats flapping, Tabitha dragging her bag with a sulky look on her face. I withdrew out of sight behind a parked minivan until she had passed. I didn't want to talk to her, partly in case I blurted out what I had seen in the shower. She would think I had lost it completely.

I let myself into the house and stood for a moment, listening to the silence. Then I set about cleaning the kitchen after my culinary attempts of the previous evening, removing every speck of dust and smear of grease, occasionally glancing out of the window as my neighbours went about their routines. With the windows still open, the quiet was punctuated at regular intervals with the sounds of south-west London: planes flying overhead at regular intervals; emergency vehicle sirens in the distance; playing, shrieking and laughter as the playground nearby filled and then emptied with the school routine.

By 11 o'clock, I had exhausted all possible household chores and sat in the lounge, hands gripping a cup of tea that had long gone cold, staring at nothing but the pictures in my head.

With jarring insistence, a shrill ringing interrupted the stillness. The home telephone in the hall. Very few people used the home number any more. My heartbeat shifted up a gear, remembering previous phone calls on this line. It was rarely good news. I put my mug down on the table and approached the phone, as though any sudden movements would make it strike out at me like a viper. My hand hovered above the handset, then slowly lifted it.

'Hello?'

'Hello, is that Mrs Pullman, Grace's mum?' a polite, efficient female voice filtered into my ear.

My heart started to race as the floor dropped away from my stomach.

'Yes?' I said, my voice cautious.

'Oh, hello there. I'm calling from the Richmond Music Trust – you applied for piano tuition for your daughter... from my notes quite a while ago, it seems...' I could hear the faint rustle of paperwork in the background. 'We got your message asking for an update and I'm just getting in touch to let you know that a space has become available if Grace is still interested? I'll send out a letter with all the details, but since you phoned last week anyway, I just wanted to let you know.'

I sat down heavily on the stairs, clutching the handset with white knuckles, my breathing shallow.

'Mrs Pullman?' the voice persisted.

'Um, yes... I, er... she... I didn't ring last week.'

'I'm sorry, it's a terrible line – did you say you didn't ring us? I'm sure you did, left a message?' the voice persisted. 'Anyway, how about I send you the details and you can get back to us – as soon as possible please – if she would like to take up the offer.'

'Um, yes... that would be fine,' I managed to choke out.

'Excellent, have a good day. Goodbye.'

I dropped the handset without saying goodbye, but remained sitting on the stairs. I focused on the dust dancing in the stream of sunlight filtering through the window. I considered the purple orchid on the hall table, its smooth, vivid petals velvety against the white walls, and made a mental note to water it. I noted the small flecks of dirt on the mirror that I had missed when I last cleaned it, avoiding my reflection, wide-eyed and haunted. I didn't want to consider the possibility that I was finally losing my grip on reality. Had I really phoned asking about piano lessons? When? After too many drinks one afternoon? And the shower glass? Who was that? Me again?

The doorbell rang once with purpose, jarring and loud in the silence. Through the frosted glass panel I could make out Scarlet's familiar, welcome shape in a haze of blurred purple spots. I quickly got to my feet and opened the door, wearing what felt like my first real smile of the day.

'Well, hello there!' she exclaimed brightly. Then she frowned, 'You okay? You look a little peaky.'

I stood to one side to let her in, then closed the door firmly behind her, shutting out the world.

'It's nothing, just a weird morning.' I replied.

'Want to talk about it?'

'I don't know. It might be nothing, just me being silly. Come on through, there's something chilling in the fridge,' I said, quickly.

She led the way, went straight to the fridge and grabbed a bottle of prosecco while I took out two glasses – a well-practised routine now.

'Tom and I had dinner together last night. Not out, but at least at the table together. It's been ages since we did that,' I said, avoiding what was really on my mind.

'Oh? How was it?' she asked.

'The steak was good – and I did an excellent mushroom and cream sauce,' I replied wryly as I tore the foil off the bottle, my hands trembling still.

She rolled her eyes. 'Come on, spill. Is that why you're upset?'

I twisted the metal ring, feeling it cut into my skin. 'No, yes… I tried, really I did, but I can't tell you what we talked about. It was…' I paused, trying to find the right adjectives as I pulled and tugged on the cork, '… polite, mundane.'

With that, the cork gave way with an impressive pop.

'But you did it. You sat next to each other and connected, even if only for a little while,' she suggested.

'Technically, we sat opposite each other.' I caught her exasperated expression as I poured the prosecco. 'Yes, okay, so maybe I'm feeling guiltier than I should. I just wish...' I stopped.

'What? Wish what?'

'Nothing.' I clammed up.

'Come on, Ron, wish what? You can't stop there.'

'I wish I had let him in more, you know? I know what he wanted to talk about, but I couldn't. I couldn't give him what he wanted, not yet,' I said. 'But...'

'What?' she probed, reaching for a glass.

'It's just... it felt like he was holding back too. Not like we normally are – you know, avoiding each other because we don't know what to say. It was more like he wanted to say something, but couldn't. I don't know what I'm trying to say. It just felt stilted for more reasons than usual. Maybe he didn't want to ruin all the effort I had gone to or something. Anyway, I need to focus on the fact that we actually did sit and talk, even if it didn't set the world alight.' I sighed, turning the metal cage over in my fingers. 'I just worry that if I start talking to him, then I'll never stop, you know? The words will just keep pouring out of me and I'll say the wrong things, then it'll be out there, real, and there'll be no taking it back. It's probably best not to say anything at all and to carry on living like we are.'

'But if you avoid it, you'll never get past it.'

'True. It's the emptiness that scares me the most though. I just felt deflated this morning, like someone had let the air out of a balloon, and sometimes I can't shake that feeling. It follows me around.'

'Oh come on, you're being too hard on yourself as usual. Chill.' She looked at me carefully. 'Or has something else happened to put you in this mood?'

I paused. 'Just some weird stuff has been happening lately – I've been finding things… I don't know, some days I think I'm just going mad, that's all. You're right, forget I said anything. Too much wine last night I think.' I plastered my smile back on my lips and took a drink. Something was holding me back from mentioning the phone call.

'Okay, well, I have news.'

'Oh? Go on then, put me out of my misery.'

'An old boyfriend got in touch the other day. I was mad about him when we were younger, but he hooked up with a friend of mine. I was heartbroken – you know, the usual story of teenage angst. Anyway, to get my revenge, I bided my time, then slept with him when he was still going out with her.' She was so matter-of-fact about this detail that I almost didn't register what she had said.

'That's harsh! For the friend I mean, not him.'

'Why? She knew I liked him at the time.' Scarlet shrugged. 'Anyway, she never found out about our fling – it was my sweet little victory more than anything else – but they went on to get married.'

'It's funny, that reminds me of Felicity.'

'Why? It wasn't her boyfriend I slept with.'

'No, it's just that when we were at uni, Felicity was actually supposed to be on a date with Tom and she asked me to go with her because she was nervous. He brought Ian along as a double date, but Tom and I hit it off straight away and Felicity ended up snogging Ian at the table.' I paused to take a drink. 'She was seriously pissed off with me the next day for hooking up with Tom though, but she had already arranged to meet up with Ian again, so couldn't really complain.'

'I haven't met Ian, but I think you got the better deal by the looks of the photos of Tom you have around the house. He's a bit of all right, isn't he?'

I smiled. 'Ian is lovely, but quite bland I suppose. His heart is in the right place though. Anyway, so how did this ex get in touch?'

'Through Facebook.'

'I have a profile, but haven't looked at it in months,' I admitted. 'I haven't had much to shout about lately.'

'You should just make stuff up like everyone else. It's all make-believe, all those status updates about how amazing their kids and husbands are, when in actual fact most of them are miserable, their kids are underachieving brats and their partners are having affairs. It's all about one-upmanship, another way for us all to feel inadequate. You must be curious though, about what people get up to?'

'Not really.' I swirled the remaining drops around my glass.

'You could post photos of bottles of wine – you're an expert on that and we are single-handedly propping up the prosecco export market,' Scarlet teased.

'And Ocado!' My daytime beverage deliveries were a regular occurrence now.

'Come on, where's your iPad? Let's have a quick look. It could be a laugh.'

The iPad lay abandoned in the lounge and as I half-heartedly went to retrieve it, I said over my shoulder, 'So tell me more about the ex then – what did he want?'

'Oh, just digging I think. Turns out he divorced my old friend recently and was wandering down memory lane – a bit of "what if", which is never a good idea. I'm more of a "no regrets" girl. Once you've made your bed, lie in it and make it as comfortable as you can or get a new one, but don't cry about it, you know?'

'Regret can sometimes keep you company when you're lying alone in that bed you made for yourself,' I replied as I came back into the kitchen and saw her roll her eyes.

'Lighten up!'

'Sorry. I don't know if this thing is even charged.'

Scarlet refilled our glasses while I turned on the iPad and opened the Facebook page. The cursor flashed above the password box.

'Don't tell me, you don't know your password.'

'My password is always the same for everything.' Since she was born, it had always been 'Grace01'. I would never forget it.

The Facebook page loaded and I noticed the 'notifications' icon light up.

'What about you? Any dodgy ex-boyfriends in your past?' Scarlet asked.

'No, not really. A couple of boyfriends, but nothing serious until I met Tom. He was considered the Golden Boy, I guess, so I won the star prize – or that's how I saw it then. I was the woman you would've hated, the one who got the guy. Funny how things work out. Look at me now: I don't work, I'm not much of a wife, I wear beige and hardly leave the house. Sometimes I think deep down he wishes he had ended up with Felicity instead of me.'

'His life wouldn't be any more peaceful though, would it? I bet she's seriously high-maintenance. Be careful, Ron, anyone might think you still love him if you care this much about what he thinks,' she teased.

'I do still love him,' I said emphatically. 'There's just… stuff…'

'Then change the "stuff" if it means that much to you. If you keep hanging out with me, maybe some of my fighting spirit will rub off on you.'

'Some stuff you can't change.' I had seen flashes of this stubborn positivity in Scarlet and part of me envied her for it. She was a woman of contradictions – more likely to change her mind than admit she may have been wrong about something, and dangerously loyal. I could imagine she was quite a force of nature as a young woman. She still was now and I loved her for it. I needed a tornado to sweep through my life and shake things up because the quiet was killing me slowly. But to make a change, you had to have the will and the energy; I was still lacking in both.

I turned back to the Facebook page in front of me. The notifications alert immediately flashed red in the corner.

'It seems someone has been trying to get in touch with me.'

I clicked on the notifications and opened up a friend request.

The kitchen swirled around me as I looked at the picture in front of me. I could hear Scarlet talking to me from a distance, but I was struggling to maintain my equilibrium.

Grace's face stared back at me. Someone had created a Facebook page for her.

'Ron? Ron, are you okay?'

I threw the iPad onto the kitchen counter and darted for the downstairs loo. The glass of prosecco came back up and I was left feeling shaky and cold, kneeling on the toilet floor.

Scarlet tucked her head around the door. 'Hey, what happened?' She crouched down next to me.

Could I tell her what was going on? Or would she think I was mad? No, I needed to process this myself first.

'Sorry, too much prosecco too quickly, I think,' I mumbled.

'Okay, I'll give you a minute and I'll put the kettle on.'

She pulled the door closed behind her and I took another minute to try and steady myself. My brain whirled and dipped, trying to comprehend all of the little coincidences of the day. Was someone trying to wind me up? Did I do this? No, I couldn't have. A little voice said, *Well, you do go on the school run still*, but I didn't want to acknowledge it. But why had Scarlet been so insistent that I look at my Facebook page? Did she have something to do with this?

When I returned to the kitchen, Scarlet was tapping away at my iPad.

'Let's look at Felicity's Facebook page.'

If she was acting, it was Oscar-worthy.

'No, it's just going to annoy me.' I wanted her to leave, but didn't want to have to explain why.

'Oh come on...' She pulled up the page, ignoring me. I took in some more air, not wanting to look at the screen but feeling compelled to all the same.

I pulled my eyes away from the red notifications alert to concentrate on the page Scarlet had opened. Felicity's thumbnail was a photo of her and Ian standing arm-in-arm against the backdrop of a beautiful beach. As Scarlet scrolled down, the status updates all seemed to involve how far Felicity had run or details of apparently regular date nights with Ian. Then Scarlet clicked on Felicity's photos and the timeline was full of images of Tabitha riding horses, hanging out with friends, eating ice cream on holiday, interspersed with Felicity and Ian in romantic clinches. She was very good at portraying the perfect wife and mother.

'Okay, that is nauseating,' Scarlet said, grimacing.

'Told you.' I was thoughtful for a minute as I studied the photo in front of me. Felicity was standing gazing up at Ian as he handed her a glass of champagne at a garden party. The tag was *My thoughtful, gorgeous man looking after me as usual*. I was surprised at the bilious hatred that bubbled in me and washed away the earlier trepidation.

'She thinks she's just perfect, doesn't she?' Scarlet said.

'I could tell her a few home truths,' I replied venomously.

'Oh, really?'

'I can safely say her and Ian are not what they appear in these photos.'

Scarlet's face ignited at the idea of proper gossip. 'Oh?'

'I don't want to talk about her.'

Scarlet looked annoyed, but I ignored it. My eyes

continued to scroll though the photos as we travelled further back in time with Felicity. Now the photos were more familiar and my face started to appear, smiling, happy. Then I saw Grace's face in a photo from one of Tabitha's birthday parties, grinning at the camera with a plastic tiara on her head and cake icing around her mouth. I quickly turned the iPad over so that I couldn't see any more.

'You keep alluding to this "thing" that happened. Am I allowed to ask what it was yet?'

Part of me desperately wanted to tell her, but would our friendship metabolise into pity if I did? And what about the niggling doubt still casting its shadow?

I plunged in, my voice small. 'I had a daughter.'

'Yes, I know – Grace.'

'She was in an accident last year.'

There. It was out and the ground hadn't opened up and swallowed me whole.

Scarlet was quiet for a moment, then leant over and took hold of my hand, breathing out as she did so.

'What kind of accident?'

'She was hit by a car. The driver was drunk at the time.'

'Wow. I don't know what to say.'

I shrugged, looked away.

'I wouldn't begin to know where to start dealing with something like that. Why didn't you say anything sooner?'

'I didn't want you to look at me differently. People do that. Once they know, all they see is that, like a black pity cloud hanging over me, like it's contagious or something. I want you to see me as more than my circumstances.'

'I get that. For what it's worth, I can't see the cloud, but I can see a true friend. I'm not going to ask if I can help or tell you I'm sorry – even though I am – because that won't help. But I can listen if you need to talk.' She patted my cold fingers.

'Well, I may need you more than ever in the next few weeks. It's her birthday soon – the first since the accident.'

I could feel my insides tugging and pulling, as though my head and stomach were in a jousting match.

'What about the rest of your family?'

'I don't have any close by. My parents have retired in Spain and Tom's family is miles away in Australia. They were all here after the accident, but I couldn't ask them to put their lives on hold for me.'

'Well, I'm here, whatever you need, but especially if you need someone to take your mind off it all. You shouldn't have to feel alone.'

'One thing I have proved over the last few months is that it is so easy to live like a hermit these days. You don't need to leave the house anymore.'

'That's a bit sad though, isn't it? And I wouldn't say healthy.'

'Sometimes it's necessary.'

'You know, if it wasn't for me, you'd be a right misery all of the time. Speaking of which, you need another night out – so tonight, Mrs Pullman, you're coming with me. We need to blow off some steam.' She pulled her best Austin Powers villain face, one little finger to her mouth. 'Life is too short to be good all the time, isn't it?'

'I don't know. Today has been hard.' I grimaced.

'Exactly, so yes, tonight! You have credit in the bank with Tom for last night, so ride the wave and use it. We'll go out, have a dance and a laugh, take your mind off it for a bit. It'll be great! You had fun the other night, didn't you?'

She came around behind me and put her hands over my eyes. I recoiled, not sure what she was doing and immediately ill at ease.

'Relax.'

I sat ramrod straight, barely breathing.

'Can you hear the music?' Her voice was really close to my ear and I could feel her breath tickling my earlobe. I turned my head slightly, but she said in a low tone, 'Na-ah, keep 'em closed. Just remember the beat and how it felt to let go the other night, the music reverberating through you, the sounds of laughing. It was fun, that's all. No thinking, no worrying. Now, open your eyes, refill that glass and let's do it all again.'

That was her answer to everything and I desperately wanted to feel some of her enthusiasm, even for just a moment, so I ignored the prickles of doubt and gave in.

Tom

As Tom put his briefcase down in the hallway and threw his keys on the table, he looked up to see V standing in the kitchen doorway. She was swaying gently on her feet, but he hoped it was because she was wearing ridiculously high heels and not from alcohol. She was dressed in a pair of skin-tight black jeans that he hadn't seen before and a purple top adorned with sequins that caught the light as she moved. He had to admit she looked amazing. Her hair was piled up, showing her long neck, and subtle make-up gave her a sense of drama. It was so unlike how she would normally dress that he was momentarily dumbstruck.

He recovered himself and said, 'Going somewhere? You look... amazing.'

'Yes, Scarlet and I are going out tonight.'

It was on the tip of his tongue to say 'Again?'

She teetered towards him and grabbed a wrap that was draped over the banister. 'Don't wait up – Scarlet wants to make a night of it.'

'Can I drive you somewhere?' He was suddenly nervous about letting her go. 'Where are you meeting her?'

'At the new Mexican place in town. It's okay, I've booked an Uber.'

'No, let me drive you. Please.'

'It's fine, really. You've just got home. Relax.'

'Wait!' He couldn't explain his unease. 'How much do you really know about this woman? Is she a mum from school? You're spending so much time with her...'

'No, she's not from school – thankfully – and I know all I need to, okay? See you later.' She seemed rattled by his question and moved to the door quickly, before pausing and turning back. 'But thanks – for worrying about me.' She kissed him lightly on the cheek, grabbed her throw and clutch bag, and opened the front door. As she was closing it, he could've sworn she said over her shoulder, 'Be careful not to wake Grace when you go up.'

He stood for a moment, his eyes on the closed door, willing her to come back and say she had decided not to go. He had an ominous sense that his world was shifting underneath him again, but pushed the feelings aside and headed into the empty lounge. The lamps were lit, but there was an air of abandonment, a lack of life. It was spotlessly clean, not an ornament out of place, but it had no soul. Tom walked over to the bay window and pulled the curtains aside to watch V walking down the driveway, her heels clicking faintly on the paving. His mind swirled in a hundred different directions, pulling him from last night to memories of when this room was full of colour and laughter, and back to tonight and her casual, throwaway comment.

He slumped into the armchair next to him and sighed as the silence of the house settled around him.

Shifting his position to undo his tie, he heard a metallic rasping sound coming from the armchair. He reached down the edge of the seat cushion and his hand caught on something shoved down the side. He stood up and lifted the cushion. Stuffed below were four pill packet sleeves, the pills all missing. He looked at the writing on the other side and recognised them as the sleeping pills the doctor had prescribed for V after Grace's accident. He thought she had stopped taking them; in fact, he had suggested she stop because he was worried about her becoming dependent on them.

He heard a car pull up. Through the gaping curtains he saw V get into it. The door slammed shut, the car pulled off and she was gone. Clutching the pill packets in one hand, he replaced the seat cushion on autopilot.

More movement outside caught the corner of his eye. Felicity was in her front garden, with two lurid orange traffic cones in her hand. The cones were a long dispute that had rumbled on for over a year. Never able to find a space outside her door, Felicity had started placing parking cones in the street whenever she moved her car. V and Tom used to laugh about it, especially as they knew it annoyed many of their neighbours who struggled even more to find parking spaces when the cones were out. Tom and V had off-street parking, which wound Felicity up somewhat in return. Now the humour of the situation was stale as Tom had listened to Felicity moan and rant about it far too much. She could latch onto a topic and suck the life out of it if you showed the tiniest bit of interest. That's what their pillow talk had eventually turned into: her moaning about middle-class trivialities and him fighting the urge to run screaming for the door. So why had he kept going back there? Because when she wasn't talking, she was a lot of fun. Because it was a good way of distracting him from his feelings of abandonment, ridiculous as they were at the time.

V mustn't have seen her when she left (or had chosen to ignore her), but Felicity would've seen V no doubt. Tom could just imagine her gossiping going into overdrive on the school run tomorrow as they all speculated about where V had gone, and he had another flash of momentary pride at his wife for getting out there and starting to live again. He was under no illusions about V and Felicity's relationship these days. There was an underlying current of tension that had probably always lain dormant, but was now fully awake. He didn't think it had anything to do with the affair. Rather, it was more likely that V had distanced herself from her old friends as much as she had her husband in a weird form of self-preservation.

He realised he was staring at Felicity, who had now noticed him and was summoning him over. He considered her for a moment, the pill packets still clenched in his fist, then reached over to pull the curtains together and headed into the kitchen, his thoughts in freefall.

V's iPad was lying face down on the counter and he picked it up while shoving the pill packets into his pocket. Perhaps her search history would shed some light on what was going on with his wife these days. The screen came to life and immediately loaded Felicity's Facebook page. He scanned her status updates with a sardonic shake of his head, then clicked the back button.

He froze in shock when the page created in his daughter's name filled the screen. Who had done this? Veronica?

Felicity's words rang loud in his head as he scrolled through the images and status updates. If V had created it, then Felicity was right and she really did need help. The updates made it sound like nothing had happened. Grace was apparently going to parties, taking part in music festivals and behaving like any 9-year-old girl would.

He turned off the iPad and sat in the silence once again.

*

The glare of the laptop screen illuminates my fingers as I pour over the websites, enjoying every minute of this retail therapy. I have added the credit card number so many times now, I can recite it by heart.

Toying with her has become a guilty pleasure, certainly more enjoyable than I originally anticipated. She is making it easy too, but it is time to turn the screws and ratchet up the pressure a notch.

The call about the piano lessons was a stroke of genius on my part. It will have rattled her, but this will ensure she starts to come apart at the seams. I add a few more items to my online basket and check out one more time, making sure her address is listed in the delivery details and not mine.

Once the payment has cleared, I go into the search history and clear it, including the activity on Facebook now that Grace has her very own page. No one would think to check, but it pays to be careful.

Oh, it's all so easy. Little steps to the precipice.

Veronica

I stood in the street for a moment, waiting for the Uber to pull up. The moon was full and bathing the street in silver, and I couldn't help feeling light in spirit now that I was out. The Uber pulled up to the kerb and I could see Scarlet in the back seat already. She was dolled up to the nines in a neon pink fitted top, skin-tight, black, leather-look trousers, and white heels. As I climbed in next to her, she wolf-whistled and I giggled.

'Looking hot there, girl,' she said, grinning.

I flushed. 'Stop or I'll convince myself to go back inside and change.'

'No, you won't.'

'Maybe I shouldn't go out tonight. Tom has just got home, he's on his own, maybe...' I looked back towards the house as the car pulled away, the weight of my selfishness now clouding over my earlier good mood.

'Stop, would you? Have a bit of fun – let's go and have a laugh, a few drinks, and if after a couple you want to call it a night, then we can. Don't pull the plug yet though.' She was throwing me the puppy-dog eyes again.

I hesitated a moment longer, then said, 'Oh all right. One or two then. But make sure I hang onto my shoes!'

The driver was watching me closely through the rear-view mirror, but I ignored him and looked out of the window at the people we passed. I couldn't help wondering what was going on in their lives. One thing my recent experiences had taught me was to never assume that the mask we show in public is the same face we wear behind our own front door. Sometimes there is a bigger fight going on inside than we care to admit and that, after noticing Felicity tonight, as she staked her claim to a few feet of tarmac for her precious 4x4 that had never seen a drop of mud, sometimes we stress about the little things too much. I looked over at Scarlet as she gazed out of the window and I had a moment of pure affection for her, my only friend. Then close behind that was a writhing worm of self-doubt: would she be there for me if tragedy struck again? Hopefully lightning doesn't strike the same place twice, but considering how distant I now was from my old friends, how did I know she wouldn't react in the same way? Or that I wouldn't? She had been supportive when she had heard about Grace, but could I take it at face value? She didn't seem to have a serious bone in her body.

Most of my old friends had taken the approach that

I would come to them if I needed to talk and that I just needed time. Others had struggled to find the words, preferring to retreat politely rather than feel any awkwardness. It was easier for them that way, but not easy for me to deal with the overwhelming seclusion, as though I was a lone black cloud in a perfect blue sky, with everyone hoping it would just blow over.

'You're quiet. Not stressing about something, are you?' Scarlet asked.

'No, just wondering where all these people go and what their stories are.'

'Sorry, love?' the driver asked suddenly as he peered through the rear-view mirror again at me.

'Oh, um, nothing, thanks,' I replied. He turned up the radio and I lowered my voice.

'I love a bit of people-watching,' Scarlet said, watching the sights in the street.

I sat quietly, aware of the driver's eyes flicking between me and the road. I met his glance and he looked away quickly. Scarlet babbled on next to me as we drove through the streets. I nodded here and there, letting her fill the silence. After ten minutes, the driver looked up to ask where we wanted to be dropped off.

'Outside El Chihuahua's would be good, thanks,' I replied.

The car pulled up to the kerb and we clambered out. As I went to close the door, the driver looked back at me and said, 'You okay, love?'

'Yes. Looking forward to a night out with my friend,' I replied.

'You go easy, okay? Be careful.'

'Um, thanks…'

'Come on, you. Let's get in there!' Scarlet said over my shoulder.

I gave the driver a quick smile, then stepped back as the car pulled away.

The bar area was almost full to capacity, with revellers swilling carnival-coloured cocktails. Scarlet led the way, weaving through the bodies in the general direction of the bar. Generic Mexican music played in the background and the air was heavy with citrus, masking an undertone of something acrid. As I drew closer to the queue at the bar, I noticed a neon sign towards the far end of the room that read 'The Dirty Sombrero', with an arrow pointing down some darkened stairs.

I leaned into Scarlet's ear and said, 'I wonder what goes on down there then,' pointing the sign out to her.

'Curiouser and curiouser,' she said, still surging forward.

We hovered near the back of the queue for a moment and, just as I was wondering how in hell we would get served, Scarlet grabbed my arm and pushed me forward roughly, saying, 'Get me something with tequila in it.'

I threw her a startled look just as I collided with a

tall man standing in front of me. He turned abruptly and glared at me as I stammered out, 'Sorry, I tripped.'

Just as quickly, his glare softened and he said, 'No worries, babe. Trying to get to the bar?'

I threw a glance at Scarlet, who gave me the thumbs up, before replying, 'Yeah, no chance right now though, right?'

He smiled, then said, 'Tell you what, when I get served, hopefully next, I'll order for you as well. How's that?'

'That's very sweet of you, thanks. Two Tequila Sunrises please.'

'You'll owe me though.'

'Oh, I'll give you the money obviously,' I said, affronted.

He chuckled. 'No, I mean the next time you're at the front of the queue, you'll have to get my round in for me.'

'Oh!' I said with a shake of my head and made a mental note to relax a bit. 'Of course.'

A small part of my brain had registered his twinkly eyes, dimples and the way he had leant in to be heard, his aftershave lingering between us, but the uptight, married part of me promptly slapped me back into place.

I heard him order three pints and the cocktails, so I scrabbled in my bag for my purse and pulled out a few notes to reimburse him. Scarlet stood to the side of me, scanning the room. Every now and then, her eyes would alight on a face and I could almost hear the gears turning as she considered the options in the room. I started to panic that she would end up meeting someone and would leave me to fend for myself. The idea caught in my throat. Then my knight in a shiny shirt turned back towards me with the two drinks in his hands.

'There you go, ma'am,' he offered with a smile.

'Thanks so much. Here...' I handed over the money, hoping he wouldn't argue about taking it. As it was, he happily accepted it, although protested that I had offered too much and handed a fiver back with the promise to look out for me later when his round was due.

I turned back to Scarlet and followed her towards the stairs I had seen earlier. She had spied an empty nook that we could settle into, with our backs to the wall and a perfect view of the revelry playing out before us.

'He was nice,' Scarlet said, pointedly not meeting my eyes, but with a cheeky grin on her lips.

'Very charming, but I'm a married woman and you are my chaperone. Don't get any ideas of hooking up with anyone cos if you leave me to my own devices, God knows what I could do.'

'Yeah, cos you're such a party animal,' she teased.

'You're right – I would probably slink off home for a cup of cocoa and an episode of *Poirot*.'

We laughed as I took a long pull on my straw. The cold, sweet cocktail flooded my mouth, making me wince. 'Wow, that's sweet. I can hardly taste the tequila.'

'There's probably none in there – they charge you for it, but put half a tot in. Just means we can drink more though. Or we switch after this and go for a naked tequila shot.'

'But then the drink is over too quickly, don't you think? One gulp and it's gone. Are we playing the long or short game tonight?'

'Oooh, look at you getting lairy!'

We clinked our glasses together and settled into perusing the room again. I noticed a few people disappearing down the mysterious stairs over the next half an hour, and could hear different music filtering up every time a door at the bottom opened.

'I want to know what goes on down there,' I said to Scarlet.

'So ask someone.' Everything was black and white for her, no anxiety about talking to strangers, fumbling her words or creating the wrong impression. I envied her that too. It was a new experience for me to be in a relationship where I was the envious one, and I wasn't sure how comfortable I was with it.

Our drinks were empty, and the inevitable fight back to the bar loomed. I scanned my immediate surroundings and couldn't see my aide from earlier but did notice a waitress weaving through the crowd wearing a Wild

West gun belt slung with bottles of tequila. I caught her eye as she poured some shots for a group of eager student-types, and indicated that we should be next.

'Naked tequila it is,' I said to Scarlet as the waitress finally approached.

She was a tiny slip of a girl, who looked weighed down by the bottles. She also had an enviable pair of legs poking out of a pair of crotch-skimming hot pants. 'How many?' she asked.

'Two please,' I replied, grabbing more money in the process.

'Authentic or gold?'

I looked at Scarlet for guidance, who merely shrugged in reply.

'It'll have to be gold, I guess,' I said uncertainly, handing over the cash.

'Okay, gold it is.' She grabbed two plastic shot glasses from a pouch on her left hip and, in a well-practised move, held them in one hand while deftly pouring with the other. She passed me the two shots, before spiriting a small tub from another hidden pouch containing a neat pile of lemon slices and a small salt cellar.

Scarlet immediately responded, 'No salt and lemon for me, ruins the taste,' so I waved away the waitress's citrus offerings.

A closer look at the shots revealed tiny flecks of gold leaf floating in the clear liquid, which reflected a rainbow of colours from the neon sign above us. I was mesmerised, watching the light twirl and dance, before Scarlet clinked her shot to mine and said, 'Bottoms up!'

The shot went down smoothly, then kicked back with fire as heat floated through me.

'Wow,' Scarlet said with a slight croak to her voice. 'What's next?'

The waitress had only just turned away from us before I was calling her back and ordering two more. This time she suggested we try it the 'authentic Mexican way', with a shot of hot sauce mixed with pomegranate as a chaser. I wasn't convinced this was entirely authentic, but Scarlet was well up for the experiment. Before I knew it, the waitress had shoved two shot glasses in my hand – one with the unmistakable smell of tequila filtering from it; the other containing a thick, alarmingly fuchsia liquid. With some trepidation, I knocked back the tequila and swiftly followed it with the chaser, which washed away the sting of the alcohol and left a sweet, but spicy and very pleasant taste behind.

'Now that I like!' I pronounced.

It was only once the waitress had weaved back through the crowd that I realised that in my haze of tequila excitement, I had forgotten to ask her about the downstairs bar.

An hour later and the evening had turned fuzzy around the edges. We had managed to worm our way through the crowd closer to the bar and had secured one barstool at the edge. Scarlet was happy to stand, one stylish foot propped on the bar rest, another cocktail cocked at the ready. I positioned myself on the stool with my back to the bar, while Scarlet looked over my shoulder and pointed out the interesting patrons.

I ordered a couple of packets of crisps and a bowl of peanuts, and we settled into the people-watching, concocting stories about the couples around us. Mid-sentence, I felt a tap on my shoulder and saw Scarlet raise an enquiring eyebrow.

I turned to find my drink-saviour from earlier smiling down on me.

'Hey there,' he offered.

'Hi,' I said with too much enthusiasm.

'I see you're in prime ordering location now, very handy,' he replied, indicating my barstool.

'I am indeed. Need a round?'

'That's okay, it's not as full up here now.' I looked around and noticed that the crowd was thinning. 'Everyone's heading downstairs, you coming?'

'My friend and I were talking about that before and wondering what goes on down there.'

'It's a basement dance club, a lot of salsa, a smattering of blues... It's a laugh. You should come down. Free entry until 11 p.m., but then you have to pay a cover charge, so best be quick.'

I looked at my watch and saw it was already 22:50.

'See you down there,' he said as he headed for the stairs.

I followed him with my eyes.

'So, a basement dance club. Fancy it?' I said to Scarlet.

'Do I ever! Let's cut some shapes, baby!' She grabbed my arm and propelled me towards the stairs.

It was all I could do to concentrate on not tipping forward on my heels with alcoholic vertigo down the dark, steep staircase. They weren't kidding about basement. It felt like we were descending into the depths of hell – the bass beat vibrated through our toes, neon fluorescence reflected off black walls ominously decorated with Day of the Dead skulls adorned with pink hair bows and smoking cigarettes. The air got heavier and thicker the lower we went. I pushed against a heavy black door at the bottom and burst into a kaleidoscope of colour and activity. The small room was crammed with writhing bodies, all bouncing to a salsa beat; our ears were immediately assaulted by laughter, shouting and merriment; and the smell of sweat and alcohol was intoxicating. I turned to look at Scarlet, beaming, and shouted, 'Perfect!'

We muscled further in and I noticed a small DJ deck set up in the corner, with a dreadlocked man spinning discs. We hovered in the doorway for a moment, taking it all in. The walls were pitted with crevices holding booths with miniature disco balls above each one that reflected neon shards of light off the dark walls.

Garlands of illuminated flowers and chilli peppers were strung across the ceiling, and on the far wall, a tiny bar was a hive of activity as people flashed money, knocked back shots and gesticulated loudly to the one waiter on duty. The wall behind him was shelved with what looked to be an infinite amount of different tequila bottles; that seemed to be the only thing on offer down here. I nudged Scarlet and indicated I was heading that way.

Bank card in hand, I attracted the overworked barman's attention, set up a tab and got down to the business of sampling what was on offer. Another shot down and Scarlet and I were tearing up the dance floor. The eclectic music moved from salsa to blues to pop classics to club. It was exhilarating. I spotted my new friend across the room and he acknowledged me with a raised shot and a wink before he got down to the serious business of gyrating against a young blonde in a tight vest. Surprisingly, my heart fell, but then the song changed and an eighties classic began to play and my disappointment was immediately forgotten. Before long, sweat pearled my brow as the tequila loosened my limbs. The balls of my feet ached in my shoes, but I was in my own world, swirling to the beat.

We took a change in the tempo of the music to look for a booth. As luck would have it, a group slid into their jackets just as we were scouting around, so we manoeuvred into their vacated seats and spread ourselves out.

'This place is wild!' I shouted at Scarlet, grinning infectiously. My ears buzzed – from the music or tequila I wasn't sure – and my heart was pounding in my chest. We'd been in the booth all of five minutes before a man sidled in next to me.

'Hey,' he said, pressing close up to my side. I moved over. 'I've noticed you hanging out. Having a good time?'

Scarlet watched with narrowed eyes from across the table. I took in his interested face, with a thick hipster beard obscuring most of it and making his expression difficult to read. His lips were thin and dry amongst the facial hair.

'Yeah, we're having a good time. You?'

'Yeah, I am.' His voice was heavy with hidden meaning.

I longed for another drink, just to give myself something to do to avoid his intense stare.

He leaned into my ear unnecessarily. 'You wanna go get some air?'

'Not really, I'm okay here, thanks.' I shifted over again and was now trapped into the corner of the booth.

'I was watching you dance – looks like you know how to move.'

Fingers of creepiness tickled the back of my neck and I concentrated hard on not grimacing in disgust.

'Look, I don't mean to be rude, but you're not my type. I hate to think what's lurking in that beard, for a start.' I could see Scarlet sniggering across the table. 'So how about you move on and leave us to our drinks.' My pulse was racing in my neck.

He narrowed his eyes, went to reply, then changed his mind and shrugged out of the booth without looking back.

Scarlet laughed out loud. 'Jesus! Persistent or what? Loved your beard comment!'

'I only seem to come up with these things when I'm with you! God, I need another drink.' I waved over a hovering waitress and ordered another round.

Once the drinks had arrived, I took hold of the glass and brought it to my lips. The acrid smell of alcohol hit my nostrils and I felt my stomach heave unpleasantly. I quickly slammed the drink back on the table and took in a gulp of stale air.

'Ugh, I feel sick.'

'You ok? Go outside for five – it's really stuffy in here. I'll keep the booth.'

I went to grab my bag from under the table and felt the handle catch on the heel of my shoe. Leaning over, I could see my personal detritus spilling onto the dirty floor – lipstick, used tissues, a lone tampon. I quickly gathered together as much as I could see before the nausea returned, then abandoned the bag on the table and staggered out none too gracefully towards a door marked 'Toilets' in the far corner of the room. It led to a long, narrow corridor winding past a now-dormant kitchen and two non-descript doors. Choosing the New Orleans-style image I thought looked most like a woman, although was very much open to interpretation, I pushed through into a dark cave of a bathroom. I rushed into the cubicle and closed the door behind me. Kneeling on the cold tiles, I waited to see if anything would come up, but the nausea had passed.

I emerged from the cubicle to be confronted by my own face in the mirror above the sink. My eyes were wide, pupils dilated, cheeks red with exertion. The reflection swam in front of me, at once in focus then a Picasso image of eyes and nose. I still needed air.

I left the bathroom and headed back towards the stairs to the outside and the crisp street air. It was deserted, with only a few parked taxis at the kerb waiting for the bars to close and their night-time trade to kick in. I wandered down the street a little way, breathing deeply and feeling my dizziness subside and my pulse slow.

I turned to head back to the bar, but felt a large hand grab my arm and spin me around. The beardy guy towered over me and, catching me off-guard, I felt him pull me roughly towards a small alley next to the bar door.

He leaned into me, his weight pressing me against the brick wall, and my heart rate inched back up in giant leaps. His breath was sharp with alcohol.

'You think you're a bit of all right, don't you?'

I was struggling to compute what was happening. I considered the flaky skin on his lips, watched as if in slow motion as they came closer and I felt him press them against my mouth. I could feel his tongue trying to force its way into my clamped lips. It wasn't erotic or exciting, if that's what he was aiming for. His hands started to roam over my body, searching for a way in, and I felt my blood pump faster as I realised I may be in a bit of trouble. One arm then pinned me tightly across the shoulders to the bricks as his other arm carried on roaming.

I didn't feel scared though. On the contrary, adrenalin suddenly flooded through me like a hit of caffeine and I felt more alive and in control than I had in months. If he was hoping to terrify me into submission, he'd picked the wrong night.

He pulled back to look at my face, searching for the anguish and dread that he needed to see, but the wide, demonic eyes that looked back threw him momentarily off guard. In that second, his grip loosened and I twisted free. The anger that had been bubbling under the surface for months rose up with ferocity and I felt myself jab the flat of my hand up and under his nose. Blood immediately flowed down into his beard and he staggered backwards, his hands clasped over his injured nose.

'Fuck!'

I moved towards him and pushed him back against the opposite wall, then went in low and grabbed his crotch in an iron-clad fist. He exhaled sharply and he released his nose to grab at my fingers.

'You don't know who you're messing with. I've had to deal with a lot worse than the likes of you recently, so if you want to come out of this with both balls still in place, you'll back away quietly.'

'Fucking bitch,' he spat at me.

I gave a squeeze of my hand for emphasis and relished the strangled groan that escaped from him, before I let him knock my hand away and stagger off into the night.

The grin on my face felt frozen in place as I turned and headed back into the bar.

I returned to the booth, but Scarlet wasn't where I'd left her. The lurid skulls painted on the wall, with their cavernous eyes and menacing grins, peered down on me lasciviously, making me feel twitchy and watched. I was still high on the adrenalin and blood rushing through my body and wanted another drink to extend the feeling. I felt alive, strong, dangerous – poles apart from the numb emptiness of the past year.

The crowd had thinned and waiters were starting to stack the chairs on the tables. Looking around, I saw Scarlet sitting on the bar, legs dangling, singing loudly to 'Piano Man' by Billy Joel. I floated up to her, performing an impromptu expressionist dance routine across the floor and laughing hysterically. A few of the clean-up staff were watching me with wonder – or disgust. I didn't care. I leaned in and told Scarlet about the Beardy Man and she high-fived my bravado like a high-school cheerleader. She jumped down to join me and we weaved and swayed around the dance floor.

Eventually, when I staggered and fell against a table, one of the waiters gesticulated to an unseen body and a big, burly, suited man emerged to casually suggest he call us a cab, which I accepted with an exaggerated sigh and booing from Scarlet. I tried to focus on my watch face and I think it said 03:19, but I couldn't be sure.

We grabbed our bags and lurched up the now fiercely lit stairs, through the empty bar above and out into the chilly night air, the man holding a steadying hand in the small of my back. This time, the cold air slapped me full in the face and everything went blank, due to a lethal combination of alcohol and shock I expect.

The next thing I knew I was pulling up in a cab outside my house. I found some cash in my purse and handed it over, before trying to scrabble out of the car with a bit of forceful help from Scarlet and the driver, who helpfully said, 'Straight in, miss. And watch yourself.' He didn't hang around to make sure I was okay but sped off, possibly in case I threw up on him.

I offered to walk Scarlet home, and she replied that she would then walk me home, at which point we collapsed in hysterics at the idea of us walking to and fro between our houses, but never finishing the journey, like a warped *Alice in Wonderland* satire – 'Curiouser and curiouser,' she had said earlier. Indeed, it did sometimes feel like I had fallen down a perverse rabbit hole.

It was all we could do to stand up; as it was, we were using each other as stabilisers. Before staggering off in the opposite direction to me, Scarlet spotted Felicity's perfectly placed parking cones ready for duty. She looked at me, winked naughtily and tiptoed over to the cones while loudly shushing me with a finger to her lips. I teetered over, giggling.

'Have you got any make-up on you?' she asked in a loud drunken whisper. She grabbed one of the cones as I sat down heavily in Felicity's perfect plant pot of pansies and lavender, which fitted my bottom perfectly and was astonishingly comfortable.

I found some bits of old, abandoned make-up in the back pocket of my handbag and Scarlet began applying eyeliner, mascara and eye shadow in the shape of a crude face to the orange plastic, all the while with her tongue poking from her mouth in concentration. Her face reminded me of someone, but I couldn't think who in my intoxication.

In a final flourish, I handed her the red lipstick lifted from our first outing together and she added a demonic, grinning mouth to the mask. She stepped back and presented the cone to me with a 'Ta-da!'

It looked sinister and evil – a huge smiling but crooked red mouth, big black-rimmed eyes with heavy blue lids and rosy cheeks.

She staggered over to Felicity's front door and placed the cone on top of the perfectly trimmed olive tree that stood to the side. I pushed with my feet to stand up, but instead heard an alarming cracking sound and felt the tub give way underneath me. Scarlet roared with laughter as I hit the ground hard, then held out a hand to try and help me up, but we had both gone beyond hysterical laughter. The exertion of standing proved too much to bear as the taste and smell of tequila rose in my nostrils. I suddenly retched and vomited right onto Felicity's doorstep. Horrified, I stepped back, just as the outside light above her door illuminated. We turned on our heels and scrambled to hide behind the nearest car.

As I crouched on the ground, Scarlet handed me my bag, gave me a quick thumbs up, proudly proclaimed, 'Nice one!' then turned and disappeared into the night. I leopard-crawled towards my own door and darted inside without a second glance.

The throbbing in my head woke me and I struggled to peel open my eyes. There was a distant ringing in my ears and I felt like I was lying under a very large, heavy object. I looked over to Tom's side of the bed, but it was empty.

Slowly, body consciousness filtered in. I appeared to be naked from the waist down, my jeans and knickers tangled together in the middle of the bedroom floor, but was still wearing my bra and top. My necklace had wound around my throat and threatened to garrotte me. One shoe lay abandoned in the middle of the cream carpet and I could tell from my desiccated eyes that I had scrambled into bed without removing my contact lenses.

I peeked over at the clock on the bedside table and it took a few seconds before the numbers came into focus. It was already past 10 a.m. I couldn't remember what time I had got into bed.

I slowly pulled myself up to sitting, then wished I hadn't as the room kept moving around me. Nausea hit me and a foul-tasting burp rose in my throat. I launched myself towards the bathroom and made it just in time before I threw up violently into the toilet. Once the heaving had stopped, I knelt, then lay on the floor with my burning cheek against the cold tiles. My head was pounding more than ever with the exertion – a steady, rhythmic thud behind my eyes. I peeled the dehydrated contact lenses from my eyes and threw them into the toilet bowl, then lay still again.

I don't know how long I stayed there. It felt like hours; the tiles weren't cold against my cheek any longer, but I was shivering.

Eventually, I dragged myself to standing, wrapped

my mouth unceremoniously around the tap in the basin and swilled brutally cold water, before drinking as much as I could handle without throwing up again. Then, on very unsteady legs and with one arm outstretched to steady myself against the wall, I crept back to bed and pulled the covers over my head.

When I next opened my eyes, I noticed a cup of tea on my bedside table, steam still uncurling comfortingly. The fog in my brain was lifting by small degrees. I could hear distant sounds of Tom pottering around downstairs. My stomach dropped and a thin casing of shame fell over me at the thought of explaining myself – again.

I sat up slowly, rearranged the pillows behind my still throbbing head and reached for the tea. As I brought it to my lips, the faint smell of milk made my stomach lurch again and it was all I could do to get the cup back on the table without spilling it before I was propelling myself to the toilet again. This time nothing came up, but the retching seemed to continue for ages.

I was left on my knees panting, tears of exertion running down my cheeks and the smell of alcohol in my nostrils. I wiped my face and this time I crawled back to bed, the act of standing proving too challenging.

Propped up against the plump pillows again, I closed my eyes and tried to remember the details of the night before. Some of our conversations filtered back to me and made me chuckle despite my condition. I vaguely remembered someone offering to call us a taxi. I also remember walking relatively steadily to the door of the bar, then feeling the cold night air hit me like an ice sheet. After that, the details faded into misty uncertainty, but the cold air had clearly brought my inebriation rushing to the surface. I reached once more for the tea, hoping the caffeine would settle the tremor in my hands as I tried to dredge up what I had done next.

An image of the Beardy Man and his scaly lips pressed against mine reared up and coldness washed over me, quickly followed by the heat of anger. I pushed on past and conjured up flashes of other moments – the taxi journey, snippets of conversation, terrible singing – and then the memory of the parking cones and my special gift for Felicity rushed in along with mortification.

I sighed as a voice in my head started lambasting my behaviour. *What kind of a mother was I? What if Grace had seen me in that state? What if Beardy Man hadn't surrendered so easily?* Then I remembered Scarlet drawing the face – she could surely share the blame for that stunt, hilarious as it was at the time.

My thoughts were a jumble: Voice 1, the prosecution, accusing and scolding in Tom's rich, lecturing tone (the one he saves for telling Grace off); Voice 2, the defence, vocalising that I am allowed to let my hair down once in a while (not surprisingly in Scarlet's lyrical, righteous lilt). I couldn't remember the last time I had laughed as much – or suffered as much the next day – but I did have fun. Then my innate sense of responsibility, borne from nearly a decade of being a mother, kicked in and Voice 3 joined the baying crowd (sounding very similar to my own mother) to chastise me for getting that drunk and out of control, and putting my own safety at risk.

I dozed off with the voices arguing amongst themselves.

I was woken by the sound of the front door closing. Tom going somewhere no doubt. Looking at the clock, I realised that I had missed the morning completely and it was now just after 3 p.m. I lay for a moment in consideration, then decided that I was indeed feeling less shaky and nauseous. My head was still pounding though. Looking over, I saw that my still-full mug had been replaced with a tall glass of water and a couple of paracetamols. He had his moments, I'd give him that.

I sat up gingerly and reached for the glass. It was cold and wet and all I really needed right then. I threw back the pills and gulped some of the water, hoping it would all stay down.

Equilibrium partially restored, I gingerly climbed out of bed and headed for the shower, still feeling jaded and fragile. I turned on the water as hot as I could handle, in the hope of blasting some life into me, and kept my eyes averted from the glass screen in case there were more mist messages I didn't want to read. The steam started to make me feel light-headed after a while, so I emerged into the foggy air of the bathroom and groped for a towel. I dried myself slowly, my head pounding even more when I bent over to wrap my hair in the towel. Everything was proving a feat of pure exhaustion.

Downstairs I heard the doorbell ring. My first reaction was to ignore it. I wasn't expecting anyone and certainly didn't want visitors, not even Scarlet. It rang again, more insistently, so I grabbed my robe off the back of the bathroom door, tying it tightly as I headed towards the stairs. From the top of the staircase, I could see a shape through the frosted glass of the door, but it didn't look like Scarlet. I hesitated, unsure whether I had the energy for this, until the letter box flew open and Felicity's eyes peered straight at me. My heart and stomach fell.

'Veronica, open up!' she called.

Knowing that she had seen me, I descended the stairs wearily and pulled open the door. Felicity was standing on the step in her blue Lycra running capris and a ridiculously tight vest, eyes glistening.

'Felicity, what a nice surprise. Going for a run?'

'Veronica.' I could feel her bristling in front of me. 'We need to talk about last night.' Her voice was so cold, I imagined seeing puffs of her breath in the air.

I knew I had a choice to make: denial or admittance. *What would Scarlet do?*

Felicity tapped her foot, expecting me to say something, but I hadn't chosen my method of attack yet.

She eventually broke the standoff. 'You know what I'm talking about.' Her arms were folded tightly across her ample chest, making her boobs look like they were making a bid for freedom from the Lycra.

I felt a giggle rise in my throat.

'About what exactly?' I managed to say.

'I heard and saw you!' Her voice was rising and her boobs heaved in tandem, jiggling in her incredulity. I couldn't help but stare and wonder if one of them would break loose if she got really wound up. They were challenging me – and I accepted.

'Doing what?' Pulling my eyes away, I leaned against the doorpost and folded my arms in defiance. I was aware that I was still wearing a ridiculously bundled towel on my head and a robe in the middle of the afternoon. But gone were the days when I gave a shit what Felicity thought of me, it would seem.

She rolled her eyes and shrugged her shoulders melodramatically, with a huge sigh. Boob 1 and Boob 2 undulated. 'So it wasn't you drunk on my doorstep last night? You weren't defacing my traffic cones? I got the fright of my life when I opened the door and saw that face this morning!' Her mouth was pulled into a grotesque mask of disgust. 'Thank God poor Tabitha wasn't with me when I collected the milk this morning. She would've been traumatised,' she continued.

'Oh, I doubt that,' I muttered. 'She's probably seen – or done – worse.'

She threw me a stony look, then continued her rant. 'Then I saw what else you left! For goodness sake, Veronica. Not only did you break my flowerpot, but to vomit on a neighbour's doorstep is possibly the biggest insult you could come up with. We've been friends for a long time – I deserve better than this. Tom couldn't have been with you. He would never have allowed this to happen.' She gesticulated at me vaguely. Her voice had risen an octave, and Boob 1 and Boob 2 were dancing as her hands waved in emphasis.

I started to giggle.

'How can this possibly be funny?' she screeched.

'Oh come on, Felicity. If you think about it, it kind of is,' I said in between chortles.

'No, it bloody well isn't.' She was now shouting and using her height to tower over me in a manner she thought was threatening. But all it did was give me an even closer view of Boob 1 and Boob 2, making me snigger some more.

Then she started to jab at me with one long-nailed finger, while spitting words at me. 'Have you no shame? Think about your husband. Think about your daughter.'

And at that point, my mirth vanished as she overstepped the mark.

She continued jabbing away, 'I'm only pleased that I had time to tidy up your mess before Tabitha saw it. I would not have liked to try and explain to my impressionable young daughter – and your goddaughter – the seedy side of alcohol and what happens when a woman loses control, like you have so clearly done. She is naïve, innocent and bright, and I would hate that to be sullied by the likes of you.' Tiny drops of spittle settled on her lower lip as the vitriol dripped from her tongue. 'You are a disgrace, Veronica, and you need to sort your head out. It's no wonder our friends have washed their hands of you. I don't know who you are anymore. Grace would be ashamed, as I'm sure Tom is.'

Once was an insult; twice a challenge. I felt a snap in my head and, as if from a distance, watched my hands shoot out in front of me to shove at her, pushing her back and away from the doorway. She stumbled under the sheer force of my reach, then overbalanced on the step and fell hard onto the pathway.

'Don't you ever mention Grace to me again.' My voice was low and icy. 'Tabitha has never been a patch on her and you are not worthy of speaking her name, you paranoid, arrogant bitch. You sit there in your perfect house with what you think is a perfect daughter, looking out your window every day and passing judgement from the safety of your fucking Laura Ashley lounge,'

I spat back at her. 'We've been friends a long time, but you've always looked down your – quite substantial – nose at me. You've spent years putting me in my place and bullying me to make yourself feel better and more in control, but no more. I don't need a lecture from you – and I certainly don't need your pity, because you have nothing that I would want.'

My voice was a low monotone, almost unrecognisable, and my heart was pounding, the blood thudding in my ears. I reached down to where she still lay sprawled and grabbed hold of her jaunty runner's ponytail, then yanked her up as hard as I could. She shrieked, her feet scrambling to find purchase on the path.

'Now, I'm a little unpredictable at the moment and possibly slightly unhinged,' I snarled, 'so for your own safety, I suggest you get your bony arse and ridiculous tits off my front step before I slap you back to yours.' I released the ponytail with force and she retreated down the path, tears prickling her wide eyes.

As I glared at her retreating back, she turned around and said, 'This isn't over, Veronica. Not by a long shot. You don't know the half of what's coming to you,' all the while sounding like a movie villain.

I lunged towards her, my gown gaping open. I heard her shriek again and dart away, before I sneered at her, 'Oh, it's over. This so-called friendship is over.'

Then I turned away and slammed the door.

I looked down and saw my hands were shaking.

My mind was blank, refusing to compute what had just happened, but I could feel the adrenalin buzzing through my veins like fizzy bubbles. I pulled my robe tight around me, then walked into the kitchen and took a can of Coke from the fridge, thought for a moment, then replaced it and headed to the booze cabinet instead.

Pulling the vodka from the shelf, I unscrewed the lid and took a gulp straight from the bottle. The liquor burned as it hit my throat. I had never raised my hand to anyone before and in the space of a few hours I'd assaulted two people, both of whom deserved it, but still. My propensity for violence was starting to scare me. I took another healthy gulp, before wiping my mouth on my sleeve and returning the bottle to its place. The shakes were subsiding, replaced by a feeling of crackling electricity in my fingers.

I had the urge to call Scarlet. She would be proud of me. I headed back into the hallway to see if my handbag was there. I saw it lying on the floor under the hall table, but when I opened it, there was no phone inside. I cast my mind back to the bar and remembered dropping my bag at some point under the table, then scrabbling around for the bits that had spilled out onto the floor.

To double-check that I hadn't taken my phone up to bed with me, I raced up the stairs two at a time, my altercation with Felicity suddenly filling me with a burst of energy. There was no phone on the bedside table or dresser. I headed back to the top of the stairs and was about to bound back down when I was struck with a sudden case of vertigo on the top step and I had to clutch onto the handrail in case I toppled forward. I closed my eyes against the dizziness as a fresh wave of nausea hit me. Sitting hard on the step, I took a moment to breathe deeply and hang my head, the towel slumping forward and pulling on my hair, bringing some clarity.

Once the dizziness had subsided, I slowly descended the stairs, all the while hanging onto the rail, then grabbed hold of my bag again for one more futile search. Another thought struck me and I grabbed my purse and opened it. My bank card was missing too and I distinctly remembered handing it over for the tab earlier in the evening. With a sigh, I knew I would have to return to the bar.

I sat in my car for a moment across the road from the bar. My hands gripped the steering wheel and it took a second of concentrated thought to get them to let go. Nausea swept over me once more and I breathed deeply. So much for hair of the dog – the vodka felt like it was suspended in my throat.

With a mental push, I got out of the car and walked slowly through the dingy car park, my scruffy Converses kicking up puffs of dust and my still damp hair sticking to my cheek in the breeze. There were loads of people milling around, looking decisive, going about their business. I felt like I was in a thick fog, my head pounding, walking through treacle.

Approaching the bar, my eyes flicked to the alleyway briefly, then zoned in on where I needed to be.

I pushed through the glass doors and looked around. Snippets of memory flooded back, the conversations I had been involved in, laughing, lots of drinking. I was surprised at how spacious and airy the place was during the day; last night it had been packed full and resembled a cavern.

There were a few people enjoying afternoon drinks, but for the most part it was quiet. I approached the corner of the bar where we had taken up residency last night and looked around the chair legs and floor to see if I could see my phone lying anywhere obvious, perhaps kicked into a corner. No such luck.

I leaned on the bar, waiting patiently, and after a moment one of the bar staff emerged from the back room, the huge box of crisps in his arms obscuring his face.

'Excuse me,' I called as he bent over to put the box down.

'Yip,' he replied, standing up and turning towards me. He studied me for a second, then said with a smirk, 'You look how I feel.' My green-tinged pallor was obviously giving me away.

'Probably,' I replied. 'I think I left my bank card here last night? I opened a tab with it, then we kind've got distracted...' I trailed off, realising that I probably hadn't even paid my bill.

'Okay, it'll still be here then. Name?' he replied.

'Veronica Pullman.'

His voice was muffled as he rummaged on a shelf behind the bar. 'Nope, can't see anything, but it may be downstairs. I'll go and have a look.'

'Thanks – um, also... did anyone hand in a mobile phone?' I continued, a blush creeping up my neck.

'Jeez, you had a good night, didn't you? Let's see – the cleaners were in earlier, so they may have found something. Give me a minute.' He started rummaging again, then disappeared.

I sat heavily on the same bar stool that had propped me up for some of the previous evening, and let my heavy head fall into my hands. The strain of having to hold a conversation was starting to take its toll and I had an overwhelming urge to just rest my forehead on my arms and go to sleep.

Forever.

Just for a second I felt relief at the idea.

The barman returned and I pulled myself upright again.

'Good news: I've got your card. The bad news is you haven't paid your bill, so owe us £57. I also found a phone that was handed in downstairs, but how can I tell if it's yours?' He dangled the device in front of me, teasing, enjoying my obvious discomfort. I could see straight away it was mine from the crack in the top corner of the screen where Grace had dropped it once.

'I can tell you my number – if you look in the contacts at the top, it should list the number of the phone. Or if you look in the photo gallery, you should see some pics of my daughter and me.'

'Nah, you're okay, I believe you. I think you could do with going back home, so I won't torture you anymore. Besides, your daughter is probably wondering what mum got up to last night,' he said with a wink.

'I doubt it,' I replied.

He turned away towards the register to sort out my tab. Another wave of nausea hit and I almost had to make a run for it, but he handed over the card terminal, which forced me to focus as I entered my PIN, a number that was hard to forget, being the year Grace was born, but one I couldn't bring myself to change. Card returned, phone in hand, I muttered a 'thanks' and retreated from the bar at a sloth's pace.

I climbed into the car and slammed the door shut as utter exhaustion flooded over me. I just sat, staring out of the window, unseeing. Time ticked by – five minutes, ten. The phone that I had hastily thrown on the seat started to vibrate and ring next to me, and I looked at it snaking its way across the seat. I could ignore it. I wanted to. But it could be Tom wondering where I was and he deserved to hear something after last night.

I picked it up and answered it without checking the caller ID, then heard Scarlet's voice in my ear.

'Finally you answer! Before you say anything, I am so sorry. You must hate me – and so you should.'

Relief flooded through me. 'Why would I hate you?'

'Oh my god, do you not remember how we closed out last night? Me vandalising Cruella de Vil's parking cones; you hooching on her doorstep! She's going to kill you!' I could hear the twisted mirth in her voice and knew she wasn't sorry at all.

'She's already got to me today. It was bad.'

'Aagghhh! Tell me everything! I'm coming over.'

'I'm not at home. I had to go back to the bar and get my phone – oh, and pay the bill. Give me half an hour and I'll be home. Tom's not there anyway.'

'Excellent – hair of the dog it is!'

The smell of alcohol still in my nostrils, my stomach lurched in response.

I spent the erratic drive home going over Felicity's words in my head. The anger returned thick and fast, and my foot responded by pressing harder on the accelerator. One phrase kept repeating over and over in Felicity's self-righteous, squawking voice: 'Grace would be ashamed of you.' It repeated louder and louder until my head was screaming. Tears began to leak from my eyes and stream down my face; snot ran from my nose.

I couldn't see clearly and swiped at my eyes with my sleeve, all the while pressing harder on the accelerator in a bid to outpace the voices.

Suddenly I saw a flash of colour in front of me. A woman on a pedestrian crossing. I was going dangerously fast. I slammed on my brakes and stopped with the nose of the car just over the line. A car behind me blared its horn as the pedestrian glared at me through the windscreen, frozen in position. I raised a shaky hand in apology, waiting for her to be well clear of the crossing, before slowly pulling away again. I didn't want to think about how close I had come to hitting her. The shakes were back and I was relieved to turn into my own street a few minutes later, the tears shocked into submission.

I parked the car and stood resting against the car for a moment, taking some steadying breaths. Walking towards my front door, I noticed a police car round the corner and pull up to the kerb behind me. My heart started to thud. Had they just witnessed the pedestrian crossing incident? Good luck explaining this one to Tom.

A tall, young policewoman and a podgy, older man climbed out of the car and headed straight for me. I put the key in the lock and opened the front door, pointedly ignoring them in the hope they were heading elsewhere, then heard the policewoman say behind me, 'Veronica Pullman?'

I turned with what I hoped was a casual smile. 'Yes? Is everything okay?'

My cheeks were burning, but my hands were icy cold. I fiddled with the key as it stuck in the lock, resisting the urge to run inside and slam the door in their faces.

They were both holding out identification that I didn't bother to look at. 'May we come in? We've had a complaint raised that we need to talk over with you.'

'Oh?' I said, feigning innocence. 'Um, yes, please do.'

Freeing the key, I pushed the door open further, then stepped aside for them to pass. 'Please go through to the kitchen – do excuse the mess. I haven't had a chance to straighten up after my daughter had breakfast this morning.' I gestured with my arm towards the kitchen, then closed the door behind them and took another fortifying breath.

They stood just inside the kitchen door and I could see them glance at each other. I then saw what they could see: completely clear countertops, no sign of dirty cereal bowls or milk splashes, everything immaculate.

'Silly me,' I said with a chuckle. 'I must've been on autopilot this morning. Can I offer anyone some tea?' I sounded like I was hosting a coffee morning rather than about to be questioned by the law.

'Perhaps we should get to the point, Mrs Pullman. It seems that a neighbour has filed a complaint with us regarding your behaviour.'

'Gosh,' I jumped in, inwardly cringing and wondering

if I would start calling them 'chum' soon. It had to be bloody Felicity. My mind scrambled for purchase. Did they just see me get out of my car? Would last night's excesses have worked through my system by now? Did I put the vodka bottle away earlier? Oh god, if they were behind me at the zebra crossing, they would definitely breathalyse me. The irony of being done for drink driving. Unforgiveable. But I didn't have enough vodka this morning to be worried, surely? 'I'm really sorry about that, I was completely away with the fairies when it happened,' I said vaguely.

The two exchanged another glance. 'I think you may have misunderstood us.'

Inwardly, I kicked myself hard. Not the driving then.

I backtracked, 'I'm sorry, I'm not myself today. Not feeling well. Please carry on – I'm not entirely sure what you are referring to, to be honest.' My voice sounded unnaturally high-pitched in my ears and my smile was starting to ache.

'We're referring to an alleged assault that took place on your property earlier today.' The policewoman pulled a notebook from her vest and flipped it open, just like they do on the TV. I could feel the giggles building. What the hell was wrong with me? I clenched my fists and dug my nails into the palms of my hands in an attempt to focus.

The woman continued. 'A Felicity Green has contacted us to say you violently assaulted her during an unprovoked attack this afternoon after she was trying to resolve a matter of vandalism on her property. She claims you physically attacked her when she implicated you in vandalising her traffic cones and...' She paused and consulted her notes '...and flowerpot, and apparently vomited on her step. Perhaps you could fill us in on your version of what may have taken place?'

How were they managing to keep a straight face during this apparent interrogation? I took a moment to sit on the stool, more because my legs had started to shake than anything else, before saying, 'It was all a misunderstanding really. She accused me of messing with her cones – which I believe she is legally not allowed to use as it is – and because of the things she was saying about my family, she overstepped the mark and I admit I pushed her off my step so that I could close the door. As it is, I was the one who feared a physical attack when she pushed into my doorway. I had no choice.' I mentally crossed my fingers. 'It was all very unfortunate since we have known each other a very long time.'

'Mrs Green claims you were drunk last night?'

'It is no secret Mrs Green has a vendetta against me – I have no idea why. She was out of control, jabbing and verbally threatening me, and, as I say, I had no choice.' My nails dug further into my palms.

'Well, since there is no concrete proof of the vandalism and you are correct in suggesting that Mrs Green is legally not allowed to have traffic cones outside her house without written consent from the council, she has agreed to remove the cones and not press charges against you, but did ask that we talk to you about your behaviour. Living in close proximity to others is hard enough without a turf war between neighbours, Mrs Pullman, so we urge you to calmly talk through your differences with Mrs Green and come to some sort of understanding as we may not be as lenient in any future altercations. Are we clear?'

'Yes, yes, absolutely. I am mortified that all of this has happened. I intend to stay well out of her way from now on.' I hopped down from the stool, hoping to indicate that the conversation was over, but there was one more thing they had to say.

In a gentler tone, the policeman said, 'Mrs Green also filled us in on recent events as background and we suggest that you seriously consider talking to an objective party on the matter.' He pulled a card from his vest and held it out. 'This counselling service may help with that?'

I started at the white rectangle he was waving like a tiny flag of surrender, but made no move to take it. Instead, my nails dug deeper like claws.

He paused, then carefully placed the card on the countertop. 'It's there if you need it.'

With that, they turned and headed back to the front door. I made to follow them on wooden legs, fists still clenched, but the policewoman turned and said, 'We can let ourselves out. Have a good day and thank you for your co-operation.'

They disappeared through the door, but I barely noticed as it shut behind them. My eyes were trained on the card, sitting on the counter like a letter bomb. Rage coursed from my toes all the way up my legs until my vision clouded. I grabbed the card and threw it towards the corner of the room, then sunk to my knees. The hard tiles bruised my kneecaps and jolted me. I looked down at my clenched fists and slowly unfolded them, noting the angry red half-moons where my nails had imprinted the pale flesh.

As I sat there mesmerised, I heard from a distance the sound of knocking, then Scarlet's voice through the letter box.

'Ron? Are you in there? Open up. Was that the police?'

Scarlet and I sat in silence initially. I stared into a mug of black, swirling coffee, trying to get my head straight; Scarlet looked on with concern, but let me take a moment to calm down. Felicity had struck a nerve earlier and opened up a raw wound, but had now declared war by setting the police onto me.

'So?' Scarlet said with a raised eyebrow.

I looked up and briefly met her eyes before looking away again, not quite ready to start talking yet. I was still raging inside and felt a glut of bubbling lava every time I thought about Felicity. My mind kept returning to what she had said about Tom and Grace, and I desperately wanted to push it aside and let it go, but I couldn't. A cold sheet seemed to wash over me and I knew she was right to a certain extent, but I couldn't accommodate such thoughts yet as it would mean facing up to others.

Tom would never say if he was ashamed or hurting. By nature, he was one of the most non-confrontational men I had ever met. It was one of the first things I had loved about him: his ability to give everyone the benefit of the doubt, no matter how much they had wronged him, and to let things go rather than take people on. He was a listener, not an orator, and terrible at addressing anything that worried or angered him, but very empathetic. If Tom was hurting, he would keep it to himself so that he didn't make it harder for me. But then, wasn't I kind of doing the same thing? He hadn't even called me to find out where I was last night, instead trusting that I was okay.

Part of me was acting like a rebellious teenager, perhaps thinking that if I pushed him far enough, he would force me to start talking, and once those gates were open, we would have to let the flood subside before we could close them again. But another part wanted to keep the gates closed, scared of the torrent I would unleash.

'Oh, come on already! Tell me what I've missed!' Scarlet pushed.

'She set the police on me,' I said, turning back to

face her. One look at the expression on her face and we both collapsed in spasms of laughter and my anger evaporated.

When it finally subsided and we had wiped our eyes, she said, 'She really was pissed off then,' which set us off again.

The laughter eventually petered out. 'Not only did I assault Felicity, I had to do the Walk of Shame back to the bar to retrieve my phone and pay the tab, then I nearly ran over a pedestrian on the way home, only to find the police on the front step warning me to back off my neighbour.'

'So all in all, a busy day so far.'

'You could say so.'

'Well, I'm proud of you, girl. You let your hair down, you had a laugh, you blew out the cobwebs – and you stood up to that psycho bitch.'

'I think you'll find I'm considered to be the psycho bitch around here.'

'Nonsense!' Then her tone changed. 'But there is a lesson to be learnt.' She had come over all stern, like a teacher telling off a small child, and I felt my stomach plummet at the thought that I had disappointed her too. 'Never shit on your doorstep.' I looked at her, wondering if there was a punchline. 'But vomiting is a different story.' She cracked up with laughter again, clearly not feeling any remorse for our previous night's indulgences.

'Those bloody parking cones.' I paused, the giggling subsiding. 'She said some stuff though. It hit a nerve. I have to admit, I nearly did hit her properly. She goes on about how I need to get a grip and how my behaviour is out of control, then says I don't talk to anyone anymore and I'm cut off from my friends, but how many of them have actually talked to *me*?' My blood was rising again. 'In the beginning, sure, they offered sympathy and brought over cottage pies, but I could see from their faces that they were all pleased it was happening to me and not them.'

'Are you sure about that?' she asked.

'What do you mean?' Now was not the time for Scarlet to play devil's advocate, not with the mood I was in.

'Well, maybe, just like you, they didn't know what to say. Maybe you misinterpreted their motives. Maybe you were signalling that you needed time and space, and they were obliging, until it got to the point that they couldn't find the right way to talk to you anymore. They couldn't find the right in.'

I glared at her. Whose side was she on, anyway?

'I'm just saying that I think you may have built your defences too high. It might be time to start breaking them down and letting somebody else in. You let me, didn't you? Although I am very persuasive.' She gave me a Cheshire Cat smile.

'Yes, and I'm starting to wonder why I did.'

'Come on,' she nudged me with her elbow. 'You know you love me,' she teased. 'There is another theory to consider though.'

'Oh?'

'That Felicity has been spreading stuff about you, talking behind your back, maybe that's why everyone is avoiding you.'

'She wouldn't, would she?'

'Who knows? I think you have to be careful.'

I chewed my lip in thought. She had a point, but a whispery voice in my head was telling me to slow down. The voice that usually popped up when I let Felicity boss me around and talk over me was suggesting that perhaps Scarlet was just as threatened by Felicity as Felicity was by her. Suddenly I'd gone from 'No Mates Pullman' to two people pulling me in opposite directions. Maybe I couldn't trust either of them. Like Tom had said, how much did I really know about Scarlet? And even though I thought I knew everything about Felicity, she had proved me wrong on occasion.

Then, just as quickly, I felt traitorous for even thinking that of Scarlet, who had only ever supported me, helped me, kept me alive these last few weeks, even if I felt close to death today. She was about the only person I felt anything for right now; for everything and everyone else, I felt numb and hollow.

But there was still a niggling suspicion hovering in my subconscious that something wasn't adding up.

'You know, at some point we have to talk more about the accident. It would probably help,' she said.

I put my mug down hard on the counter and coffee splashed over the side onto the granite surface, sullying the immaculate white expanse.

'Not now,' I said firmly and stood up. 'Tom will be back soon and I have some explaining to do, so it might be best if you go.'

Scarlet stood up slowly. 'Okay. If you're sure, but you know where I am if you need me to listen.' She stepped forward to hug me, but I was stiff and unyielding in her arms.

Tom

'I told you to let it go!' He could see Felicity through her kitchen window as he paced up and down in the garden, his jaw clamped in anger, his mobile tight against his ear.

'I couldn't, okay? I have a right to tell her she's out of line – and you admitted you thought she'd overstepped the mark! I'm tired of everyone treating her with kid gloves. What if Tabitha—'

'Oh, for God's sake, Tabitha wouldn't give two shits and you know it.'

'Tom!'

He took a shaky breath and flung himself down into a garden chair, loosening his grip on the phone a little. He suddenly felt as though the air had been pushed out of him.

'I don't have to explain to you what she has been through,' he said in a quieter voice. 'And with the court case coming up, which she refuses to even mention… Yes, she was out of line, but I dunno… something is different.' He thought of how Veronica's eyes were sparkling again, but not in youthful effervescence; more like the lingering after-effects of an illegal high. It scared him.

Tom couldn't see Felicity now that he had sat down and it helped him feel more in control. She had wanted to have this conversation in person, saying she didn't want to be talking in hushed tones down a mobile line and through the bare wooden fence separating his life from hers. She wanted to be looking him in the eye, holding his hand, forcing him to see what was in front of him. But he needed distance from her. She wanted to get back together, but he wanted to put the whole thing behind him.

Tom had been under no illusions about what all of this had meant for Felicity when it had first begun: a juvenile game of one-upmanship and he hadn't minded being the star prize. But for himself, he wasn't so sure. What had started as a shoulder to cry on and a sympathetic ear had morphed into nothing deeper than pillow platitudes. He supposed it was really down to feeling needed, pathetic as that sounded. Felicity had played to his ego, stroked it and made him feel noticed. Then she had started talking about them having a future together, leaving Ian, him leaving V, and he had panicked. He hadn't really thought through what the affair meant – and he supposed that was essentially what this was, although the label left a bitter coating on his tongue and seemed to mock the years of friendship they had already shared. If it was serious, how long it would go on for and what the complicated repercussions would be – he hadn't thought through any of it.

In contrast to the pressure from Felicity, V had now become a solitary figure and as much as he reached out to her, she pushed him back further and with more force. He felt like an intruder in his own home most days, as though he was disturbing the stale air by daring to carry on with his life. But he couldn't give up on her again. She deserved better than this and he was in no doubt that this was wrong. She may not be giving much thought to his grief and heartache, but he knew she was so consumed herself that there was no room for him too. Yet.

'Anyway, I've told you before, we can't be together.' His voice was strong and convincing, even if his heart was hammering unpleasantly in his chest.

'Tom, I—'

'No, Felicity,' he said more emphatically. 'V needs me. It's obvious what she's doing. She's looking for attention, my attention. When she shut me out, I should've tried harder to get back in, but I didn't. I gave up on her too easily. She's my priority now. You have to accept that our time is over.'

Tom ran his hand through his hair, felt strands catch on his wedding ring.

'I need you too, Tom.' He could hear the panic building

in her voice, her words scrambling to find something to say that would fix this. She had said to him the last time he had emphasised they were through that she didn't want to go back to endless days of nothing to look forward to, mundanity, staring at Ian across the dinner table, discussing the weather and tutting at the news. She had said she would go mad herself. He felt himself bend, guilt manipulating him like malleable play dough between the will of his lover and enduring love for his absent wife.

'Felicity, look, let me sort things out here, get us through the trial, then we'll talk again, okay? That's all I can promise right now. I've failed. I've let her and Grace down. Now I need to fix it. Let me fix it.' His voice was strangled.

He cut the line and it went blissfully quiet. He sat for a moment, his eyes closed, his hand holding the phone lightly in his lap. Then his breath caught and he began to cry quietly, his shoulders lurching. He forced a shaky breath into his tight lungs and tried to get himself back under control.

What if he were to just disappear? Pack a bag and pick a destination far away. But he knew that was the coward's way out. He needed to accept responsibility for his mistakes and face them head on.

He stood on wooden legs and saw Felicity moving away from the window. Swiping at the tears sticking to his cheeks like a filmy skin of glue, he took another breath. The duplicity and unfaithfulness had completely consumed him lately, making him nervous, thrilled and ashamed in equal measure. Just because Veronica wasn't taking notice of what was going on around her didn't mean he hadn't stressed about keeping it hidden from her.

The thought of her finding out what he had been doing – with Felicity of all people – made a wave of nausea crash over him, followed quickly by a tightness in his chest, like a scream trying to force its way out. He sunk back into the chair, clutched his chest and hoped it was a heart attack.

Felicity

They gathered around the low table with their skinny lattes, frothy cappuccinos and strong Americanos. Someone had sneaked a bag of mini muffins onto the tray and they were all secretly relieved because they were starving, but couldn't admit the pull of the cake. A few of them were now persisting with Virginia's diet and even their coffees were considered contraband.

Felicity looked around the table. Across from her, Penny was regaling them with facts about the plans for her new kitchen extension – should she have painted or high-gloss units; what do they think about the hob on an island with a hanging extractor fan; was a separate utility room necessary? It was all rather tedious, but she feigned interest, making the appropriate nods and grunts at necessary intervals, while secretly wanting to tell her to just shut the hell up.

'I think it's the same colour as you used in your hallway, Felicity.'

'Really? Fascinating,' she said, dripping with sarcasm.

Penny's eyebrow arched. 'I'm sorry, Penny, I'm sure your kitchen will be amazing when it is done.' She reached for her cup and took a sip.

'So what's up with you then?' Virginia asked.

'Nothing.' She had been desperate to tell them about Veronica ever since Tom had snubbed her yesterday, but had patiently waited for her moment. 'Well, it's... I had a run-in with Veronica yesterday and it's been playing on my mind ever since.'

'What do you mean by a "run-in"? Like an argument?' Virginia asked.

'You two were like hissing cats when we last met up, so I'm not entirely surprised.' Zara said, then looked around the table as if for backup.

Felicity prickled, but kept a straight face. She sat forward and pushed her coffee mug away from her. 'Look, between us, I'm worried. It seems our old friend Veronica has been getting herself into trouble. I was actually shocked at what I witnessed last night.' She paused for dramatic effect. 'I had just got back from picking Tabby up from her dance class – she's doing her exam in a few weeks and her teacher thinks she has a very good chance of a distinction. Anyway, I was about to go inside the house when I heard Veronica's door open. There she was, dressed to the nines in sky-high heels, clearly heading out for some do or other. I could hear voices, so she was with someone but it wasn't Tom.'

'Where was Tom?' Penny asked, leaning forward with interest.

'His car was in the drive, so he must've been home. But she disappeared in what I assume was an Uber, then I noticed Tom staring out of the lounge window and he looked dreadful, I have to say. Completely lost.'

They murmured in solidarity.

'I feel so sorry for him. After all he's been through – often it's the men that take it the hardest because they just don't know how to channel their emotions properly, you know?' Virginia contributed.

'So true, they feel completely out of control when they can't fix a problem,' Penny murmured.

'Not that Veronica is doing a very good job of handling that herself, mind,' Felicity threw in.

'So what happened? It's great that she's going out, surely?' Zara said.

'Well, not necessarily. So it gets to the early hours of the morning, Ian and I were asleep, but as you know, since Tabby came along, I'm a very light sleeper—'

'You know, I'm the same. The slightest thing wakes me up these days,' Penny interrupted. 'It's like once you have kids, that's the end of sleep as you know it. They can sleep like a log, but not us...' Her voice petered out as she caught Felicity's stony glare.

'As I was saying, it doesn't take much to wake me up, but last night the noise in the street would've woken the dead. Car doors slamming, laughing, raised voices, it was ridiculous. So I woke Ian up – naturally he hadn't heard a thing...'

'Of course, they never do,' Penny commented.

'...He wanted none of it, said that it was probably just drunks on their way home and went back to sleep, but I thought it sounded like a familiar voice. I had a look out of the window and, as I thought, it was Veronica, pretty much leopard crawling to her door because she was so ratted! I watched to make sure she got in the house okay, because it was the decent thing to do, and eventually went back to sleep, but it took me a very long time. I felt dreadful this morning from tiredness, but that was nothing compared to how I felt after seeing the absolute carnage she had left in my front garden before she got to her own front door. And to think I was worried about her safety!' She took a satisfied sip of her coffee.

'Why? What had she done?' Virginia asked.

Felicity placed down her cup with authority. 'Well, as I opened the door to bring in the milk this morning, I found myself staring into the most frightening and grotesque face ever.' Felicity's hands danced in front of her face, exaggerating and punctuating every word. 'She had drawn a fully made-up, evil-looking face on one of my parking cones and positioned it right where it would scare me the most when I opened the door. I have to admit, I screamed when I saw it!' She sat back for emphasis.

Zara snorted with laughter; the others looked outraged and all turned to stare at her.

'Oh come on, you have to admit it's a little funny!' Felicity flicked her an icy glare. 'Sorry,' Zara mumbled.

'That wasn't the worst of it. She had completely trashed my beautiful flowerpot on the step – the lavender was annihilated. And...' she paused dramatically, 'she had vomited on my step.'

Indignant gasps rang out.

'Now that's out of order!' Virginia offered.

Zara still looked amused. 'Well, good for her, I say,' she said. All eyes swivelled to glare at her again. 'What?' she said, looking from one to the next. 'After everything she's been through, she's allowed to let her hair down once in a while. Besides, with the trial coming up, it would be normal for her to want a drink. I can't imagine the stress she must be under. Okay, so maybe vomiting on your front step was a bit much, but I doubt she did it on purpose.'

Felicity felt rage burning her throat. Zara was defending her? 'There are still certain standards that need to be maintained. We can't all just go running amok when we want to,' Felicity retorted. 'What if Tabitha had been the first to open the door? We have our children to think of and have to set an example.'

'My point exactly, Felicity.' Zara countered. They all lowered their eyes to their cups and shifted in their seats, except for Felicity, who stared resolutely at Zara.

'Well, I didn't find it funny in the slightest. I called the police.'

'You what? Why?' Zara asked incredulously.

'Well, I went over to confront her and ask for an apology and she went absolutely nuts on me! She shoved me so hard, I fell over, then she grabbed me by my hair – I thought she was going to kill me. She looked feral! I was petrified and I realised at that moment that she isn't all there anymore. I'm seriously worried about her state of mind. So I called the police and complained, hoping that would shock her into action.' Her voice had risen a few octaves in outrage, but she contained herself and slipped back into middle-class mode before saying, 'They came over the same day, very efficient, and suggested they just have a talk with her as, apparently, legally I'm not supposed to be using the parking cones, so she would be within her rights to lodge a complaint against me ironically.' She rolled her eyes. 'A bloody cheek, considering I'm not hurting anyone! Anyway, they had a word with her and brought up the idea of counselling and I hope the whole horrible episode is finished with, but it was galling to think the police could do nothing about it.'

The table was silent for a moment, then Zara said in a low voice, 'I'm sure she's doing the best she can. None of us know how we would react if we were in her shoes. For all I know, I would be locked away by now in a padded cell.' She picked up her spoon and stirred her coffee for something to do under the heat of Felicity's gaze.

'Perhaps Veronica should be.' Spears of white hot anger shot through Felicity. 'Someone needs to do something. She can't go around disturbing the peace, vandalising property and generally being antisocial. If it were me, I would want someone to step in. It's obviously a cry for help. Tom agreed with me.'

'You told him about it?' Zara asked, frowning.

'Yes, of course. He needs to know what's going on. A lot of it he doesn't see when he's at the hospital.'

'I haven't seen Tom in ages, actually. How is he doing?' Virginia asked.

'He's been doing so much better lately. We talk all the time and he's trying really hard to move on. He's seeing a grief counsellor and I'm very proud of how he's tackled all of this.' Her fingers played with the edge of her mug and she felt her cheeks warm. She was still annoyed with him after their conversation yesterday, though. She felt cheated – and the irony was not lost on her.

'How often do you see him then? I thought he was working crazy hours at the moment,' Zara said.

Felicity backpedalled. 'Oh, no, well, just in passing really.'

'But enough for him to confide in you,' Zara persisted.

'Well,' Felicity shrugged, 'he needs a friend and we have been friends for a very long time now. You know, I was supposed to be on a date with Tom the night he met Veronica, not Ian. She just manipulated things because she fancied him.' She knew she had said too much, but couldn't get her mouth to stop babbling. 'It feels like yesterday – and if things had played out as they were supposed to, all four of us would probably be better off.'

'You really think that?' Zara looked aghast.

Felicity shrugged, then looked away. The others sat resolutely silent.

'You know, Will has been trying to get together with Tom for a drink for weeks, but he's never available. It's funny that he makes so much time for you though.'

Zara narrowed her eyes as a flush deepened and spread down Felicity's neck. 'Well, it's not that he makes the time as such. Just old friends supporting each other really...'

'Oh, you know what men are like,' Penny interjected, 'They would get together and talk about cars or football, but never about what they really want to talk about. Women are much better at that.'

'Yes, and I'm sure if Veronica wanted our help, she would ask for it?' Virginia sounded unsure.

Zara slammed her mug onto the crumb-spattered table. The others jumped. 'When have any of you offered her any help or even asked her how she is lately? You know as well as I do what date is coming up. This is not an easy time for her. Felicity, you and her are the oldest of friends, as you keep reminding us, which should mean something to you. Maybe you need to cut her some slack instead of exacerbating her problems by calling the police! Or moving in on her husband!'

There was an audible gasp around the table.

Before Felicity could answer, Zara continued her tirade. 'I'm just as bad at avoiding her, I admit. I never knew what to say afterwards. None of the words sounded right. She didn't want platitudes or pity, but I also didn't know what she did want to hear. Actually, no, I do know what she wanted to hear. She wanted someone to tell her it hadn't happened, it wouldn't hurt any more or that it was all a bad dream and because I couldn't honestly tell her that, I avoided it altogether. And she was left on her own. I'm not proud of that, but there is still time to help her. We've all known each other a long time' – she looked at Felicity pointedly – 'that should count for something.'

'Well, according to Tom, she has this new friend that she's been going out with, so maybe our friendship isn't as important as we thought it was,' Felicity said icily.

'Oh,' Zara replied. 'Is that what this is really about? Is your nose a bit out of joint then?'

'What? Absolutely not! For the record, she is avoiding me, not the other way around. I would love to meet this new friend of hers,' she replied with as much conviction as she could muster.

'Well, at least she has someone helping her through

this, even if it isn't any of us. We have to give her the space she needs and be here when she is back to her old self,' Zara countered.

Silence fell.

'I still think she should be ashamed of herself.' Felicity couldn't let it go. She had hoped for all of them to be on her side for a change. Bloody Zara. Her steely eyes glinted.

'Do you know what, Felicity? You can be a right bitch sometimes. I hope nothing as awful ever happens to you because it's times like these when you need your friends, and I, for one, am ashamed of all of us.'

"Excuse me, but-' Felicity looked outraged.

'And a word of caution: leave Tom alone. You're not being fair to either of them.'

'Okay, Zara, you've made your point,' Virginia said.

'Sorry,' Zara mumbled.

'I always got along so well with Veronica and I haven't been as supportive as I should've been.' Virginia stared into the dregs in her mug. 'I feel terrible about it. I wouldn't want to be deserted by my friends when I really need them the most and that's what we did. God forbid I am ever in the same situation.' With that, she scraped back her chair and got to her feet. 'I better go, dinner to get ready and all that.'

Penny mumbled something about needing to be somewhere and shuffled off too, leaving Felicity sitting with Zara. Her cheeks were burning and her fingers fidgeted and twitched as she realised she was desperate for a cigarette for the first time in years. She grabbed her phone from the table and made to stand up. 'I think we're done here, Zara, don't you?'

'Look, I'm sorry for flying off the handle – mostly my own guilt really.' Zara stood too. 'I was out of line there. But we both know what I'm talking about when it comes to Tom.'

'Do we?'

'Yes. I was there that night. I saw the two of you in the kitchen at V's dinner party. I know something happened between you and I hope for the sake of your friendship with V that it didn't go any further – or won't in the future.'

'You don't know what you're talking about.' Her voice was menacingly low. She turned her back on Zara and worked her way through the coffee shop to the door. Zara followed her.

'Okay, I'm sorry. Maybe I misread the situation. But I do think Tom needs to be talking to Veronica more than to you,' Zara continued as they stepped outside and walked towards the edge of the pavement. Cars streamed past in a steady line and they stopped on the kerb.

'Zara, you would probably do well to keep your nose out of it, to be honest. Meddling can be a dangerous pastime.' Her voice was like ice.

Zara narrowed her eyes. 'Excuse me?'

'You have no idea about my relationship with Tom and how important we are to each other and I am not about to abandon him now, regardless of what stupidity Veronica is up to. As you say, the next little while will be hard on him and he needs me.'

'She needs him more,' Zara replied, looking at Felicity closely. 'Maybe I should speak to her about this.'

'Maybe you should leave well alone. You really don't want anyone to get hurt, do you?' Felicity moved to step into the road, then pointed down to the pavement. 'Oh, your shoelace is loose. You should tie that in case you trip over it.'

Thrown by the sudden change of subject, Zara looked down at her feet as she stepped off the pavement, barely registering the sound of a car horn blaring.

Veronica

October 10th. One of the days I had been dreading the most, but I woke up early on Grace's birthday, as I did every year, ready to get everything prepared and the cake made. This year I couldn't decide between a vanilla or a chocolate cake, so settled on a three-tiered mix of the two: a vanilla layer sandwiched between two chocolate layers, and covered with purple icing and hand-made fondant flowers. She would love that.

Tom had already left the house when I came out of the shower. I wasn't sure where he had gone. We had barely talked since my night out. I'd told him about my altercation with Felicity because I knew she would share her version at the first opportunity. He had been shocked to start with, but then seemed saddened, although he hadn't commented. I came away feeling like I had disappointed him again and surprised myself by realising that for the first time in a long while I had actually wanted him to hold me and tell me everything would be okay. It was only when he walked away from me without saying very much, apart from a quiet, 'Perhaps I'll have a word with her and smooth things over,' that my loneliness presented itself like a thin cloud. I had the urge to shout and rant, but he had walked into the garden and closed the door behind him, mumbling something about an urgent call to make. By the time he had ended his call, the cloud vapour had dispersed and blankness has returned.

Afterwards, I kept to myself as much as ever. Truth be told, I was nervous of running into Felicity again, now that my initial bravado had dissolved. The day after, I had woken with my friend, Guilt, sharing my pillow, whispering sweet accusations in my ear, reminding me of my domestic failures. All vestiges of teenage rebellion had fizzled away, leaving behind a headache of unworthiness.

Last night he had tried to talk to me about today, whether we should do something to mark the occasion, but I wanted to do this my way. I had set out on the school run, but saw Felicity in a huddle with a number of other mums, many of whom she wouldn't normally talk to, animatedly holding court, with her arms gesticulating dramatically and her eyes manic, and with Scarlet's suspicions ringing in my ears, I convinced myself she was telling them all about what I had been up to, so I made a hasty retreat.

Back at home, I gathered the baking ingredients onto the counter, double-checking them against the recipe as I went. But as I pulled the block of butter out of the fridge, I knew straight away that there wouldn't be enough. With a blip of dread, I checked the fridge shelves for another block, then checked the margarine tub as a possible substitute, but even that was down to the scrape marks at the bottom. I closed the fridge door, cursing under my breath and wishing I had added more than just bottles of prosecco to my last shopping delivery.

A plausible idea came to me and I grabbed my phone from the counter, my snatching fingers only serving to knock it onto the floor first. Impatiently, I reached down for it, then hit redial, knowing it would ring straight through to Scarlet.

'Hey honey,' she said, her voice immediately comforting me. 'It's been a while, how've you been?'

'I'm okay. Listen,' I said, rudely getting straight to the point. 'I've just realised I don't have enough butter for Grace's birthday cake, so I was wondering if you happened to be on your way over and whether you could get me some from the shop? It would save me some time.'

'I would, but I won't be there until later as I have some stuff I have to do first. It would be quicker if you popped out yourself, to be honest. So you're making her a cake, huh?'

I wasn't used to Scarlet saying no to me. 'Yeah, she loves cake,' I replied quietly.

Scarlet started to say, 'Are you——', but I cut her off and said in a fraught tone, 'Thanks anyway. I better get this done, otherwise there will be no cake after all. See you later,' and I hung up.

At the thought of heading outside, I took a quick detour past the liquor cabinet for a sneaky sip of courage, then threw on the Converses that were lying abandoned by the door, and grabbed my purse and keys. I paused for a moment, my hand on the latch, and looked out of the side window to see if anyone (Felicity) was about. With the coast clear, I opened the door, took a breath and stepped across the threshold.

I watch her from the shadows as she steps out of her front door and crosses the street, her eyes down, her feet heavy but moving one in front of the other, as if in automation. She has told me before that she never turns left down the street anymore, that being the direction in which Grace died. Instead, she turns right and takes the longer route around the block rather than facing her demons head on.

It's Grace's birthday. The day she has been dreading. The gifts won't have been delivered yet. I doubt she would've emerged if they had. I follow her from a distance, keeping out of sight, curious to see where she is going. She seems quite in control, which irks me. I was hoping that the day would be marked by more visible emotion, but from the outside she appears resolutely calm.

This just won't do. It's not healthy to bottle it up; I need to help her with that. Sometimes you need a real friend to help you to face up to such things. Time to make her realise that she is out of her depth, floundering, that masking her emotions will do more harm than good. A little reminder of Grace's funeral perhaps; something to show respect on such an auspicious day, albeit with a hidden sting, like a wasp hiding among the petals.

I follow her as far as the convenience store and watch her go inside. I know what my next step will be. I don't have much time though. She won't be in there long and I want to be able to witness her reaction first-hand this time. I can feel a thrill of smug excitement building at the thought of it, my heart taking flight as I imagine the moment to come.

I quickly nip past the convenience store, keeping my head as low as hers was, and head towards the florist further down the road with a skip in my step.

I made it without incident to the convenience store that never seems to close. When Grace was younger, I was always nipping in there for something – nappies, wet wipes, milk – but I hadn't been in for months.

The cold air of the shop hit me in the face as I pushed open the door. An old-fashioned bell tinkled above my head and an elderly Pakistani man behind the counter raised his tired eyes from his newspaper. He did an obvious double-take of recognition.

'Oh, Mrs Pullman, it's been so long.' He struggled out of his chair and shuffled around the counter towards me. The frayed sleeves of his brown cardigan and comfortable carpet slippers contradicted his sensible necktie, but in the years I had been popping into his newsagents, I had never seen him with his top button loosened or his shirt stained. He was looking at me with such intensity that I realised he was considering giving me a hug. I immediately recoiled from him and formally held out my hand instead, giving him the message loud and clear. He stopped in his tracks with a stricken expression on his round and open face.

'How are you, Mr...' My mind drew a complete blank on his name. 'Er, and your lovely wife?' I inwardly cringed.

'Ah, who am I to complain?' he replied, shaking my hand vigorously and with such a look of pity that I almost crumbled on the spot.

With my free hand, I calmed myself with a quick fingernail dig in my palm. My other hand was still clasped tightly in both of the shopkeeper's unexpectedly cool hands.

'I'm out of butter,' I announced awkwardly. We

looked at each other for a moment, then he released my hand and stepped aside.

'Of course, of course,' he said too brightly.

I moved towards the fridges, chastising myself for my rudeness.

He returned to his stool behind the counter and when I turned to look over my shoulder, he was watching me with concern. I offered him a wan smile, and kept walking, his downtrodden, pitiful eyes on my back, weighing me down.

The fridges were at the back of the store and thankfully out of sight of the counter. I stood in front of the shelves and closed my eyes. When I reopened them, I couldn't make out any of the products. Everything was a blur. The bell above the door tinkled the arrival of another customer and cleared my head a little. I saw the butter on the middle shelf and grabbed two packs, before heading back to the till.

As I rounded the shelves, the shopkeeper was deep in conversation with a woman whose pushchair was blocking the aisle, the small child clipped into it kicking his feet with wild abandon. All three turned to look at me. With a jolt, I recognised Zara.

Part of me wanted to drop the butter and make a run for it. Inexplicably, a mental image of me tiptoeing past the pushchair to the door flashed through my head, bringing giggle bubbles to my throat, and I had to dig my nails into my palms to stop me from laughing out loud. There was no way I could get past her without being seen, and since attack is the best form of defence – or so I was starting to think – I took a rapid breath and walked straight up to her, placed the butter on the counter and said, 'Hi Zara,' in as steady a voice as I could muster.

I expected pity, sadness, patronising compassion, but instead I saw what looked like fear. She looked skittish and on edge. Her unease unsettled me. I wondered what titbits of gossip had filtered through to her from Felicity's poisonous mouth to cause such a reaction. Zara had always been the most genuine of all of them.

'V, how are you? Sorry, that's a stupid question, especially today – Grace's birthday, isn't it? It came up on my phone...' Then she added tentatively, 'But you look better.'

I was grateful that she had acknowledged today.

'Er, thanks.' I was at a loss as to what to say next. 'Um, how've you been?' I looked down into the pushchair, then noticed the unsightly grey fracture boot on Zara's foot. 'Oh! What happened?'

She shuffled a little and a strange look flitted across her face. 'Oh, this? Um, well, a silly accident really. I was coming out of the coffee shop on the high street with Felicity. Silly really, but my shoelace was loose and I wasn't paying attention... Anyway, I tripped into the road as a car was coming – it could've been a lot worse. As it is, it's just a fracture.' She laughed nervously.

'Wow, I'm glad you're okay.'

'Thanks. I'll look a right sight next weekend at Penny's fortieth – if I go...' She grabbed my arm then and I could see tears glistening in her eyes as she leaned towards me. 'Listen, I just want you to be careful. I know things are going to be tough what with today and the trial, but just try and keep your wits about you.'

'What do you mean?' She was frightening me a little, the look on her face one of distress.

'I just mean that you should keep your friends close and your enemies closer, if you know what I mean?'

I didn't. 'Zara? Are you ok? Did someone-'

She dropped her arm and looked over her shoulder, her face still a mask of panic. 'Don't mind me. The painkillers I'm on are very strong.' She chuckled hollowly. 'We will miss you at Penny's party though. Well, I will anyway.'

'Right, well... I hope your ankle is on the mend soon.' I backed up to the counter, scrabbling in my bag for my purse as I did. 'I'm just heading home to make a birthday cake for Grace, so I must dash, but it's nice to see you again.' I turned to the shopkeeper with questioning eyes, choosing to ignore the yearning look on Zara's face.

'Three pounds twenty please, Mrs Pullman.'

I rummaged in my purse, found a few pound coins that clattered onto the counter as they fell from my fingers. I accepted the change from his outstretched palm and let it fall into one of the children's charity collection boxes next to the till, then edged around the pushchair and started to back up towards the door.

'Lovely to see you, Mrs Pullman,' he called after me at the same time as I said, 'See you soon, Zara.'

'Call me. We should talk.'

I raised a hand that looked more like a salute than a wave and rushed out of the door before I made the situation any more awkward.

I walked home quickly, my mind churning the whole way after seeing Zara. She seemed to be trying to warn me about something, but I couldn't fathom what. Could she have seen me with Scarlet? Was that who she was worried about? No, Felicity had probably just told them all about our run-in and exaggerated my outburst in her typical melodramatic style. Probably made me out to be some kind of pantomime villain. But then why was Zara warning me to be careful rather than trying to get away from me? Her fear hadn't seemed to be directed at me. I couldn't fathom any of it, but I had more important things to attend to.

Reaching into my bag, I pulled out my keys, then noticed a bouquet of flowers leaning up against the front door. White lilies – the funereal flower. I looked around, but couldn't see anyone. Approaching slowly, I reached down and pulled a small white card from the flowers.

It read simply, 'Happy birthday Grace'.

Who would send something like this? Surely not Tom? I couldn't stop a moan of despair escaping from my tight throat as I grabbed the flowers and darted around the side of the house to throw them straight into the dustbin. I bolted into the house, not looking back, a thin sheen of cold sweat on my forehead.

That's better. Some actual visible emotion for a change. I almost laughed out loud when she gasped in shock. I had to duck out of sight when she turned to look around, but the euphoria as she hurled the beautiful, scented lilies into the bin! Worth every penny. It shouldn't be long before the gifts are delivered, the body blows to her sanity coming thick and fast. She'll be perched on the precipice before the end of the day. Now I just need her to take the jump.

I leant against the door. The house was quiet. The clock in the lounge ticked, the morning slowly draining away. An eerie calm settled over me. Awareness of the cold butter blocks in my hand forced me to push off from the door and wander listlessly into the kitchen. I caught a glimpse of myself in the hallway mirror and I didn't like the reflection: like a rabbit in the headlights, manic and jittery, my face white and slick with fevered perspiration.

The kitchen countertops were still littered with bags of flour and sugar, and tins of caramel; the KitchenAid was ready and waiting, but suddenly I felt completely wrung out. I put the butter next to the mixer and sat heavily on the stool. Through the window, the sun was valiantly breaking through the clouds and illuminating a cobweb that reached up to the ceiling from the corner of the window frame. I stood up and retrieved a perversely jaunty, rainbow-coloured feather duster from the top of the fridge and zeroed in on the cobweb.

As I drew closer, my eye fell on a small, opaque handprint further down the windowpane, waving ghostly at me in the weak sunlight. I stopped in my tracks, then approached slowly, as though scared I would frighten it away. The handprint was smaller than mine, but perfectly formed. In the quiet, Grace's laughter filled my ears. I couldn't stop the memory hitting me like a ghost train.

The lounge floor was covered with a kaleidoscope of wrapping paper and ribbon. I perched on the couch, a cup of tea in hand, waiting for the birthday girl, all mussed-up hair and sleepy eyes. Tom appeared in the doorway with his prized possession in his arms. She let out a squeal of delight and he released her. She lunged at me, but I held her in check.

'Careful, hot tea here.'

She immediately corrected herself and leaned in for a gentle hug instead, before directing her energy back to her dad and giving him a big squeeze.

'Daddy, so many presents! Thank you, thank you, thank you!'

Tom laughed. 'Well, you better get unwrapping then. You have to go to school soon and you don't want to be late on your birthday.'

'I think you should just pick one or two and leave the rest for later, Grace,' I said.

Her face crumpled in disappointment. 'I can be quick, promise.'

'Let's see how far you get,' Tom stepped in. 'If you're still opening in fifteen minutes, then we'll have to leave it until later.'

A compromise reached, she made her way to the parcels in front of her and took a moment to plan her route in.

She was not a ripper; instead, she meticulously lifted the tape so that the paper wouldn't tear, before setting it aside. She studied each gift carefully and dished out

278

kisses of glee complete with exuberant squeezes of delight. We didn't get to the bottom of the pile before she had to leave for school, even with Tom suggesting that she tear open the last few. No, she wanted to savour each and every one.

I closed my eyes as vertigo overpowered me, then opened them and reached out a quivering hand towards the window. I let it hover without touching for fear of smearing the perfect imprint. How had I not noticed it before? The cobweb forgotten, I returned the feather duster to its resting place and smoothed my hair with my palms.

Reaching across the counter for my apron, I rolled up my sleeves and returned to the task at hand, my mind focused again, like the ghostly handprint had wiped the residue from my eyes.

As I picked up the flour, the doorbell rang. I immediately assumed it was Scarlet turning up earlier than expected.

I pulled open the door and found a delivery man standing, laden down with boxes.

'Here you go, love. There's a couple more in the van.'

He stacked the boxes on my front step and returned to the courier van parked across my driveway. More boxes emerged and were added to the pile.

'Sign here please.'

My brain wasn't computing what was going on. Had Tom been on a spending spree?

I scribbled something that looked vaguely like my initials on the electronic handset he was holding out to me, then shuffled the boxes into the hallway, before closing the door.

The boxes were all addressed to Grace.

With what felt like one hundred little butterflies with wings dripping ice taking flight inside my stomach, I opened each and every box, pulling out clothes, books, music CDs – all the kinds of things a ten-year-old would want to receive for her birthday. The air filled with the sweet, artificial smell of adolescent lip gloss and fruity body lotions. Rainbows of light danced on the walls from the sparkles on a new dress. A sharp sting on my finger from a paper cut inflicted by the cover of a book she would love.

I left the empty boxes piled high in the hallway, their contents strewn across the carpet, and returned to the kitchen on autopilot, trying not to give my brain the room to voice the thoughts pinging around.

Instead, I concentrated on the process of creaming the butter and sugar, sifting the flour, measuring the exact amount of cake batter into each tin. While the cakes rose in the warmth of the oven, I sat on the floor and watched them change shape and colour until my behind was numb from the cold floor tiles and my legs prickled with pins and needles.

I refused to look at the boxes, but they were there in the other room, taunting me.

Once the cakes were out of the oven, I took off my wedding and engagement rings, laid them on the windowsill where they glinted in isolation, and turned my attention to the decorations. Every intricate icing petal settled my mind a little more. Soon, the counter was covered in brightly coloured daisies, handcrafted fondant roses and delicate butterflies. Far more than I could use, but I couldn't still my fingers once I had started.

I didn't hear the front door open and wasn't sure how long Tom stood in the kitchen doorway watching me before his presence filtered through to my subconscious. He had loosened his tie, dropped his briefcase by the door and was wearing a look of bewilderment. He hadn't made a sound, but the air shifted to accommodate him. I looked up once I had finished the last rose petal. I wasn't sure what I was expecting, but he didn't say anything at all, merely turned and left the room.

I found him sitting in the lounge, staring ahead vacantly. When I followed his eyes, I realised he was looking at the holiday photograph of the three of us taken three years ago in Greece, which I had framed and displayed proudly on the mantelpiece. I didn't look at it much anymore; it was just a dust-catcher. I noticed my face was now obscured by a smudged fingerprint. Three happy, carefree, suntanned faces set against the paradise of swaying Mediterranean palm trees and golden sand. Just a normal family enjoying some R&R before the world as we knew it ground to a halt. Grace, with her still childishly chubby cheeks rosy against the white of her dress, was squeezed in between the relaxed, smiling faces of two adults I hardly recognised. Tom looked younger, less strained, looser; I didn't want to draw comparisons between the holiday me and what I now saw every morning in the mirror.

'Her tenth birthday,' he finally said as I was about to return to the kitchen. His voice was low and raw. I stopped, but didn't turn around.

The silence dragged on and I knew I had to break it, but knowing and doing don't always see eye to eye.

'What are you doing?' he asked then, his voice cracking.

'I'm making a cake,' I replied simply. 'She always has a birthday cake.'

'Did you buy all that stuff?'

I turned then and glared at him. 'No, did you?'

'Of course I didn't,' he spat.

Doubt flooded over me. Had I ordered them? The thoughts that had been lingering all morning began to fuse together. The lilies; the handprint; now presents for a party that would not be held. Was I losing it? Had it all finally become too much? Part of me was strangely relieved at the idea of resigning myself to madness as I was exhausted from constantly battling unseen demons.

He sighed in exasperation, then stood and took hold of my arms firmly. 'Tell me the truth, V. What's going on? Is it the pills? Are you taking too many?'

My floury hands hung limply at my sides. 'I don't know what you mean.'

'I found the empty packets, V.'

'I'm not taking pills... I...' I faltered, not sure of anything anymore. 'I don't remember ordering anything. I'm making her a cake just to keep my mind and my hands busy, but the presents... I don't know where they came from. There's been some other stuff too... the flowers on the doorstep...'

In the back of my mind, a little voice cried out in defiance: *Someone is trying to torture you.*

'Well, someone is playing a very sick joke on you if it's not you doing this and it's not me,' he echoed. 'What about this new friend of yours?'

'Scarlet? She wouldn't. Why would she?' That angered me. How dare he accuse her when he hadn't even met her. I ignored the fact that I had accommodated similar thoughts recently. I shook my head, then retreated to finish my labour of love in the kitchen, still refusing to acknowledge the abandoned gifts.

As I carefully placed the bottom chocolate tier on a jaunty, butterfly-vibrant cake stand, then applied a layer of caramel across the moist sponge, I could hear him collecting up the boxes, scrunching up paper, and carrying everything upstairs and out of sight. What I didn't want to acknowledge was the muffled keening noises he was making as he moved around, his feelings sounding too raw and naked for me to be able to empathise with today.

So I focused my energy on layering the final two tiers with the sweet, smooth caramel. My mind remained resolutely empty as I opened a tub of vanilla buttercream frosting and slowly covered the outside of the cake with precision. My hands were now steady as I smoothed and spread. Then I artfully arranged the flowers on the top, so that the cake resembled an English country garden fit for a princess.

I stood back to admire my handiwork, then noticed Tom watching in the doorway again. We stood there like acquaintances in a flat-share, not sure what to say to each other. His eyes dropped to the cake, then back to me.

'How can you do that?' he said.

'Do what?'

'How can you pretend it never happened?' His reddened eyes reached out to me.

Is that really what he thought I was doing?

'You're baking cakes. You leave that stuff in the

hallway. You refuse to talk about it. You refuse to talk to me at all.' He looked at me nakedly. 'Do you blame me? Is that what this is about?'

I could feel a fog descending over my mind and I had a sudden urge to escape, perhaps not to come back.

My phone started ringing from somewhere in the hallway. 'My phone is ringing.'

'Don't, V. Stay and talk to me, please.' He stepped towards me, but I stepped back until I was pressed up against the counter, the space between us like a chasm.

The phone rang away to itself.

'I love you,' he said. It used to be so easy to say those words back to him, but now the words choked me. 'We need to talk – I have to talk to you.'

'Not today, please.'

'Don't you think this is hard for me too?'

He turned from me and left the room, and I heard the front door close softly behind him. I didn't begin to wonder where he had gone. I just felt relieved that he had left.

I sat on the couch, facing the window. The sunlight streamed in, stronger in this room, illuminating the dancing dust. My hands were clasped in my lap, but my fingers twitched and twisted, their palms now permanently reddened where my nails always came to rest. I felt like I was falling headfirst into a crevasse without a safety net and I knew that I needed to put my hands out to break my fall, but a corner of my mind found relief in the thought that if I didn't, it could all be over finally. Perhaps I should just let myself keep falling.

Scarlet arrived soon after Tom left. After admiring my baking handiwork, she came to sit next to me in the lounge, the couch cushions shifting under her weight. She looked as though she was dressed for a party in her girly turquoise frock.

Against my better judgement, I told her about the presents, more to gauge her response than anything else.

'So you didn't order any of it?'

'If I did, I don't remember.'

'You're not loopy, so I don't believe that.'

I looked at my hands. 'Tom suggested you had done it.'

I waited for the bomb to explode, but it never came. She merely said, 'Well, that's because he doesn't know me. Besides, it's more likely to be someone who has a sick vendetta against you. I think you should consider someone closer to home.'

I followed her eyes towards Felicity's house.

'No.'

'You sure about that?' She was always so quick to blame Felicity. Why? Was she trying to shift my suspicions away from her? All of the strange coincidences had started after I met Scarlet. But what could her agenda be? No, I was just letting Tom's words cloud my judgement. Scarlet had been nothing but a friend to me.

'Yes, I'm sure. Felicity and I may have drifted apart, but she's never been malicious like that. No, there must be a reasonable explanation. Tom's family is all in Australia. Maybe a family member sent the stuff, the flowers, someone who doesn't know.' It sounded ludicrous even to me.

'The flowers could be a misconstrued gesture, sure, but the gifts? It's a lot of stuff for a distant relative to send.'

I sat forward with my head in my hands. 'I don't want to talk about it anymore.'

'Are you okay?' she asked.

I lifted my head. 'I have to talk to him sometime, don't I?'

'You don't need me to tell you that.'

'What do I say?' I beseeched to Scarlet, to anyone.

'Once you start, I think you'll find the words will come on their own.'

'I'm not ready.'

'You are, actually. You know this isn't healthy anymore.'

I looked down at my wringing hands and forced myself to stop. Deep in my gut, a flicker of determination flared, then extinguished just as quickly. I chewed hard on my lip, drawing metallic blood into my mouth.

'No, I'm not ready yet. Not today. I don't want to ruin her birthday.' I turned to look into Scarlet's open face.

She replied with a glint in her eye, 'Then we should get you dressed for a party.'

Felicity

Felicity knew as soon as she heard the doorbell who it would be. She opened it with a look of triumph on her face, but that evaporated as soon as she saw the broken man in front of her. She stepped out onto the front step and pulled the door to behind her.

'What's happened? Did you tell her?'

'No, it's Grace's birthday. She's in there baking a fucking cake and I feel like I'm going mad. She's ordered presents!'

'Look, Ian's here,' she whispered. 'He's upstairs working, so we can't—'

'Felicity, was that the door?' a deep voice called from behind her.

Moments later Ian appeared behind them. 'Shit, Tom, you okay?'

'Yeah, no, I... er...'

'Look. Come in. I've got a cold beer with your name on it.' He pushed Felicity aside and pulled Tom into the house. 'Come on, let's be having it...'

Felicity watched the two men in her life disappear into the house, leaving her alone on her doorstep, her foot tapping in annoyance. How had the four of them got to this?

'Do I look okay?'

'Of course you do! You look amazing. I wish my legs looked that long.' Veronica slipped her arm reassuringly through Felicity's and smiled. 'Relax, they're just boys and if they're awful, we still have each other.'

Felicity felt the nerves diminish somewhat in the face of Veronica's calm. She envied her the control she seemed to have over herself.

They were standing outside a bar about to meet up with two guys for a date. Felicity had orchestrated it so that she met one of them, Tom, on campus outside her lecture hall and he had suggested a drink. Nervous at the idea of a date with such a good-looking guy, she had suggested they each bring a friend and make a night of it. Felicity immediately asked Veronica, even though they hadn't known each other that long. She figured Veronica would be good for keeping the conversation going, but not gorgeous enough to steal the limelight.

Veronica's job was to big Felicity up and highlight her obvious assets. They had talked strategy and Veronica was to laugh at Felicity's jokes, keep the subject matter away from sport (which Felicity knew nothing about) *and slouch next to her in order to amplify Felicity's statuesque frame. Veronica was briefed and ready to go, but Felicity's nerves were threatening to get the better of her. She really liked this guy and needed this to go well. She had been watching him from a distance over the past few weeks around campus and she could sense he was a keeper already. Now she just had to put her plan in motion and actually catch him.*

They found Tom and his friend chatting over pints at a table small enough that their legs were cramped and touching. Felicity positioned herself opposite Tom so that she could lean seductively towards him; Veronica squeezed in next to him as he introduced his friend, Ian, a non-descript man with messy hair, stained shirt and filthy trainers. Felicity felt a brief flutter of sympathy for Veronica – next to Ian, Tom looked immaculate with his clean fingernails and neat shirt. Ian was apparently studying a business degree, but Felicity was more interested in Tom's career prospects as a doctor and paid little attention to what Ian was wittering on about.

The conversation stuttered along for a while, with Veronica doing her bit to promote Felicity as subtly as possible, but Felicity could see early into the evening that Tom seemed drawn to Veronica. Felicity started leaning across the table more, pushing her arms under her chest for emphasis, but the more they talked, the more Tom and Veronica found commonalities. So much for sticking to her script. Soon they were chatting like old friends, while Ian and Felicity were mere spectators. After a few pints of courage, Ian started a charm offensive on Felicity, but she was too distracted by what was playing out in front of her to discourage him.

How dare Veronica steal her date from under her very eyes? She started to pick at what Veronica was saying, contradicting her and steering the conversation onto topics she knew Veronica knew very little about. But Tom seemed to find her naivety charming. Felicity then tried talking over her and drowning her out, but his eyes were only for Veronica, who seemed oblivious that Felicity was upset.

As the evening was drawing to a close, Felicity made a desperate last-ditch attempt to get him to notice her by snogging Ian in the hope of making Tom jealous, but Tom merely laughed and suggested he escort Veronica home as Ian was clearly needed elsewhere. Veronica had looked at Felicity with delight, as though Felicity had given her permission, and wandered off into the night with Tom.

Their fates were sealed that night. Felicity had tackled Veronica about the failed date the next day, but she merely said that once she saw Felicity with Ian, she figured Felicity had made her choice. Of course, she had apologised, and since Felicity had quickly come to lean on Veronica as her only friend at that godforsaken university, she had forgiven her, but logged it mentally.

The bond between Tom and Veronica became unbreakable very early on and they grew to be inseparable. Felicity's only option was to stay with Ian so that she could at least shadow them, making sure she was never too far away in the hope that one day Tom would notice her. But then Tom asked Veronica to marry him and Felicity felt the first seed of bitterness take root. Ian followed soon after with his marriage proposal, spurred on by the happiness of his best friend, and Felicity had no reason not to accept: he was nice enough, he had a promising, if not boring, future ahead of him, and he worshipped Felicity.

Over the years, Tom and Veronica had grown in strength and status while her and Ian had stagnated. Ian's first attempt at running a consultancy business had failed and Tom had had to bail them out. Tom was still a silent partner in Ian's business now, which was in trouble again. When the house next door to them had come on the market, Tom had even lent them the money for the deposit, which Felicity took to be serendipitous. They were both pregnant with the girls at the time and she had sold it to Ian as needing to be close to Veronica so that they could support each other and raise their children together.

And now look where they all were; quite the dysfunctional family.

She could hear the two men talking in low tones in the kitchen, their voices and the sound of chinking beer bottles filtering along the corridor to where she still stood on the front step. Her eyes caught on the car keys lying inert on the hallway table and she reached in and grabbed them. With determination, she walked over to where Veronica's car was parked in the driveway, almost taunting her, and casually carved a deep line into the shiny paintwork along the driver's door. The squeal as the sharp key dug in sent icy darts through her ears and deliciously set her clamped teeth on edge. Then she turned and casually retraced her steps, closing the front door firmly behind her.

Veronica

New evening, new bar; this one more for the trendy, after-work types in loosened ties and power suits. Laughter, interspersed with unrecognisable music and clinking glass, gave the place a carnival feel, as though the worries of the entire global economy had been checked at the door. I expected the bar inside to be full, but it wasn't. Most people were standing outside on the pavement, smoking cigarettes in the cool night air, so there were a few empty tables inside for us to choose from. Scarlet and I picked one in the far corner of the room, facing out as always to give us a good view of the action as we settled in for some people-watching.

The barman had looked up as we walked in, then returned to wiping glasses. Once settled, I left my bag and jacket on the table with Scarlet to watch over them and approached him, these days unfazed at ordering drinks and hanging out in such places, compared to when I'd first met Scarlet. He was young enough to make me feel old, but old enough to be working in a place like this. Clearly channelling his inner Bieber, his longish blonde hair was styled into a quiff, tattoos snaking around his biceps underneath a grey T-shirt and loose-fitting jeans. He looked me over and asked, 'What you drinking?'

'Can I get a bottle of Pinot Grigio please?'

'Sure thing,' and he wandered off. I looked back at Scarlet, who waved enthusiastically like a kid at sport's day who suddenly spots their mum in the crowd. I rolled my eyes at her, then turned back as the barman placed a cold bottle of wine in front of me. 'Can I run a tab on this?'

'Sure. How many glasses?'

'Two, thanks.'

I handed over my card and he passed me a tab number in return.

Ten minutes later and the people-watching was in full swing. Scarlet and I were immersed in our favourite bar game of concocting stories about the patrons around us. The wine was filling me with warmth and I felt almost delirious, all thoughts of birthday cakes, presents, flowers and handprints melting away. Tom's pained expression still haunted me, like a black cloud over my sunshine, but getting my five a day from a bottle of wine would help that to fade eventually too.

Scarlet leaned over. 'For all intents and purposes, this is a celebration, right?'

'It is indeed,' I replied.

'So I think we need something manlier than a Pinot. We're playing it too tame here.' She pushed the bottle to one side, clearly plotting something, and scanned the room. Her eyes stalked the barman as he went about his business. With a flourish, she announced, 'Tequila!'

I laughed, but felt a flicker of apprehension and my mind flashed to Beardy Man and the smell of tequila on his stale breath.

'I can't – not after the last time. Don't think I could stomach it.'

'Okay, vodka then. We have to toast this birthday properly! Go girl, go!' She shoved me hard off my chair and I made my way back to the bar.

The barman came right over and said, 'More wine?'

'No, we're feeling a bit more dangerous than that. Two vodkas on the rocks, I think.' He looked at me as though trying to work me out, then nodded and turned away. On a whim, I said, 'Nice shirt,' in a vague attempt at flirting. In actual fact, the T-shirt was nothing noteworthy – non-descript, with some surf company logo in silver writing that only someone in their twenties would recognise. I immediately felt daft saying it, but he politely acknowledged the compliment with a slight nod of the head.

'I'll bring them over,' he said.

'Thanks,' I mumbled, feeling ridiculous, and returned to the table, my ankle twisting in my skyscraper heels. Collapsing into my chair, I rubbed my ankle. 'Don't let me lose any belongings this time – or my dinner,' I said to Scarlet.

'Can't promise,' she replied with a laugh as the barman approached with the drinks.

'Quiet in here tonight – for now anyways,' he said conversationally as he put the drinks down.

'It is, which means you could join us for a drink,' I said bravely, indicating a third empty stool at the table. I ignored Scarlet's delightedly shocked expression and the voice in my head that asked what the hell I was playing at.

He contemplated me for a second, then said with a smile, 'Maybe later...' and headed back to the bar. Halfway there, he looked back over his shoulder with a half-smile and my stomach turned over.

Scarlet was attempting to look horrified, but there was glee there too and I laughed.

'What's got into you?' she said.

'The birthday spirit,' I retorted, but sensed something shift in my brain as I raised my vodka glass and gulped it unceremoniously.

'You're scaring me... and I like it!' she replied.

I shifted in my seat and pulled my uncharacteristically short skirt down lower over my thighs, my ankle still throbbing. I hadn't seen Tom again before I fled the house earlier. Instead, I had left a cowardly note in the kitchen to say I was heading out with Scarlet and not to wait up. To be honest, I was relieved he hadn't returned. I had a feeling I wouldn't like what he had to tell me. Not only did I not want to pursue our conversation and see his disappointment again, but in the back of my mind, hiding behind all the good intentions, I recognised that I had dressed as provocatively as I could tonight, given the limitations of my conservative wardrobe, because I knew he would object. The teenage rebellion was back and Scarlet was my wingman. He may question why Scarlet was my friend, but I didn't.

Whistling her affirmation, Scarlet had convinced me to add the killer heels that dated back to my uni days – shoes that Grace had uncovered one day when playing dress-up in my wardrobe and had immediately loved, as only a pair of purple suede platforms with tiny silver stars would appeal to a little girl. Looking down now, I liked that my top was pulling tight over my chest and my legs looked longer in the heels. Mild discomfort from a throbbing ankle was a small price to pay. Bizarrely, Beardy Man had boosted my confidence and given me a weird high I wanted to feel again, although in possibly less dangerous circumstances. Pity Tom wouldn't get to see me like this. It would certainly shake him out of his sensible chinos.

I could feel my quiet politeness and middle-class manners evaporating in a cloud of vodka fumes. I caught the barman's eye and he smiled in my direction. I signalled for another round of shots.

We sank the second vodka quickly, then got stuck into the wine again. I noticed the barman throwing casual looks our way as we chatted and laughed. The bar was starting to fill up properly as the later crowd came in post-dinner. Laughter and loud music pulsed from every corner. I can't remember what Scarlet and I talked about, but whatever it was, it was superficial and shallow, just what I needed.

Sometime later, I retrieved my bag from under the seat and excused myself to go to the toilet.

'Wait, I need it too.'

'We'll lose our table though,' I replied, looking at the vultures circling.

'Just leave your jacket draped across the table with the wine bottle in full view and it'll be fine,' she said.

I did as she said, then we weaved quickly through the bodies to the corridor leading to the cloakrooms.

'You know, that barman followed you with his eyes the whole way,' Scarlet teased as we pushed through the cloakroom door.

'Don't be daft. He's probably thinking, *She's old enough to be my mother.*'

'And he'd be right!'

We collapsed into giggles.

I emerged from the loo a few minutes later to wash my hands in the sink. My eyes caught on the face in the mirror in front of me and for a split second I didn't recognise myself. There was a hardness around my mouth that I hadn't seen before and emptiness behind my eyes.

Scarlet came up next to me, washed her hands and started reapplying her lipstick. I looked over at her and had a strange sensation of déjà vu, not in the sense that I felt like I had been there before, but in that I felt I knew her from somewhere else, but couldn't quite put my finger on it. Something in her perfume or her facial expressions when she didn't know I was looking at her.

'What's that perfume you're wearing?' I asked. 'It smells really familiar to me, but I can't quite place it.'

'It's Anais Anais. Why? Do you like it?'

Then it hit me and I had to grip the sink as my legs wobbled under the weight of the realisation. That was the perfume Grace and Tom had bought me for Mother's Day a few years ago. Tom had said that Grace had taken the process of choosing the right one so seriously that she had sniffed so many, she had given herself a headache, but she had made the perfect choice. And that's who Scarlet suddenly reminded me of: Grace – but not ten-year-old Grace; rather the woman Grace would resemble in thirty years' time. The eyes in particular and the way she brushed her auburn-red hair away from her face.

Scarlet looked over at me and said, 'That ankle still

bothering you? You've gone all squiffy.' Those doubts that Tom had tried to seed before bloomed suddenly, along with the thought, *How much do you really know about her?* Then it was gone as quickly as it had arrived and the familiar face I had grown to love was looking back at me once more.

'Um, no, a bit of vodka vertigo,' I said with a shake of my head. I needed to get a grip; the emotion of the day was clearly taking its toll. 'Come on, let's hope our table is still there.'

As we emerged back into the bar, a man had made himself comfortable on the spare stool.

'Dammit, someone's taken it!' I moaned.

'Don't worry, I'll get rid of him sharpish... unless he's cute of course.' She ducked around the table and sat down, but the predatory look that appeared on her face told me our new guest wasn't going to be dismissed after all.

I sat down next to her and saw that it was the barman in the seat, pint in hand and a smirk on his lips. I went to stash my bag under the chair in a bid to hide my smile and took a sneaky glance at my mobile to see if Tom had called; he hadn't. I couldn't tell if I was more hurt or relieved.

'My shift is over,' he said by way of explanation, then raised his glass in salute.

We picked up our wine glasses and drank in return. 'Cheers,' I replied.

'So what's your name?' he said to me.

'Veronica, but Ron will do.'

'And I'm Scarlet,' she volunteered next to me, then muttered under her breath, 'Only has eyes for you, it seems.' She kicked me under the table, catching my sore ankle and making me wince.

'I'm Mark.' He took a sip, then said with narrowed eyes, 'You're intriguing.'

'I'll take that as a compliment, shall I?' I countered, not sure what to make of it.

He pointedly looked at my left hand. I looked down too and noticed I hadn't put my rings back on after baking.

'I'm starving. Crisps?' he said, pushing up from the stool. His T-shirt rode up to show an inch of tight stomach. I nodded and watched as he swaggered away. What the hell was wrong with me?

As soon as he was out of earshot, Scarlet leaned in. 'Look at you! Acting the wanton woman. I've taught you well,' she said proudly.

'I know, what am I thinking? He's half my age, for God's sake!'

'And way too cute for you,' she teased, nudging me. She fiddled with her drink, looking suddenly quite staid. 'Look, all jokes aside, are you sure you know what you're doing? After last time…'

'I'm not doing anything.'

'Okay, I'm just... you know... we laugh about this stuff, but...'

'I'm having fun. That's what you wanted!'

She looked at me, her eyes boring into mine, then laughed. 'You're right. Well, if you need me to disappear, all you have to do is say.'

'What? Look, I'm sorry I snapped.'

'No, I mean it. You don't need me here as a third wheel. I'll go so that you can have a drink and a chat, a bit of a flirt, then head home. Come on, it'll be good for you – blow out the old woman's cobwebs and all that. I'll make myself scarce.'

What scared me wasn't the idea of sitting in a bar with a stranger and playing a dangerous game, but my feeling of nervous excitement and the realisation that Scarlet wouldn't have to work too hard to convince me into it. I thought about Tom for a fleeting second, my stranger of a husband, then my teenage alter ego pushed the old lady back into her rocking chair and closed the door on her. I needed to feel that high again, the darts of adrenalin and the thrill of hanging onto control by my fingertips. Guilt tickled my earlobes at how quickly I was prepared to dismiss Scarlet though. Were my recent doubts about her clouding my judgement?

Before I could stop her, Scarlet stood up, put her jacket on and grabbed her bag. 'Call me and I'll come straight back if you need me.'

'Ok, Mum.'

'Seriously, do you have a safety word?'

'A what?'

'A safety word. You know, a word for when you're in trouble. All good wingmen need one, especially you after the other night. I don't want you getting arrested for assault or anything.'

'Okay, how about something like... strawberries?' I winced at my hearts and flowers suggestion.

'Really? That's what you come up with?' she mocked. 'I think it should be something more... meaningful, so that if I see it in a text, I immediately know something has gone tits up.' She paused again, then said, 'Like *Grace*.' Her eyes flashed as she looked down on me; I felt like she had stolen my breath.

She smiled – a broad, toothy grin, wicked around the edges – and reached out a hand adorned with red Halloween talons to affectionately stroke my cheek. Sweet and sour in equal measure.

'That's the one,' she said. 'Right, bye,' and she began to push through the crowd, before she turned back and said, 'Oh, and no running down the road naked wearing Felicity's parking cones.'

Then she was gone.

I felt weird sitting there without her, exposed and naked, as though someone had stolen my security blanket. My hands were cold and started their familiar dance of wringing and clasping, my state of mind not helped by Scarlet bringing Grace front of mind again when tonight was mostly about trying to forget.

Before I could bolt, Mark was back with crisps and more wine.

'To break the ice,' he said, indicating the fresh glasses. My head was already spinning from the vodka, but I didn't object. I told myself I didn't have to drink all of it.

He sat down opposite me, looked at my frantic hands. I sat on them to force them to stop.

An awkward silence fell. I shifted in my seat; he scanned the bar. I had hoped for something more electric than this. Maybe I should've left with Scarlet after all. But what was there at home? Silence and ghosts.

I took a deep breath. 'So, tell me something interesting about yourself,' I offered. A lame opener. At first he didn't hear me and I blushed as I repeated myself over the music.

'Not much to tell. I work as a barman, I live in a tiny flat up the road... and I love salt and vinegar crisps.' He tore open the packet and placed it in the middle of the table. 'Help yourself.' He grinned.

I studied him as he ate – his blonde, Bieber quiff, chunky hands and wide shoulders. So much of him was the complete opposite of the man waiting at home for me. Middle age had made Tom even more good-looking in his salt and pepper level-headedness, but distance was our marriage's buzzword and he wasn't here right now.

'I used the tab, a bit presumptuous, but hope that's okay? Struggling manual labourer and all that...' He shrugged unapologetically, then flashed me a supermodel smile and I heard myself saying, 'Yes, yes, that's fine.'

The sharp smell of vinegar filled my nose and my mouth started to water. Since I had bought the crisps, I figured I could eat them, so I grabbed a couple to give my hands something to do. All the while I was conscious of not making too much noise or looking suggestive as I chewed. It was times like these when I realised how long it had been since I had flirted with anyone. Before panic could set in, I reminded myself that he didn't know anything about me. I could claim to be anyone I wanted to be and he wouldn't be any the wiser. My heart shivered in my chest.

He took a long pull on his beer. 'So what's your story?'

'No story.' I reached for the crisps again.

'Hmmm. Well, here's to finding out more about you then,' he replied and lifted his glass.

I raised my eyes in what I hoped was a seductive way and lifted my glass to meet his. His gaze shifted imperceptibly to the Tag watch on my wrist.

Our glasses clinked and I heard myself say, 'To new friends and strange friends.'

The wine flowed freely, despite my intention not to

finish the second bottle. We laughed and joked easily, the alcohol clearly helping. He had a faint accent that I spent ages trying to place in a childish guessing game that he instigated, while I gave away as little truthful information about myself as I could. I wanted to shut my other life away and concentrate on the here and now. No thinking about Tom, Grace, Felicity, Scarlet – none of them. I fed him lies about my life and career – a freelance photographic journalist was the persona I went for – and he seemed to fall for it. I heard myself asking questions and making small talk like a normal woman would in a bar with a stranger, and he was attentive and engaging in return. His opinions were interesting, but tinged with the naivety of the young who think they can save the world. By the time you reach my age, you learn there are some things that can't be saved.

I could feel the heaviness in my head as the alcohol took over my senses. At one point, Mark put his hand on mine and I shuddered. It felt heavy, hot and rough to the touch. I looked down at his bulky hands, so different to Tom's. It felt alien to be touched by a stranger, but not entirely unpleasant.

He tried to steer the conversation towards my family, digging for more clues, but I ducked and dived expertly. Then he tried compliments, telling me I had lovely 'soulful' eyes – that much I knew wasn't true. By then, his hand was starting to get too hot, claustrophobic, with his damp skin pressing down on mine, so I subtly freed myself and reached into my bag to check my phone. No missed calls, no texts. Fair enough.

The conversation began to lurch between random topics and I noticed Mark's face was lopsided with three eyes that swam and floated. It was like I was watching myself from afar, part of me knowing I was very drunk but curious to see how this played out. I didn't want to know what time it was or how much money I had put on the tab, but I was strangely content as the alcohol kept the demons at bay.

'Another one?' he asked.

I wasn't ready for the evening to end yet, but I had drunk enough. Although there was always room for one more.

I hiccupped in response. 'I better go to the loo first.'

'Okay, go slow,' he replied, with a smirk over his shoulder as he headed to the bar.

I stood up, then quickly sat down as the bar swam in front of me.

Taking a fortifying breath, I tried again, narrowly avoided another head rush, and staggered to the bathroom.

Leaning on the sink, I peered through hazy eyes at my mirror image. Tom used to always comment on the sparkle in my eyes. There was no sparkle there now. I pulled my thoughts back to Mark: his youth, his swagger, like the male equivalent of Scarlet – or was that just what I wanted him to be? My inebriated self was convinced he was what I needed right now because he was different. I didn't want the past with its complications and tragedies. I wanted a future, or the hope of one at least – not with Mark as such, but just the hope of a life where I was moving forward, not just treading water. I immediately felt guilt swamp me for even daring to believe I was entitled to such a thing. I could feel my tongue heavy and swollen in my mouth, but my thoughts were disconnected between past and present. This was all still harmless fun, right?

I staggered into a cubicle, wrestled with my tight skirt, finished what I had to do, then tried to look sophisticated and in control on the long walk back to the table. I was fooling no one.

As I approached, Mark was talking to another man. Tall and skinny, he radiated animosity and scurried away like a rat as I took my seat. A fresh, cold glass of wine was on the table in front of me and I immediately grabbed it.

'Friend of yours?' I asked.

'Yeah, kind of. He's given me something that should really liven things up, if you're up for it?'

I frowned. 'What do you mean?'

He held out his hand to reveal two tiny blue pills lying in his palm like sweets. Each had a childish smiley face stamped on the surface.

'What is it?'

'You've never tried E before?'

Drugs had never been our thing as students, so I was very naive on that score. I started to feel ridiculous, old and out of my depth, sitting there in my suffocating skirt, with my make-up starting to run. Some of the lustre went out of the evening, but not wanting to sound like a fool, I answered on reflex, 'Yeah, course. Just a bit drunk, that's all.'

'That's the best time to take it.'

'I dunno, I may call it a night.'

'No, please, I'm really enjoying this, us… If we take this, we can carry on for hours still.'

I looked down at the pills again. They looked so harmless and friendly with their powder-blue smiles. Scarlet would approve; Tom wouldn't. But if he wanted to accuse me of popping pills…

'Okay, let me have one then.' I swallowed it quickly with a gulp of wine and waited for something to happen, not sure what to expect. He was more relaxed at taking his, clearly an expert.

We carried on talking, but I started to feel like I wasn't confined to my body any longer. Instead, I was floating above it, like an omniscient camera filming a scene for a movie. I wanted to stay in control, but could feel myself losing my grip. Mark was talking, but it was as if his voice was on fast-forward, rattling through the words, but coming at me through cotton wool. The surf logo on his shirt started to writhe and twist, and I was captivated.

He had stopped talking and was looking at me so earnestly that I started to laugh, then couldn't stop. When I managed to stifle my hilarity, I started to talk at him, the words tripping over themselves to escape from my mouth first.

'I think you need coffee. My flat is just up the road.'

It sounded like the most sensible suggestion I had ever heard.

Sounds filtered through the mental fog as consciousness started to build. A tap dripping rhythmically; muffled traffic noises; a pneumatic drill in the distance; a whirring of air close to me. My physical presence became apparent, heavy like stone. I was lying on my side on a soft mattress, but my neck was aching as it was propped up on too many hard pillows. I could feel a sheet constricting my legs and I half-heartedly tried to unravel myself. It was the sheet that did it – *when do I sleep under sheets? Oh God, where am I?*

My head was pounding. I didn't want to open my eyes because I knew the glare would sting, as would reality. My mouth was papery. I breathed in deeply and slowly opened one eye, then closed it straight away. Somewhere nearby, a phone vibrated on a hard surface.

How much did I drink last night? I was too tired to

think. It must've been a lot because I was surely on the edge of death. I lay statue still and willed the darkness behind my eyes to stop spinning and tilting.

There was a soft snore beside me and my eyes flew open. I looked over my shoulder and saw a hairy, muscled arm. With every ounce of strength, I slowly turned onto my back.

Ruffled blonde hair over a sleeping pubescent face; a detailed tattoo of a blue-tinged miniature dragon covering an exposed bicep. My mind was slow to react and panic jabbed at me until I could remember: the barman. What the hell was his name? Matthew? Mike? Mark. The panic ebbed slightly, but not for long when awareness of my own body took over. I was naked under the sheet.

I groaned inwardly and rubbed my hands over my eyes, trying to kick-start memories of the night before, but my head hurt too much and I couldn't get past the throbbing. Very slowly and quietly, I unravelled myself from the sheets and slid out the side of the bed onto my knees.

Goosebumps sprung up all over my body as I felt an intermittent blast of cold air. Still kneeling, I wrapped my arms around my waist, feeling exposed and vulnerable. A fan slowly rotated recycled air across the bed. I focused on it, feeling the cold awaken the rest of me, then I dared to look around and take it all in. I was in a non-descript, minimally decorated bedroom that contained a wardrobe with its doors ajar, a chair holding a haphazard pile of clothes, a sports bag regurgitating kit and random items of men's clothing strewn across a beige carpet.

I focused on a flash of pink and noticed some of the clothes I was wearing last night thrown into the mix. The bed behind me took up most of the floor space, but I was frightened to turn and look at that again. The cream wall in front of me was dominated by a large, framed poster of a Mexican tequila advertisement. 'Lick the salt, shoot the tequila, suck the lemon' shouted out at me in red letters. Even with my reduced mental capacity, the irony was not lost. In front of me were two doors, both open. One looked to lead towards a kitchen area and the source of the dripping tap; through the other I could glimpse white porcelain. I struggled to my feet and tiptoed towards this door, picking up the bits of clothing I recognised as I went. They weren't all here, but it was a start.

Very gently closing the door behind me, I rested my head on it and took a steadying breath. Just that slight movement had my stomach churning. I didn't want to think, but my brain kept repeating to itself, *What the hell have you done?*

I turned around and considered the bathroom. It was surprisingly clean. I was expecting a dirty toilet and toothpaste-splattered basin, but instead saw a neat, organised space with matching blue towels hanging haphazardly and toiletries standing in clusters on a small shelf in front of a mirror that was clearly positioned for someone much taller than me. I bent over the basin and splashed some cold water on my face, then braved my reflection. I could just make out the top half of my face peering from the bottom of the mirror: dark, wide panda eyes, jaded complexion, lips stained an unnatural pink and what looked to be stubble rash on my chin. I looked away. My swollen brain was now doing somersaults, banging against my skull as I tried to figure out how I got here, but there was a void where knowledge should've been.

My chest started to heave in panic. I knew I had to get out of the flat before Mark woke up. I couldn't face him, could hardly face myself. I dropped my head onto my chest and gripped the edge of the sink with white knuckles. Did I sleep with him? All the evidence was certainly pointing in that direction. I really hoped we used protection if we did.

This realisation proved one too many to bear and I rushed to the toilet bowl and threw up disgracefully. I immediately felt physically purged; mentally would take more work. I remained on my knees for a second, but the cold of the tiles forced me to stand up. I moved back to the sink, rinsed some water around my mouth and drank a little down in tentative sips. I felt dirty, like there was a thin film of grime on my skin, and my pores smelt musty. Part of me wanted to climb into a scalding shower; another part of me relished my discomfort. Moving as quickly as my physical distress allowed, I started to dress in the few items of clothing I had collected – pink knickers and my skirt; the rest was still AWOL.

I turned back to the closed door and began to psyche myself up into opening it in case I had woken him with my violent puking. What was I going to say to him, especially wearing just a skirt? I gripped the handle, eased it down and slowly opened the door. He was still in bed, but had turned away from me and was apparently still sleeping the slumber of a young, untroubled mind.

Holding my breath, I tiptoed into the bedroom, frantically scanning for more clothing. There was none immediately apparent, but I did notice a torn condom wrapper on his bedside table. One mystery solved. It didn't make me feel any better, just dirtier.

I headed through the other door and gently pulled it closed behind me. Then I allowed myself to release my breath.

I was in an open-plan lounge and kitchenette, again minimally decorated, but marginally neater than the bedroom. A leather couch was strategically positioned in front of a large, flat-screen TV unit that also housed various gaming paraphernalia, all alien to me. A coffee table was covered with sports magazines and CD cases. The kitchen had a few cups and plates washed and stacked on a drying rack. Everything shouted bachelor.

There were no signs of femininity, no cushions, flowers, photographs even. The only hint of disorder came from my sparkly top and jacket that were tossed near the door and my shoes lying abandoned in the middle of the carpet. Looking closer, I saw my bra dangling from the arm of the couch. That told a story of its own right there. I cringed and let the shame, remorse and disgust claw its way to the surface.

I steadied myself as my stomach churned and my head carried on with its incessant drum solo. It wouldn't do to throw up on his carpet before I left. I picked up my top and bra, then wrestled myself into them. I was still missing my handbag, which had everything I needed to take me home: money, keys, phone. My head pivoted as I searched frantically.

To complicate matters even more, I had a sudden urge to pee. In my hungover stupor, I hadn't gone when I was in the bathroom, but I couldn't face going back into the bedroom again. I pushed the urge from my consciousness with a quick jig of the hips, mind over matter.

I couldn't see my handbag anywhere and could feel panic rushing up my throat, hot on the heels of a wave of nausea. I could hear sheets rustling, but couldn't leave without my bag. How would I get home? Besides, mind over matter wasn't working and I would have to go to the toilet before I went anywhere.

I was going to have to go back in there.

I pushed open the door, praying he was still snoring. He was lying on his back, one arm draped over his eyes and I couldn't tell if he was awake or not. I crept past, towards the bathroom door, and thought I was in the clear, but just as I gripped the handle, I heard, 'Hey.'

I went cold, shoved the door shut behind me and sat down heavily on the toilet, considering my options. I would have to face him, be strong, admit it was all a big mistake, then leave. I sat on the toilet for longer than was necessary, but I knew I couldn't put off the inevitable. Reaching for the handle, I pulled myself up to my full, unimpressive height and opened the door.

He wasn't in the bedroom. I could hear sounds emanating from the kitchen. Through the doorway, I watched him pour steaming water into mugs, wearing just a pair of shorts, his impressively naked torso reminding me of my misdemeanours. He turned, saw me and held out a mug. 'I was about to send out a search party there. You rough?'

I walked towards him and took the mug, considered it, then set it down on the counter as my stomach heaved. 'Listen, last night...'

'Hey, look...'

'No, let me finish. It was a mistake. I'm married, it's been a fucking awful year and this' – I gestured between him and I – 'this is not me. I'm sorry, I have to go.'

'But you said...' He actually looked hurt.

I looked away. 'Yeah, well, I lied...' I started scrambling around, looking for my bag again, then noticed him pointing to the far end of the room where it was lying on the carpet, its contents strewn across the floor.

I hastily shoved everything back in, noting his silence behind me, but as I headed towards the front door, he said, 'I'll call you.'

I froze. *Fuck, he has my number? When did that happen?*

I legged it, albeit unsteadily, from the flat and found myself standing in a hallway of doors, like a bizarre carnival ride, not knowing what was behind each one but hoping to hell none of them opened at that moment. I must've look the worst kind of pathetic: wide-eyed, make-up shadows like bruises, unbrushed hair thick with hairspray, wearing last night's clothes and clutching a bursting handbag like my life depended on it.

There was a stairwell at the end of the hallway, to which I headed, but I had to stop as nausea engulfed me again. I breathed deeply, wishing I had a bottle of water to take the edge off. I stood at the top of the stairs, white knuckles gripping the handrail, staring down, and for the briefest of moments I could feel my grip loosen and my body tip forward. I could picture in my head the slow-motion tumble, my body turning over and over, the agony as I slammed into the concrete stairs, then blissful peace... I righted myself, the bilious feeling passed and I was able to scramble unsteadily down the stairs in my ludicrously high heels that had seemed such a good idea the night before. At the bottom I was greeted with fresh air through an open glass door and the noise and bustle of people hurrying to work, oblivious to the churning in my head and body. Looking in both directions, I tried to ascertain where I was, but in my panic it was all melding into a fusion of take-away outlets, charity shops and dry-cleaners that could be any high street in England.

Feeling the last embers of fight starting to extinguish, I turned left and dived into an alley between a kebab shop and a letting agent. This time when my stomach heaved, I knew mind over matter wouldn't work. I dry-retched fumes until I was gasping for air, then slumped into a crouch. I considered having a good cry, but knew it wouldn't help. I had to get myself home, preferably to crawl into the safety of my bed, but also to face up to what I had done. I hadn't allowed myself to think beyond escape as yet. What I did know was that this couldn't go on any more.

Crouched in a grimy alley, with the stench of uncollected garbage bags and urine assaulting my pounding head, I felt filthy, like I would never be clean again, no matter how many showers I took. Part of me wanted to stay in this alley, maybe find an off-licence, buy a bottle of amnesia and disappear. It seemed that

Felicity was right after all; I wasn't fit to be a mother. Things happen for a reason. This was my wake-up call. A tremor of fear that accompanied the relief in this thought forced me back to standing.

Think, Ron, I ordered in my head. *What would Scarlet do?* I could safely say she wouldn't be crouched in a dirty alley, weeping and wearing day-old knickers. I could call Tom – he would normally be my go-to knight in shining armour – but I couldn't bring myself to acknowledge last night in my own consciousness, let alone admit to him that I had quite possibly slept with a stranger but couldn't actually remember it. There was a name for women like me and it wasn't pretty or endearing.

I needed to get to Scarlet. She would help.

I sat on the hard, cold ground and immediately felt the damp creep into my clothes. Opening my bag, I took stock of what was inside. A packet of tissues, my purse and keys, a few loose mints from a random restaurant and the lipstick that still stained my lips. I immediately unwrapped the plastic from one of the mints and popped it in my mouth, then dug down further in search of my phone. At the very bottom, among the loose raisins and stale biscuit crumbs, I felt something metallic and cold. Thinking it was loose change, I pulled it out, but it was one of Grace's glittery pink hairclips, complete with a tiny plastic princess tiara. I looked at it as a vice tightened around my chest. The mint tickled my throat and I started to cough. Closing my fist over the clip, I refocused and grabbed my purse. I apparently had £2.23 in loose change – enough for a cup of tea while I considered my next move.

As I emerged from the alley, I could feel eyes judging me in my crumpled party clothes and fuck-me shoes. They didn't call it the Walk of Shame for nothing. Was I imagining their knowing smirks? I turned left and ducked into a small, inconspicuous coffee shop. Taking a seat at a table at the back, I put my head in my hands. An uninterested waitress strolled over and raised an enquiring eyebrow.

'Tea, please.'

I knew I had to face the glare of my phone screen and man up to the inevitable missed calls and messages eventually. My left hand still clung tightly to the hairgrip, the metal cutting into my palm. The other dove into my bag again and this time fell on my phone. Three missed calls and two texts – all from Tom. The first text was polite, enquiring whether I needed him to arrange a taxi to collect me; the second was a brief 'Call me when you get this, I'm worried', sent at 6a.m. I noted the time now – 7:05 – not as late as I had feared when I woke up, but late enough to be cruel.

With location services making it impossible to be truly lost these days, I established where I was, but my mobile battery was in its dying stages. Without thinking too much about the words, I fired off two texts: the first to Scarlet asking her to meet me; the second to Tom saying I was fine and would be home soon.

I picked at some dirt under my nail, plaited a strand of hair – anything to stop me ruminating on last night before Scarlet arrived. A tiny fleck of skin was sticking up from the corner of my thumbnail, so I picked at it, pulling with my teeth, feeling the sting as it tore and a bead of blood welled in its wake. Not content with seeing the blood, I chewed harder, making the raw patch grow.

The waitress returned with a small pot of tea, a mug and a ginger biscuit on a saucer. I muttered my thanks at her retreating back. I wasn't even remotely hungry, but I nibbled on the biscuit anyway, just to give my restless hands something to do, and sipped on the tea, keeping my head down.

I was onto my second pot when I heard a familiar voice. 'So do tell. I want all the gory details.'

Scarlet stood next to me, wearing what looked to be a long coat made out of 1960s fabric cut-offs. The loud swirls and bright flashes of colour assaulted my eyes. She shrugged the coat from her shoulders to reveal a simply styled blouse with a big bow at the neck in vibrant red chiffon. She was all about contradictions. Her ability to hold herself ransom to a fashion colour chart was limitless.

She slid into the chair facing me, then said, 'You look like shit.'

'I've fucked up this time,' I said simply.

'Okay,' she replied with her trademark sardonic eyebrow lift.

I procrastinated by pouring more tea, adding milk. 'I think I slept with him,' I said eventually. The admission was like a cold slap in the face.

'You think or you know?'

'I can't remember, but I saw a condom wrapper.' I put my head in my hands.

'Maybe you changed your mind. Anything could've happened – you could've just talked all night for all you know.'

I looked up at her. 'Come on, let's be serious. We both know what I did. And if I didn't, I cheated just by putting myself in that situation.'

'Fuck, I should never have left you.' She paused, then said, 'Hang on, if you were that drunk, what the hell is wrong with that guy? Who takes advantage of a drunk woman? Isn't that ra—'

'Don't say it. Please.'

I stared into the cup, but drew no comfort from it, my thoughts swirling, at times forgiving and berating, absolving and blaming, but not settling. Until now I had been very good at shutting out the things I didn't want to face, but an inevitability loomed over me, like a tsunami of truth.

I swallowed to try and rid some of the bitterness on my tongue. 'I did this. No one else.' I stirred the cooling tea. 'Tom doesn't deserve this. He never has, but now, with the trial – I mean, he is single-handedly dealing with all of that because I can't – or won't.'

Scarlet said nothing, just listened.

I laughed, a hollow, empty sound. 'I even tried drugs for the first time last night. Talk about having a mid-life crisis, if this is what it is.'

I looked around. The place was near empty.

I started to speak again, then stopped, not sure what I wanted to say and whether I was justifying my behaviour to myself or Scarlet.

I fiddled with the biscuit wrapper, twisting it this way and that. 'Last night... I went too far.'

'Yes, you did.' Her eyes were hard. 'I warned you. But you said you knew what you were doing. I knew he was trouble, but you knew better – or didn't want to hear it.'

I wasn't expecting her to berate me. 'But you said live more, have fun!'

'I didn't say sleep with a total stranger, take drugs, put yourself in danger. It's bad enough, but he could've done much worse. You must realise how reckless you've been. I'm all about living, but not if it means putting myself in physical danger.'

Mortification brought on a wave of anger. 'Why didn't you stay and keep an eye on me then?'

'Don't make this my fault. You're a grown woman, not a child.'

'I know that, a grown woman with a child.'

'No, you're not.'

'What?' My voice dripped ice.

'You don't have a child anymore.'

I stared at her with venom. 'How dare you.'

'It's time someone made you see sense. I love you, Ron, but you've brought this on yourself.'

She was right, of course, but it didn't make it any easier to hear. I wasn't ready to hear it. 'Was it you?'

'What?'

'The presents, flowers, the Facebook page, all of it. Was it you? Just tell me – some sort of weird way of making me face up to it? Some twisted sense of duty as my friend? Please, just be honest with me.'

'You really think I would do that to you?' Her face was twisted in shock and I knew I was way off the mark.

'No. No, I don't think it was you. I have never really thought it was you. I don't know what I'm saying any more.' I slumped back in my chair and closed my eyes, not wanting to acknowledge the hurt shaping her features. 'So where do I go from here, Scarlet?'

'Well, it seems to me you know exactly what you need to do.'

I could feel my throat constricting, panic building.

'You need to be talking to Tom, not me. It's time to tell him everything.' She was now the voice of reason amongst the whisperings of discord. When did that happen?

'It may be too late. This could finish us.'

'It could, but honesty can be a great healer. He deserves the opportunity to make that decision, especially after last night. Unless you don't want to fix things.'

Did I? I realised the hairclip was still clutched in my hand, now warm, but still cutting into my palm. I unfurled my fingers and considered the pink tiara.

'You have to ask yourself whether he is worth fighting for. I know you think the two of you are strangers, but in your head, you've known all along that he would be there for you if you asked for help. You've just never asked. Now imagine going through all of this if he hadn't been there in the background, ready to catch you. Can you honestly say you would be better off alone? Because if you don't fight for him, that's what will happen.'

'And if it is too late?' I looked up, pleading with my eyes for her to tell me everything would be okay. Of course, nothing would ever be okay again, but an improvement would be nice, if I could accept that.

She merely shrugged. 'You won't know until you try.'

I stirred the now cold tea obsessively, getting faster and faster. Scarlet reached out her hand and stilled the spoon. Last night's red talons had gone and her naked nails were startling in contrast. I looked back up at her face and noticed the garish make-up and loud lipstick had gone too. She was barefaced in front of me, but she was still beautiful.

'I'm sorry.'

'I know. Now drink your tea, then we'll get a cab home.' She smiled at me and let go of my hand. 'It's time.'

I lifted the teacup and noticed the tremor as I did so. The liquid quenched my parched mouth. All I wanted was a hot shower to scrub away the physical and mental evidence of last night, and then to crawl into a tiny, dark place and close my eyes, but I couldn't. It would've been easy to do that at the beginning, but now the discovered hairclips and fading handprints were propelling me forward a tiny bit more every day rather than pushing me down. It had all been building to this.

One more look at the pink tiara, then I tossed it back into my bag and made a deal with myself: I would talk to Tom, lay it all out for him, try to get him to understand what had happened and why. By the end of it, if he walked away, then I would start planning an exit strategy. Scraping back the chair, I got to my feet. The loose change clattered onto the plastic table-top. I watched one of the coins spin on its side a few times in defiance before settling on its back, heads up.

'Scarlet? Are we okay?'

'Yeah, we're okay. Besides, what would you do without me?'

I followed her out of the door.

*

I didn't know where to start. I stood facing my own front door like a salesman with a tale to tell, all nervous energy and fidgeting digits. I considered the pavement for a moment, the weeds pushing through the bricks, a shimmering snail trail, all so normal, procrastinating as long as possible. A plane flew low overhead, rattling my skull.

Before I could put the key in the lock, Tom opened the door, his hair on end and his feet bare beneath his jeans. I forced myself to meet his searching eyes.

'I need help.'

His face betrayed that this wasn't what he was expecting to hear, but he didn't say anything in return, just stepped aside. Scarlet's hand in the small of my back pushed me forward and I brushed past him. Once inside, I hesitated, unsure where to go next. The house smelled of coffee, with a faint undertone of cloying air freshener supposedly evoking freshly mowed grass. It was familiar and safe, but at the same time I felt as though I was in someone else's orderly hallway, like a dirty fly twitching on the wall. Everything and nothing had changed. The sunlight in the hallway dimmed and I heard the door click shut behind me.

I perched myself on the edge of the couch, feeling absurd in my party clothes, my ridiculous shoes clasped in one hand. I could feel the heaviness of Tom's eyes on me and I looked up.

'I'll put the kettle on. Why don't you go and get

changed, then we can talk,' he said, as though to a small child. He turned and walked away.

I let out a breath I didn't know I had been holding.

Tom

He had spent another sleepless night trying to track down his errant wife. He hadn't expected to pass his evenings like this until his daughter was a teenager, but it turns out his wife could be a bigger rebel than them all. He had made the first phone call at about 2 a.m., then each subsequent call had grown more frantic. What was initially anger had morphed into fear somewhere near 4 a.m. When Tom had heard the cab just after 8 a.m., he knew who it would be.

Hours earlier, lying wide-eyed and alone in bed, he had already decided what he was going to say to her. This had to stop. The only way to make that happen was to talk, tell her the truth, make her see sense, listen to what she had to say, if anything. Then they could decide where they went from here, together or otherwise. He had been avoiding it for too long enough, as had she.

But she had looked so wretched and scared when he opened the door that his steely determination crumbled, his angry questioning about where she had been evaporating into a soundless vapour. Shoes in hand, pathetically thin frame swamped under cheap glitter, looking far from her best, he was reminded of Grace caught playing dress-up in her mother's wardrobe. Then when she had said those three pathetic yet mobilising words, the diatribe he had planned was ruined.

He stood washing mugs that weren't dirty, just so that he had time to collect his thoughts and figure out what he was going to say to her now. The truth was he would do anything for her. She had always been his weakness – the feisty, spirited, argumentative girl he had met in university had captivated him. Then when Grace was born, his family was complete and they were happy for a while. They had wanted more children, but the elusive sibling for Grace had never materialised and they had accepted that theirs would be a unit of three. But nothing lasts forever, so they say.

She had always been a dreamer, full of grand plans and ambitious goals, but she had put it all aside so that Grace could have at least one parent who was always at home when she finished school every day, rather than a ghostly apparition appearing in the corridor every now and again before vanishing to an apparently busier and more interesting life.

She never complained and he knew how much she adored Grace, who had never wanted for anything. Grace became her whole life, to the point where he had felt overlooked, obsolete. Felicity – well, she had made her intentions very clear and the contradictions between her and V had made the idea of her all the more attractive. She had paid him the attention he was craving, pathetic as that was.

Then the unthinkable had happened and V had been cast adrift, her sole purpose in life snatched away from her. He had passively stood by and observed V slowly fade away until he could hardly recognise the woman living in his house. She became a mouse, barely speaking, flinching when he touched her, rare laughter never quite reaching her eyes, lost. She built an iceberg around herself as a defence and everyone caught a cold from it.

Yes, he had stood by and watched, not really knowing the best way to break through, but he had been trying to cope too. He had tried different words, but everything he said seemed to exacerbate the distance between them. It got to the point where he preferred the quiet hospital corridors at night to the acres of pristine white sheet between them in bed.

Then it looked like she had turned a corner. She started talking again and he had hoped against hope that she had started seeing a counsellor as he had suggested repeatedly. He was wrong about the counsellor. It turned out it was a new friend who was making a difference and that was fine with him because there was conversation again and he was grateful for the fractures in the silence. One morning she came downstairs wearing red nail polish on her toes and he could've wept with joy at this nod to frivolity.

But he had also ignored the scarier edge to her new friendship – the drinking; the strange outbursts; her apparent hallucinations and memory lapses; the empty pill packets. He should've asked more questions, found out who this woman was. Then yesterday, with all those presents… He desperately wanted to believe that V was the victim of a cruel prank, but he knew it was more likely that grief was finally taking its toll on her.

His hands swirled in the scalding, soapy water, checking for an errant teaspoon or a stray cup, but he had washed everything he could find. He pulled the plug and watched the soapsuds swirl and disappear. As he looked up and out of the window into the crisp morning, he could see Felicity in her garden checking the washing on her line. He watched her for a moment, his mind remembering fingers tripping over skin.

Once upon a time, the very idea of a fling with her would've been absurd amid his perfect world, but things change. Felicity was dominant, self-confident and, most appealing of all, she didn't need saving – well, not by him anyway. She needed distraction from her dull, monotone life. Even in the last few weeks as the life had begun to creep back into V's pallor, the distance between the two of them had remained, pushing him closer to Felicity, but he had resisted. That had to mean something.

THE ACCIDENT

He watched her take an armful of clothes off the line and then stride purposefully back indoors. Tom stared after her for a moment, regret in every breath. Then he reached over, flicked the switch on the kettle and started to get his confessions in order. Time to come clean.

Veronica

I took longer than I should've to change, trepidation, not style, making me question my outfit repeatedly. But I also knew that all the delaying tactics in the world wouldn't make this go away. The shower had washed away any surface dirt, but that was all. Scarlet suggested I play the victim with plain clothes, naked face and simple ponytail. I allowed her to act as the puppet master. Eventually I descended to my fate, bare feet matching his, with only chipped nail polish on my toenails left to remind me of the previous night's excesses. Exhaustion hollowed out my legs and the hangover of earlier had settled into a thin coating of nastiness on my tongue. My mind kept conjuring up the smiley face on the blue pill, taunting me.

Tom was waiting for me in the lounge, with a prim pot of tea on a tray, and I felt like I was presenting myself before the headmaster to be reprimanded for smoking behind the bike shed. He sat in the armchair, legs crossed, looking tired and pale. My conscience prickled again. He looked up as I sat on the couch. I had asked Scarlet to stay and she disappeared into the kitchen. There would be time for introductions later.

He didn't speak immediately, just reached forward and poured the tea, before handing me a mug. If his choice of cup was deliberate, he didn't give any indication. It was from the pottery shop, hand-painted by Grace's chubby hands, all splashes and flicks of colour blending together to create a montage that only a toddler could identify and only a parent could love. I shrunk back, my eyes searching his expression, then reached out to accept the cup. I could feel the heat burning into the pads of my fingers and I lowered it hastily to the side table.

Neither of us wanted to speak, but the silence was oppressive.

Eventually, Tom said, 'Where were you?' The 'this time' hovered unsaid.

'Just out,' I replied, knowing that that wouldn't suffice but hearing it crawl from between my dry lips anyway.

He immediately dropped his head and shoulders. 'That's all I get? We should've been together, especially on her birthday.'

'You're right, I...' I paused, picked up my tea, burnt my lip, put it back down and returned to chewing on my ragged thumb. 'Um, I went out with Scarlet, we drank too much.' I chuckled, 'You know me and spirits – not a good mix.' Nor drugs apparently.

A clock ticked, a car accelerated past the window, normal morning routines unfolded around us.

'Where did you go?'

The million-dollar question.

Before I could explain, he said, 'Look, that's not important. We need to talk. I need to talk. God, I don't know where to begin.'

I frowned. This wasn't what I was expecting. The confessions were supposed to be coming from me.

He held his head in his hands for a moment, then muttered to the floor, 'I've been having an affair.'

Heat rushed up my neck.

He looked at me, his eyes pinpricks in his dejected face.

'I've been having an affair,' he said with more conviction. 'It's over now, I've finished it, a while ago, but I need to explain... why...'

I started to laugh great gulps of mirth at the irony of it.

'Ron, stop.'

I couldn't. The laughter sounded wild and feverish and I could feel cold tears streaming from my eyes.

'Ron!' he shouted.

Hearing him call her by that nickname jolted her. The laughter died as suddenly as it had started. I looked at him properly for the first time in a long while. He looked older, shattered.

'Who?' I needed him to admit all of it.

I could tell he was dreading that particular question. 'Felicity.'

I snorted again.

'Things before Grace – we had drifted apart a bit, you were busy, she took up all of your time. I don't know, it sounds lame, but the best way I can describe it is that I felt like I was intruding on your little partnership. It's no excuse and I know I've hurt you on top of the grief you're already living with. But that's the thing – we don't talk, we had stopped talking even then. We used to – years ago – but then family life took over, responsibility, and we stopped.'

He paused for breath. When he spoke again, his voice was weighed down with regret. 'You have every right to be angry. A part of me wants you to get angry, because at least then we would be talking and you would be reacting. We've never really talked about what happened, any of it, but it's constantly there between us, in everything we do, like an elephant in the room, and I need it to be over.'

I shook my head, incredulous, trying to clear the picture hovering in my mind of Felicity's smug face. 'Okay, my turn.' Tit for tat.

I sat forward and rested my arms on my knees, mirroring his pose.

'Last night...' But I couldn't get the words out. Everything I wanted to say sounded empty and hurtful, like a woman scorned.

He was peering at me through intense eyes, betraying the effort it was taking for him to remain composed.

'What? Say something. Anything,' Tom pleaded.

'Okay.' I dragged my eyes back to Tom. 'I guess I was feeling...' What exactly? My vocabulary was still failing me. The words in my head sounded chaotic and misaligned. 'Yesterday, when I was making Grace's cake and after all those presents, you had this look on your face as though you thought I was mad, like I had lost the plot. You immediately assumed the worst of me, instead of contemplating the fact that someone else may have been involved—'

'That's not true, I said as much—'

'No, your face gave you away. You thought I had finally tipped over the edge. And I don't blame you. There have been so many things that have happened that I haven't been able to explain. And even I don't know what to believe of myself any more. Every day I seem to be doing something that I would never have even considered before. Hell, I even thought it was you for a minute – the flowers yesterday...'

'What flowers?'

'It's not important. Anyway, I didn't want explanations and theories from you; I just wanted you to be there for me and to listen. Scarlet? Well, she understands that. She humoured me, dressed herself for a party, said the right things, so I decided that a party was what we would have.' I could remember the flare of defiance I had felt. 'We went to a bar, we had a lot to drink...' I paused.

'So where did you spend the night? At her place?'

'Um...' A lie leapt to my tongue, but that would be too easy.

'Look, that's twice in as many weeks you've put me through hell, just for a couple of drinks with your new mate. Who is she?' His voice was edgy. I could see him physically attempting to calm himself down, a deep breath, a steadying of his hands. Then in a calmer voice, he said, 'It's great that you've found someone that you can hang out with and talk to, but it's gone too far. You didn't even act like this when we were at university. Talk to me. Please. I'm really worried about you.'

I raised my eyes to scan his face. He looked so wretched.

Tom was still talking, his pent-up angst finding release in words. 'It's the silence that hurts the most. We've never talked about Grace. You still won't talk now.' I hated the way he said her name with such reverence. He had canonised her, but to me she was still my little girl. 'I would rather you were angry, lash out, throw something, I don't know... use me as a punchbag, but don't keep locking me out. I hurt too. I've wanted to talk to you, needed to talk, but I haven't because I thought it would make everything worse, but it can't get any worse than it is right now. You don't even seem angry about this thing with Felicity. You don't even seem surprised.' His words were tumbling over each other, and I put my hands over my ears.

'I... I don't...' I blew out some air. I could feel my control slipping away, like retreating sand in an hourglass. I had to get my thoughts in order, but the sand was accelerating. All I wanted was to put my hands up in defence and back away, run for cover, hide in a small, dark place. But the sand had momentum now and I knew once the last grain had filtered through, the truth would spill out along with all the hurt and grief.

'You want me to get angry?' My voice was low, dangerous, as I felt my mind struggling to hold onto the conversation. I looked at the carpet, the beige neutrality of it, and wondered how much dirt it was hiding deep in the thick pile. 'That's about all I feel these days. If I'm not angry, I'm numb. Yes, I feel angry – at you, at Felicity, at the world. But the anger scares me, so I lock myself away so that I don't hurt anyone else. But Scarlet, she lets me be. She doesn't judge, ridicule, remind me, pity me. She just lets me be me, whatever that is on any given day.' I looked up at him again. 'You'll like her, Tom. She's funny, outrageous,' I smiled, knowing she would likely be eavesdropping and wanting her to hear. 'She reminds me of what I used to be like, before us, before this' – I indicated the sensible suburban room around us – 'before...'

'Look, don't get me wrong. I know we've struggled to talk about everything and I'm really glad you've found someone to confide in, but this all seems so... extreme. You have to admit, you've gone off the rails a bit.' There was relief in his tone now, his voice lower than it had been.

He started to speak again, but I held up my hand, 'No, let me finish, please. I need to. There's so much more I should be saying.' I took another deep breath. 'In the beginning, I felt like I was drowning. Life was carrying on around me like nothing had happened. You had your work, our friends all carried on with their family life – I know they could do nothing else, and you needed to swamp yourself in work to cope, but I felt... cheated – like it wasn't fair – and then angry. The constant questions about whether I was okay that I didn't want to hear in the beginning stopped coming, the casseroles weren't offered any more, no one knew what to say to me, so they left me to myself and said that time would heal everything and it would get easier. But it didn't. There are reminders everywhere. It gets harder to wake up and breathe every day, to swing my legs out of bed, to put on a happy face. I can't just carry on doing the dishes and wandering around the shops, not without Grace there.

'Then Scarlet came along and she has shared the load a bit. She seems to know what I'm feeling and when I need to talk – or when I need to be distracted. I've been to some dark places, but she steers me away – and she's saved me, made it easier to carry the blame around.'

'Blame for what?' he interrupted.

'Sometimes, I think what if it was really me in that accident and that this is actually hell? Part of me thinks that all of this is just rightful punishment and I deserve to suffer.'

'I don't understand.'

I ignored him. Words were tumbling out of my mouth in fits and starts, with no order or reason, but now that I'd started, I didn't want to stop.

'Last night there were too many drinks, and' – I shook my head again – 'I took some drugs, stupidly, recklessly, and woke up this morning in a man's bed with no idea how I got there.' I rushed it out. 'What I do know is that this is not about hurting you or blaming you; it's about me finding a way of channelling all of this anger and grief and... I'm sorry. You have no idea how sorry I am.' I was wrung out.

Tears tracked slowly down his cheeks and it was his turn to look away. He got to unsteady feet. Approaching the window, he stood, looking out. I waited. While my hands started their wringing dance again, his were still, clasped prayer-like.

When he eventually spoke, his voice was croaky. 'Give me a minute. I need a minute.' He left the room.

I slumped back into the couch cushions and closed my eyes. I felt the cushions shift next to me and opened them again to see Scarlet looking at me in concern. She rested her hand lightly on mine.

'You okay?'

I just shook my head. Before I could reply, he was back. He didn't seem angry, just disillusioned, beaten, which cut through me deeper than any rage would have. He was so focused on my face, he didn't acknowledge Scarlet at all. 'You're wrong, you know. It has always been about blaming me,' he said. 'You think I didn't do enough.'

'No, I... Is that what you think?'

He interrupted forcefully, his eyes firing. 'You had your chance to speak; let me have mine now.'

Scarlet had retreated to the far corner of the room, as though hiding herself from the bullets of hurt and recriminations that were shooting around.

He composed himself somewhat. 'I've never heard you say the words since it happened, you know. Most of the time you don't even say her name.'

'What words?'

He returned to his seat and leant forward, looking purposefully into my eyes so that I couldn't look away. 'Grace is dead.'

It was like a knife stabbing, twisting, inflicting searing pain. I put my hands over my ears again, but he crouched in front of me and grabbed them, forcing them into my lap, holding them hostage.

'She's dead and you have to face up to it, but

you won't let yourself. In your heart, you think I should've saved her. I know you do. You think I should've done more, but I couldn't. The car was going too fast. The driver was drunk. No one could fix her. But don't blame me – I'm a doctor, not God, and I wasn't on call that day. To be honest, I'm glad I wasn't. I couldn't have been her doctor that day. I was her dad instead.

'What you did last night' – he paused, hurt etched into the lines of his face – 'it was you taking out your anger by trying to hurt me, and I get it. But it has to stop. Both of us have to stop this, stop trying to punish ourselves, each other. I thought you were on the mend and that was my mistake. I was so wrapped up in my own grief, I was just trying to get through each day myself and I couldn't prop you up as well. But I failed you. All of this is a cry for help – and I will help you, if you let me.'

'There's more,' I said.

'What?'

'I knew.'

'Knew what?'

'I knew about the affair.'

Grace

Tabitha was being mean as usual. Every picture Grace drew was met with a spiteful comment. They had never liked each other, so why their parents thought they should play together all the time was weird.

Right now, her dad and Felicity were downstairs talking about something 'important' apparently and they had been sent up to Tabitha's room with snacks and instructions to 'play nicely', but that was never easy when Tabitha was in one of her moods.

Today it was because her dad had said she couldn't have her own pony. Grace didn't know what Tabitha was making such a fuss about; she was allergic to horses anyway. But Tabitha liked to create a drama and Grace thought it was just to make the grown-ups uncomfortable, so that they got that panicked look on their faces, then generally they would give in and let her have whatever she wanted.

Grace carried on colouring in her pretty montage

of flowers and butterflies, ignoring Tabitha as much as possible. Pink, she needed more pink in this picture.

She reached across the carpet for the raspberry pink pen, but Tabitha snatched it from her fingers.

'I need it.'

'Can I use it when you're finished?'

'Maybe; maybe not.'

'Please, I want to finish off this butterfly.'

'In that case, no you can't.'

'Why are you so mean?' Grace could feel tears prickling behind her eyelashes.

'Why are you such a goody two shoes?' Tabitha wore an ugly scowl on her face. As quick as lightning, she reached over and pinched Grace hard on the arm. 'You gonna cry now? Run to daddy? Go on, why don't you go and see what they're up to downstairs?'

Grace didn't want to cry in front of Tabitha because that usually made her worse, but her arm was stinging and she didn't like the threatening look on Tabitha's face.

'My mummy and your daddy are in love, you know,' Tabitha said in a low voice.

Grace was confused. Daddy was in love with her mummy, not Tabitha's.

'No, they're not.'

'Yes they are. I saw them kissing.' Tabitha started writhing on the carpet and making smooching noises.

'Stop it! Don't say that!'

'It's true! Maybe they'll get married and you'll have to come and live here with us.' Tears streamed down Grace's cheeks, but she didn't notice. All she saw was the malevolent look on Tabitha's face and she just wanted to wipe it away. She slapped her hard, then sat back on her hands, as though not trusting that they wouldn't strike out again.

Tabitha's hand flew up to her cheek and she was stunned into blissful silence. It didn't last long. She started screaming at the top of her lungs.

Grace could hear footsteps thunder up the stairs and her dad and Felicity appeared in the doorway, both looking anxious.

'What happened?' Daddy asked.

'Tabby, darling, are you okay?' Felicity crouched down next to Tabitha and swept her into her arms.

'She hit me, Mummy, really hard.' Tabitha turned the volume up on her sobs.

'Grace! Did you?' Her dad looked at her with shock.

'She was saying stuff, Daddy...' Grace choked out, her heart feeling like it would implode when she saw the disappointment in her dad's eyes.

'Felicity, I am so sorry, I don't know what's come over her.' He turned back to Grace. 'You and I are going home right now and you need to explain yourself. But first, I think you have something to say to Tabitha, don't you?'

Grace turned wide eyes to Tabitha and mumbled

an apology, before making her way downstairs with heavy legs. She was relieved to be going home, but her mind was doing somersaults trying to understand what Tabitha had said. Surely it wasn't true. She could think of nothing worse than having to come and live with nasty Tabitha. And where would Mummy live? How much would she see her? She desperately clung onto the thought that Tabitha was lying just to be mean; it was the kind of thing she would do, after all.

Grace went to get her shoes from the cupboard under the stairs and could hear her daddy and Felicity through the small gap in the staircase above her head, calming Tabitha who was in full pity mode now.

'Tabby darling, you've had a shock. Go and lie on your bed with your favourite panda bear and I'll bring you a lovely hot chocolate,' Felicity was saying in a sing-song voice.

'Can I have sprinkles, cream and marshmallows please?' Tabitha replied in a woeful voice punctuated with repressed sobs.

'Of course you can, my angel.'

She heard her daddy and Felicity descend the stairs above her head, then they stopped halfway up and continued talking in hushed tones.

'I'm so sorry, I don't know what that was about.'

'Sounds like a cry for attention if you ask me, Tom.'

'I'll talk to her, find out what's going on.'

'And what about us? We need to finish our conversation.'

'It's finished, Felicity. I've explained to you, we can't do this anymore. You and I need to go back to the way things were. I love V; you love Ian. We can't be together any more. There's too much at stake.'

'But Tom, I…'

'No, Felicity. Please, just leave it.'

'You'll change your mind, Tom, you always do. You'll be back in my bed, holding me, kissing me.'

Grace didn't like the new tone of Felicity's voice. It sounded like they did on the television when her mummy told her to cover her eyes at the soppy bits. And why were they talking about kissing? She crept quietly from the cupboard and peeped around the staircase.

Felicity was stroking her daddy's face like he was a dog in need of petting and it made her feel very confused and sad inside, her mind jumping to what Tabitha had said. She went back to her shoes and put them on as quickly as possible.

Minutes later, her dad appeared behind her with a stern look in his eyes.

'Right, madam, you have some explaining to do.' He marched her out of the front door without a glance back at Felicity.

As they walked away, he said, 'What was that about?'

Grace didn't want to tell him what Tabitha had said, partly because she didn't understand it herself. She wanted to talk to her mummy first, maybe she could help her understand it. 'She wouldn't let me have the pink pen,' she replied instead.

'That's no reason to hit her. I know she can be difficult sometimes, but the better person will always ignore rather than reacting, Grace. Never hit, okay?' He crouched down at her height in the street and he looked so much like the daddy who kissed her mummy goodbye every day that she burst into tears of confusion and shame.

'Hey, hey, no need for that.' He gave her a big, firm hug and carried her home. 'Maybe you need some hot chocolate too.'

That night, Grace couldn't sleep. All she could think about was Felicity, her daddy and the nightmare of having to live with Tabitha. She had visions of being made to sleep in their cupboard under the stairs like Harry Potter or having to clean horse poop off Tabitha's riding boots every day like Cinderella. By the time morning came, she was feeling even more sad and confused, and knew she had to talk to her mummy about it.

She dressed carefully and brushed her teeth before coming downstairs. Her mummy was sitting at the dining room table tapping on her laptop and talking into her mobile phone.

'No, we need at least 500 hamburgers – there's always a rush at the end of these things, especially if the bar has done well.'

'Mummy, where's Daddy?'

Mummy placed a hand over the mobile mouthpiece and said, 'He's gone to work, Grace. Get yourself some cereal please,' then carried on talking.

Grace wasn't hungry, but she did as she was told. She poured a handful of Cheerios into a bowl, then retrieved the bottle of milk from the fridge. It was full and very heavy, but she carried it carefully over to her place at the island.

Her mummy had finished her phone call, but was still tapping away at the keyboard.

'Mummy, can I talk to you about something?' she said in a quiet voice.

'Hmmm?'

'It's about Tabitha.'

'Yes, your dad told me what happened. He's right, you can't go around hitting people, even if they are being mean,' she said, her eyes still on the screen.

'Well, it's about what she was saying.' She unscrewed the lid off the milk bottle.

She heard her mummy sigh impatiently and finally look up from her screen. 'I'm really busy with the arrangements for the school quiz night, princess. Is it important?'

'I think so. She was saying stuff... about Daddy and Felicity.'

'What kind of things?'

'That they are in love and that I might have to move in with them and live there instead of here.'

'Well, that's just ridiculous, isn't it? You live here with me and Daddy. She's just trying to wind you up and because you reacted, she won, didn't she? Now eat your cereal.' She turned back to her computer.

But Grace had the sudden feeling that this really was important and that she should try and get her to listen.

'She said she'd seen them kissing. And I heard them talking yesterday in funny voices... Felicity said something about them kissing too and being in bed together and I know only people who love each other kiss, so...' She stopped. Her mummy was watching her closely and she felt overwhelming relief that she had done the right thing when she saw a look of fleeting realisation pass over her mummy's face. She had heard her this time.

Then the look was gone and was replaced by anger.

'That's an awful thing to be saying to me, Grace. It's simply not true. Felicity is a friend of ours and now you are being hurtful by saying such things. You're as bad as Tabitha!'

Her mummy's harsh, shouty words made her start crying and she whipped her hand up to wipe her eyes, knocking the milk over in the process. It pooled out towards her mummy's laptop as if in slow motion.

'Grace!' her mummy hollered. 'Be careful!'

Grace leapt from the chair, indignation colouring her vision, and ran from the room. She paused in the hallway, unsure where to go, as her mummy bustled in the kitchen wiping up the spill and muttering under her breath. Grace thought fleetingly that it would be great if the laptop was broken, then she ran for the front door. If Tabitha could do things for attention, then so could she. If she ran into the street, her mummy would have to follow her, wouldn't she? Maybe then, she could get her to take her seriously.

She grabbed the door handle and pulled it open before tearing off down the street in her bare feet. She could hear her mummy call to her, but she kept running, her vision blurred by tears and her brain clouded in confusion.

Veronica

'I remember watching her like it was all in slow motion, like I was swimming through quicksand to get to her. She reached the end of the street and stepped off the kerb into the road. I was almost there and I reached out a hand, but there was only empty air. There wasn't a screech of brakes or anything like that, just a dull thud that I felt in every nerve ending of my body and a sudden quiet. Then a noise like a fox wailing, but it was coming from me.'

Tom slumped onto the couch next to me, not saying anything, but processing it all.

I sagged into myself, suddenly exhausted. Scarlet stood across the room, her hand covering her gaping mouth. Tears made her irises glisten.

'But you said...' Tom trailed off, then stood up with such force that I was thrown to the side of the couch as his weight shifted from my side.

He started to pace in circles.

'She didn't see us, you know… did she?' His voice was strangled.

'No, no, she didn't, but she needed me to listen and to believe her and I didn't. I shut her down. I wasn't there when she needed me.'

A moment passed while he processed it all. 'I need to understand this. You said something about a shop – I thought she was walking to the shop.'

'I couldn't bring myself to tell you the truth. Cowardly, I know. And part of me didn't want to admit it.'

I stood and walked over to him.

'I don't blame you if you can't forgive me, but I am sorry.' My voice cracked as tears left trails in my still made-up face.

I could still see the conflict on his face, the angels and demons in his mind fighting to be heard and to lay the blame somewhere.

'But I am as culpable as anyone then,' he said.

'That's not why I'm telling you. If anything, I'm to blame for not being the mother she needed. Sometimes that is what I struggle to accept the most. I didn't want to believe what she was saying about you and Felicity, but now I know she was telling the truth.' I sat down heavily again, my legs not able to hold me up. 'It was my job to look after her. It's funny, I spent so many years worrying about her well-being, the food she was eating, whether the toys were educational enough, was she getting enough sleep. But in one second my lack of care ended up killing her. I have to live with that.'

He came to sit next to me. 'You can't keep blaming yourself. I'm as much to blame as you. She should never have been in that situation and I put her there.' I could see it was physically paining him to hear the role he had played. 'But even so, it doesn't change the fact that neither of us were driving the car. The police said he was going too fast, he was drunk. He didn't even brake. He killed her, not you, not me. A sober person would've braked, would've been able to stop.'

We sat in silence.

Eventually, he said, 'We've got to stop doing this to each other. Especially now, with the trial coming up.'

'The trial.' A chance to have it all replayed in a public arena; a chance for everyone to hear my culpability – up until now, I had refused to contemplate what that would be like.

'Yes, the trial.' His voice broke and quivered. 'The bastard will be found guilty and we can start getting our lives back, can start trying to forgive ourselves.' He looked down again. 'Do you remember what you said to me on the morning of the funeral?' His tears were flowing freely now.

'No, I don't remember the funeral at all,' I admitted.

'You said, *Why couldn't you save her? You're a doctor and you've saved hundreds of others, why not her? And*

I couldn't answer you, so you walked away and didn't come back. I lost both of you that day.'

'I don't remember. I... that wasn't fair of me.'

He swiped at his tears, then pulled me into his arms. It felt strange and yet familiar. I felt stiff and unyielding, even though I wanted to fold into him.

Eventually, he released me and I noticed Scarlet standing to the side of the room. I'd forgotten she was there.

'So I should probably do the polite thing and introduce you to Scarlet now.' In all the drama, Tom hadn't noticed her.

He looked puzzled. 'Now?'

I looked at Scarlet, who smiled back at me. I shrugged.

'Well, it's rude to carry on ignoring her,' I said to Tom.

'You're right. You're spending so much time with her, the least you could do is introduce me. When is a good time?' He smiled wearily.

My brain was obviously struggling to process the stress of the day on top of a monumental hangover and it was all starting to take its toll, because I wasn't grasping what he meant.

Feeling silly, I indicated Scarlet to my left, 'Tom, meet Scarlet; Scarlet, my husband, Tom.'

Scarlet approached him, her hand extended politely.

He laughed, but didn't take her outstretched hand, then stopped abruptly, studying my face. 'I don't get it,' he said, head cocked to one side, his standard look when trying to figure me out.

Scarlet lowered her hand, looking affronted.

Up came my anger again, bubbling and roiling. 'Tom, please. I know you're hurt and angry, but it's not like you to be rude to guests.'

He didn't look cross though, just bewildered. 'You've lost me, Ron. Is she in the car? Go and get her then. There's still tea in the pot.'

I raised my hands in question and turned to Scarlet, who had sat down next to me dejectedly. 'She's right here, Tom.' My voice rose an octave. 'You're being ridiculous.'

Scarlet was wriggling her fingers at him in a childish wave, like a three-year-old trying to attract her dad's attention.

'Ron, there's no one there.' His voice was low, his expression one of sudden realisation.

The air in the room pressed in around me. The clock ticked on the mantelpiece and the ice-winged butterflies in my chest took flight again.

'Of course there is.' I frowned at him, the anger turning to embarrassment at his behaviour. This was so unlike him; he was normally the epitome of manners.

Tom was pale. 'What does she look like?'

I was clearly missing a vital piece of a puzzle I didn't know I was solving. Now it was my time to humour him. I sighed. 'She's beautiful, auburn hair, lovely heart-shaped face, the most bizarre choice in clothes... a beautiful wreck.' I looked over and smiled at Scarlet, who stuck her tongue out at me. 'She reminds of what Grace would've looked like,' I whispered.

Tom just stared at me, like I had something unspeakable on my face.

Suddenly, he stood up, then moved around to where Scarlet had been sitting. 'Ron,' he said slowly, 'There's no one here.'

The room tilted beneath my feet. I looked past him to where Scarlet had been moments before, but the space was empty. I could feel his thigh pressing against mine, smell his aftershave in my nostrils. I looked around, searching for her, but there was just the two of us in the room. That feeling of slipping sand in an hourglass returned, but this time it was my sanity filtering away.

'But... she was... did she...?'

She couldn't have moved that quickly without me seeing her. It was physically impossible. My mind whirled from one side to the other, reasoning, doubting. Tom was saying something, but I couldn't hear him through the traffic in my head. Images were coming to me – of people watching Scarlet and me with polite disbelief, her food growing cold on her plate, never getting to see her house. I had assumed observers were eavesdropping on our colourful conversations, that she was always on a diet, that perhaps her house wasn't as grand as mine. Now the synapses were connecting. I felt sick, bile rising in my throat. Tom had taken hold of my hand at some point and was still talking, but I pushed him away and ran to the kitchen. I reached the sink as the bile rose, the acidic malodour creeping into my nostrils and helping to purge my head and my stomach. I was panting for breath. Tears streamed down my cheeks.

Tom came up behind me, reached out and lightly pulled my hair back from my sweaty face.

After a moment, he said, 'Don't shut me out. Talk to me, explain it so that I can understand.'

'I don't understand myself,' I choked.

I couldn't still my thoughts. Out of the cacophony in my brain, one lyric kept repeating on a loop: *She has to be real. She has to be real.*

'Where's my phone?' I choked out.

'Why?'

'Please, find my phone.'

He left the room and returned moments later with it. He passed it to me gingerly and I checked my messages with shaking fingers. There were the texts from Scarlet, but the number they were sent from was my own.

More images fired through my mind: the lipstick case; Felicity's face as we jumped on the trampoline; the polite sideways glances as we chatted in coffee shops. It all started to click into place and the chorus changed to *She's not real. She's not real.*

I turned and stared, not seeing, out of the kitchen window, my hands clutching the countertop for stability.

Life was carrying on regardless out there: a fly batting against the window pane in a vain attempt to escape; a bird rooting in the grass; a red blouse flapping in the breeze on Felicity's washing line.

Quietly, but with a sting like salt in a wound, I said once more, 'Help me.'

I felt his arms wrap around me and the energy dissolve from my legs as I collapsed into him. His assured presence broke through the last of my defences and I turned into him, sobbing, gasping for breath, my mind still a hurricane of images as I tried to figure out what had been real and what had been concocted by the peacekeepers in my head. We sank to the floor and sat like that for what felt like an eternity, him gently rocking me as I shuddered and wailed.

Eventually, as my breathing began to even out, he pulled me to my feet and we returned to the lounge to sit close together on the couch, closer than we had been in a year, my chest still involuntarily spasming, his hand stroking my hair with the lightest of touch.

Finally I found a voice. 'She was there one morning, in the rain. It was the end of the school run and I had been watching the stressed mums dragging their kids to school, everyone miserable and shouting, and I kept thinking how lucky they were that they could do that. I wanted to shout out of the window at them, tell them to be grateful. And then she was there, in front of me, and she was... happy... carefree... vivid.'

I looked down at my fingers as they resumed their fidgety dance, picking and pulling. 'It was shortly after I'd had that meltdown in the shoe shop. Felicity was there and I just... Anyway, after that, we bumped into each other a few times – come to think of it, mostly when I was struggling to cope. She would ring the doorbell, we would open a bottle of wine and talk – about anything and everything, sometimes deep stuff, but mostly not. Mostly it was a way of not thinking about Grace.

'She made me feel like I could carry on, could laugh again, try and do normal things. It was like a huge weight that had been pressing down on me was suddenly more manageable – not gone, but that bit lighter because she was helping to carry it.' The words were coming faster and tumbling into each other, but I had to get it all out.

'It got to the point where I found I needed her so much that I couldn't get through the day if she wasn't by my side. She would tell me what to do, what to say, because I couldn't rely on my own brain any more. She kept the horrible thoughts away too – and there have been some.' I looked up at him then, open and honest.

I flicked stray tears from my cheeks. Tom rested one hand on my knee; the other reached over to still my fingers and remained there. I looked down at this familiar hand, so different to the hand that had touched me the night before. I shuddered.

'I never thought… it never occurred to me…' I shook my head, closed my eyes. 'Then things just spiralled. We started going to bars, drinking too much. But if I was drinking, I wasn't thinking, you know?' I looked back at Tom's face, wanted to see if he was getting it. He nodded almost imperceptibly and I carried on. 'Like you said, when it all happened we didn't talk much, you and I, because I couldn't. If I put it into words, then it had actually happened and I thought I would go mad.' I laughed at the irony. 'And look at me now.'

'You're not mad,' he said with conviction.

'I've managed to create and spend time with an imaginary friend for the last few months. A therapist would have a field day with this. Maybe all the rest – the gifts, the flowers, all of it – maybe it was me after all.'

I wanted him to understand what she had meant to me, how she had helped me to cope and live with the overriding remorse at what happened, but I didn't think words would do her justice. Instead, I sat quietly, numb.

'Where do we go from here?' I asked, scared to hear the answer.

'We get help – for you, for us. It'll take time.'

'Is there an "us" still?'

He didn't reply immediately and I was surprised at

how much I wanted him to say we still had a chance. But it was a lot to ask. We had both done some damage.

'I know I've hurt you, done unforgiveable things, but I need you. I can't do this alone – apparently, if I have to conjure up an imaginary friend just to make it to the supermarket.'

He laughed a little at that. 'Yes, there's still an "us". We owe it to Grace to try and fix this.' His voice dropped to a whisper. 'Let me be your Scarlet.'

The agony in my chest had now been replaced with emptiness, the same feeling that was there after Grace died, but this time Scarlet had been added to the pyre and I was grieving for her too.

'I'm scared, Tom,' I admitted.

'Me too,' he said and pulled me towards him again. 'I know you don't want to hear it, but Felicity has been really worried about you. Let her help you too.'

I shook my head against his chest and buried it a little deeper, but he pushed me away gently.

'Look, her and Ian have been our oldest friends for as long as we've known each other. We need to talk about where we go from here. Ian doesn't know – and I don't know if I want him to. His company is in a bad way again. I know you don't owe her anything, but... what about Ian? She really was worried though – she phoned me to tell me about the message in the shower and really wanted to help.'

Something niggled at me, a realisation that was just out of reach.

'What?'

'She said you were acting strange, talking about something you had written on the shower door or something? She said she'd calmed you down, so I wasn't to say anything as it would set you off again.'

I went cold. I pushed away from him sharply, my mind whirling.

'What? What have I said?'

I rushed into the hallway, threw a pair of shoes onto my bare feet and pulled open the door, ignoring the questions Tom was firing at my back.

He grabbed my arm and I turned to him with frantic eyes.

'Ron!'

'Get Ian out of the house – I need to talk to Felicity.'

My hands were shaking as I knocked hard on Felicity's door. Tom hovered in the street, shifting nervously from foot to foot.

'V! This is a nice surprise, how are you?' Ian pulled me into a gentle hug, but I stiffened and he released me quickly. 'Come in, both of you.'

'Oh, that reminds me, Ian. I still have your leafblower – it's at home. Come with me and we'll grab it. V wants to chat to Felicity anyway,' Tom improvised in a thin voice.

'Oh, sure, go on in V. She's upstairs, but I'll tell her you're here. She's getting Tabby ready for yet another party...' His voice trailed off as he noted the look on my face.

I stalked past him and perched on the edge of Felicity's couch, knees and jaw clenched, trying to steady my breathing. Confronting her outright wouldn't help – she'd just deny everything. I needed to somehow get her to admit it herself. My knee-jerk reaction to march straight over here meant I hadn't given much thought to what I would say to her.

Ian flitted around me, offering cups of tea and making polite small talk before heading out the door after Tom.

I heard muffled footsteps, then Felicity strode in, exuding authority in her own home.

'Veronica, this is a... nice... surprise.'

'Felicity, how are you?' I kept my tone as low and neutral as possible.

She began to shuffle around me, straightening magazine spines and flicking imaginary balls of fluff from the coffee table. Once so welcome in her home, I now felt like I was cluttering the otherwise immaculate room. I coughed subtly as a whiff of cloying jasmine tickled my throat from the pointy sticks in the reed diffuser on the side table next to me.

A clock ticked. I cleared my throat.

Before I could speak, a pint-sized girl burst in, eyes blazing.

'Momma, I thought you washed my pink skirt. I can't find it anywhere and I need it for Jessica's party later.'

With practised patience, Felicity turned to her. 'I did, darling. I laid it out on your bed ready.'

'No, you did not. You have to find it, Momma. I need to get ready.' She stamped her tiny feet in time to her demands, her fists clenched.

'You have plenty of time, Tabitha – and look, Mummy is busy chatting to Veronica right now.'

'Hi, Tabitha. You've grown so big since the last time I saw you,' I said.

The girl didn't acknowledge my presence in any way. Instead, she folded her arms defiantly and glared at her mother. 'I simply cannot be late.'

Felicity turned back to me and said, 'Bear with,' then rushed out of the room. The air was instantly more breathable.

Tabitha remained behind to hold court. I was aware of her watching me and I mentally scrabbled around to find something to say. She flounced onto the couch with a melodramatic sigh and an Oscar-winning eye roll.

'How's school, Tabitha?' I asked carefully.

'Boring.' Her eyes roamed over the room, then settled on the *Hello!* magazine on the coffee table.

'Why are you at home today?'

'Inset day.'

'Still doing well with your ballet?'

She grunted in what I assumed was affirmation while retrieving the magazine. Sitting cross-legged on the couch, she looked more like she was waiting for a Botox consultation, with her leopard-print dress pulled primly over her knee and her pink, expertly painted toenails.

Another pre-adolescent sigh as she tediously flicked the pages.

I desperately wanted to say something to her about Grace, *that day*, make her aware of the damage she had caused. But she was just a child following the example of her designated grown-up, so I couldn't blame her.

Instead, I focused on the dust-free coffee table in front of me as I tried to order my thoughts. Sitting beside the pile of interior design and gossip magazines was a cast of Tabitha's feet as a baby, immortalised in shining bronze. Bile rose in my throat again and I took a deep breath.

Then Felicity was back, pink skirt in hand, apologies at the ready.

'So sorry, darling, I had left it on your chair, not the bed.'

I could hear the muttering under Tabitha's breath as she stomped from the room.

Silence descended again. Felicity lowered herself regally into the armchair, her ballerina pumps sinking into the plush pale grey pile of the carpet.

I shifted uncomfortably against a stiff cushion.

Looking at my feet, I noticed a dark clump of mud lying next to my scruffy Converses like an accusation. I shifted my foot over it, then ground the mud deep into the carpet.

The sun pierced the bay window, its glare narrowing the pavilion grey walls.

'So?' She straightened her skirt over her knees, a mirror image of her daughter. 'You wanted to talk to me about something?' A quiet smugness settled over her sharp features.

God, I hated her. Her dust-free house, her uncomplicated life, the injustice of it – that she could end up with everything still in place while I was grasping at mere fragments of my former life. How did that happen? I had a sudden, overwhelming urge to grab hold of one of her scented diffuser sticks and plunge it into her self-righteous eye. I sat on my hands instead, reminding myself that it wouldn't help, even if it made me feel better for a minute.

'Um, yeah, I... er... First off, my behaviour has been inexcusable. I ... I've been struggling to come to terms with Grace's accident and with her birthday coming up... I've been acting out of character and I realise that my actions towards you in particular have been immature and... I'm sorry.' It galled me having to say all of this, but if she thought she had won, she wouldn't be able to stop herself from gloating. I was counting on it.

With an exaggerated sigh, she got to her feet and stood, looking down at me, her hands on her hips. 'You know, when Grace first died...' I flinched, 'I was sympathetic. I mean, I wouldn't wish that on any parent and it proves how life is so short and we should make each moment count. That's why I indulge Tabitha so much – she deserves to relish every minute she is alive. But seeing you hanging around the school gates every day, slowly losing the plot, locking yourself away, I started to pity you instead.' Each word was a poison dart. You could see in every crease line on her face that she was enjoying being in control. 'You do need to get your head sorted, Veronica, before you lose more than just your daughter.'

Just my daughter?

I got to my feet, tired of looking up at her – or rather of her looking down on me. 'I've said what I have to say, accept it or not.' I turned to leave, knowing she would want the last word.

'You know who I feel sorry for? Poor Tom. He has to deal with your breakdown on top of his own grief. No wonder he spends so much time at that hospital. You want to be careful there, Veronica, or someone may well come along and whisk him away from you.' Her eyes glinted like steel ball bearings.

I turned back to her slowly, fire in my blood. 'And I suppose you think that woman is you?' All I could picture was her and Tom, like a black and white movie replaying in my imagination, all jumpy and stuttery.

'What on earth do you mean?' She held a hand to her chest theatrically.

I laughed derisively. 'Oh, come on, since we're being so brutally honest here. I know about you and Tom. He's told me. He's also told me that it's over between you. You may pity me, but I'm a survivor and we are going to get through this. For you, Grace has nothing to do with it. You hardly had two words to say to her when she was alive unless it was to try and belittle her or use her weaknesses to boost Tabitha's confidence, even though you should've been taking notes on what a daughter should be like so that you could figure out how you are getting it so wrong.'

'How dare you!'

We circled each other like hissing cats. I hadn't heard the admission I had come for yet, so I wasn't about to back down.

'I came here to clear the air, but you still find me threatening, don't you? God knows why – I'm the first to admit I'm a mess – but all you see is the one thing you can't have: Tom. You may have distracted him when I wasn't there and he was feeling left out, but that makes you a parasite feeding on a man's weaknesses.' She paled. 'He's knocked you wide now, hasn't he? He's come back to me and you just can't stand it.' Talk about goading the wild animal.

The hatred on Felicity's face was raw and ugly. 'You know, I just don't get it. Even when you're going mad, Tom still stands by you. There is nothing you can do wrong. Yet look at you – I don't understand what he sees.' She waved a hand in front of me incredulously. 'He was supposed to be mine, not yours. I've had to stand by and watch you living what should've been my perfect life with the perfect family. Instead, I got boring Ian and his fucking spreadsheets. Even then, Mr Reliability was meant to have one job: to keep us financially secure and he failed, needed you two to bail us out, to even put a roof over our heads. I'm not actually sure what Ian has been good for, short of fathering Tabitha.'

She was pacing in front of me, jabbing her finger and wearing a mask of repugnance.

'It was a stroke of genius convincing Ian to buy this house. I needed to be able to see Tom every day, to be within reaching distance of him, because I knew he would realise sooner or later.'

'Realise what?'

'That he chose the wrong one. And he did realise, once you started taking him for granted. I couldn't keep him away – he wanted it all the time. Sometimes it was hard to keep my voice down in case Grace heard us at it.'

'Careful, Felicity, don't go there...'

'What? Don't want to hear the truth after all? About

how much he enjoyed it, how many times he told me he loved me?'

'He has never loved you. He ended it with you!'

'You can believe that if you want. We were going to come clean with you and Ian, start a new life together, but then your stupid brat of a child went and got herself run over.'

I could feel my fists clenching and my jaw stiffen.

'At first, I was annoyed – terrible timing – and the guilt was ruining Tom. But then I realised that her dying was a blessing in disguise. She was always such a people-pleaser, wasn't she? She did me quite a favour. I guess you could call it collateral damage because once the shock had worn off, Tom started calling me again, crying on my shoulder, asking to meet up.'

Her mouth was a snarl and I could feel her spittle on my face. I didn't want to hear the words, but needed to all the same.

'You were shutting him out, so I let him in. He just needed a little more encouragement, that's all, something to help him see that we should've been together all along, that I'm better for him. And what better incentive than if your wife is slowly losing her marbles?'

There it was. The dots connected in my head, all the strange coincidences and little reminders. I felt cold and hot simultaneously, shivery but feverish as I realised how deep her obsession ran, how she had just been biding her time.

'It was you.'

'The little messages from the dead? Yeah, I thought that was quite clever of me.' Her smile was villainous. 'To be honest, it wasn't planned. I should thank you really. You gave me the idea originally. That day in the shoe shop. I'd been carrying that stupid dummy around for weeks after I found it down the back of Tabby's bed one day. I was actually going to give it to Tom as a memento or something, thinking it would maybe bring on another one of his needy episodes, but there you were, floundering around on the floor, like a bag lady with your stained top and unbrushed hair. I was ashamed of you. I should've taken a photo to show Tom what his perfect doctor's wife had turned into.' She shrugged casually. 'But instead I shoved the dummy in your bag when I was helping you up, knowing you'd find it eventually. Imagine how chuffed I was when I saw you pull it from your bag in the coffee shop! You didn't quite react how I wanted you to then – there was no wailing or anything, still too polite for that – but you looked like you'd seen a ghost, excuse the pun.'

My fingers itched to scratch her eyes out as I listened to the vitriol spilling from her acid tongue.

'I knew I needed to push a little harder, so I left a message on the music teacher's answer machine. Remember how you used to moan about that piano waiting list? The photo tossed into your gym bag, the Facebook page, the flowers, all easy to explain as you losing your mind. Even writing Grace's name in the shower – Tom should've asked for his house key back really. You two look so peaceful when you're sleeping.'

I felt like a cold hand had reached up, grabbed me by the throat and was slowly asphyxiating me.

'All I needed was to nudge you towards the edge of the cliff, then stand back and watch you fall while I comforted Tom and picked up the pieces for him. And you were so close to the edge, weren't you?'

My voice was menacing. 'But I didn't fall, Felicity. I survived. You didn't win.' Then another thought struck me hard, like a body blow. 'Zara.'

'What about her?'

'It was you she was trying to warn me about.' I scratched around in my memory, trying to remember what she had said. 'She said she was with you when she fell into the street.' I was struggling to comprehend the dark depths to which she had been willing to go.

'She was far too interested in my relationship with Tom, threatened to speak to you about it. Now there's a proper friend, not like me,' she sneered. 'I have to say, she surprised me. I didn't know she cared that much about you. But then, it didn't take much to frighten her off, just a nudge... literally. Now look at you: your friends have all abandoned you, your husband is staying with you out of pity and your daughter is dead.'

Enough. An animal growl emanated from deep inside my guts and I threw myself at her, my fingers like claws reaching for her eyes. I felt my nails connect with her skin before strong arms clamped around me and I was pulled back, still scratching and growling.

'She's not worth it, Ron! Stop!'

Tom held me tight against him while I writhed and thrashed. Felicity was cowering on the carpet, holding her hands to her face. Standing in the doorway, looking ashen, was Ian, his hands hanging by his sides, the leafblower lying absurdly at his feet, now returned to its rightful owner.

Seeing his face, the fight in me evaporated and I slumped against Tom.

Felicity peeped from behind her fingers, then launched at her husband, weeping dramatically. 'She attacked me, Ian. Keep her away from me. She's crazy.'

Tom looked at her in disgust. 'You're the crazy one. Sick in the head. We heard every word.'

'How could you, Felicity?' Ian looked shell-shocked. 'Not just Tom, but how could you be so sick that you would torture your friend like that? Has she not had enough to deal with? And Zara? Bloody hell, I don't know you at all, do I?' He turned to leave the room.

Felicity wore a grotesque mask of rage, accentuated by the beads of blood forming along the deep scratch lines on her cheek.

'Jealousy has made you ugly, Felicity,' Tom said, then

turned to me, his arms reaching out. 'Come on, enough now. Let's go home.'

'At least I've still got my Tabitha.' Her voice was glacial.

I stopped. 'You must be so proud of her. Do you know that she knew about you and Tom? That she was taunting Grace with it? Does that not worry you – what she's turning into? A manipulating bully?'

'If she was enjoying tormenting Grace as much as I've enjoyed tormenting you, then yes, I am proud of her – a chip off the old block.'

All at once, I heard Scarlet's voice again, shouting incredulously in my ear, defending me still. 'How dare she? Are you really letting her off this easy? She's made you question everything about yourself, from your parenting skills to your sanity. She's praised her bullying little shit of a daughter for tormenting Grace, she even tried to kill your friend and you're just going to tell her off and leave?'

I saw a flash of red hair and heard an animal snarl before my hand was propelled onto the bronze cast on the coffee table and it was pitched with force at Felicity's smug face.

Epilogue

Veronica

The bath water was frigid, but still I sat with my knees drawn up and my arms clasping them tightly to my chest. Goosebumps stood to attention on every patch of exposed skin.

'Ron, are you okay?' Tom called through the locked door. He had taken to checking up on me constantly since our mutual confessional. A few weeks had passed and everything and nothing had changed. The house next door was up for sale. Ian had sold his company and was moving with Tabitha back to his hometown to live closer to his family; and Felicity was in hiding apparently, licking her wounds. Ian had made it clear he wanted her to have nothing to do with Tabitha after he'd come to realise that Felicity's acidity was rubbing off on their impressionable daughter. Rumour has it the large scar on Felicity's face from where the bronze cast struck her will never fade completely. Ian had convinced us not to get the police involved and besides, there was very little evidence of any wrongdoing on her part. No one was certain where exactly she was and I still looked over my shoulder now and again when a cold wind blew over me.

Tom and I were also taking baby steps forward. I couldn't blame him for handling me with kid gloves. He thought Scarlet was gone, but she was currently sitting on the closed toilet lid, listening to me voice my fears of what lay ahead.

'We'll need to leave soon,' he called again.

'I'll be out in a minute,' I called back in clipped tones.

Scarlet raised an eyebrow. 'He's just worried.'

'I know, but he's smothering me. We've gone from giving each other too much space to him not giving me any at all,' I replied in whispered tones.

'You both just need to get through this trial, then you can put everything behind you,' Scarlet replied, ever the voice of reason.

I watched the soapsuds swirl in the cold water, mirroring the feeling in my chest. The trial was starting today and I had no idea how it would go or if I could even pull myself together long enough to get through it.

'Have you seen the rosebush yet?' she asked.

'Not as such. I know he was planting it yesterday, but I can't bring myself to go out there yet,' I replied, feeling ashamed at my weakness.

Tom had planted a cerise pink rosebush in the back garden as a memorial to Grace. He had asked for my input, but all I could volunteer was that she loved bright pink. He had been stone-faced as he dug the hole, the physical exertion acting as a form of rehabilitation for him, but I wasn't quite there yet and had stayed indoors. I would be ready, soon, but not now.

'Okay, but you will. Now get your skinny arse out of that cold bath and get ready. And I'll be there, right beside you, through it all.'

I pulled myself to standing, the water trickling off my body, and I smiled at her, grateful she was still there but very aware that she wasn't. But I needed her this week; I'd worry about the implications of who she was when this was all over.

I wrapped myself in a warm towel and unlocked the door.

Tom was still standing guard, waiting patiently. 'Okay?'

'Yes, fine. I'm going to get dressed.'

*

The trial passed in a blur. I remember snippets: the musty smell in the courtroom; the monotonous tone of the lawyers as they made their case; the sound of Tom weeping quietly beside me as the driver pleaded guilty. I shut myself away mentally and let it all wash over me like a shroud, not hearing the details, not witnessing the reactions of the people around me, all the while wishing I could hide my body as I could my mind.

Scarlet kept her promise and held my hand throughout, while Tom held the other.

I refused to look at the driver on his day of reckoning. I couldn't bring myself to in case his face would be etched into my mind forever. I wanted to see Grace's face, not his. But as I heard the judge read out his sentence, I turned to look at him: a balding, hunched shadow of a man, someone almost as broken as I was. I didn't want to feel empathy for him or pity, but I could identify with his anguish. He was given the maximum sentence and was led away to spend time in a prison cell to deal with what he had done. The only difference between his cell and mine was that his had physical walls.

When we returned home from court, I disappeared straight to bed, not to sleep but to remember. Tom remained downstairs and I could hear him sobbing through the walls. We were doing it again, shutting ourselves off from one another, trying to grieve in private. It hadn't worked before and it wouldn't work now.

It took every ounce of courage I had to pull myself out of bed and make my way down the stairs. I walked into the lounge where my broken husband was and I sat down next to him.

Forcing one foot in front of the other, I moved carefully towards the four-poster bed. A fairy-tale canopy of cotton candy pink edged with lace and festooned with butterflies. I could remember with stinging clarity the moment we revealed her freshly decorated bedroom to her: bright, shining eyes peeking from behind tiny fingers and the shriek of absolute glee that followed. I lowered myself timidly onto the perfectly straight duvet, feeling the eyes of a hundred stuffed toys appraising me politely.

Here was Joey the Kangaroo from one of our first holidays as a family when we endured a hellishly long flight to take her to see Tom's family; next to it Petula the Ragdoll, hand-made for her by her granny; propped up by Roger the Monkey, a newer addition to her artificial fluffy family. I reached between Petula and Roger, my fingers creeping under the pillow until I felt them grasp thin, smooth fabric and pulled out the blanket she couldn't sleep without. The yellow of the wool was washed out from countless spins in the dryer, the left-hand corner still stained from where she had cut her head after falling against the table as a toddler. I rubbed the worn but familiar fabric between trembling fingers, then lifted it to my face and breathed in deeply. A faint essence of her was still there, like sherbet and talcum powder. I closed my eyes, finally letting myself remember. The feeling of asphyxiation lifted ever so slightly with each recalled giggle, hug and sniffle.

Then my tears came again. I felt like I had cried an ocean over the last few weeks as I sat with Tom, talking, analysing, baring our souls to each other. We were both drained and empty, but I was hopeful. I lay down with my head amongst the toys and sobbed into their fur.

Time passed – I don't know how long – but I allowed myself this moment of self-indulgence, felt myself let go. Eventually I opened my eyes and sat up, straightened the toys, smoothed down the pillow. I took another look at the blanket, then returned it to its place of safety. I looked up and saw Scarlet standing in the doorway, watching with approval, dust dancing in the sunlight like a halo behind her head. She was smiling and crying. Before I could call out to her, she lifted her hand, waved goodbye, and walked away.

In her place, Tom filled the doorway, real and tangible, broken but not beyond repair. I stood up and walked towards him.

We hope you enjoyed this book.

Dawn Goodwin's next book is coming in summer 2018

More addictive fiction from Aria:

Acknowledgements

Although written in a solitary bubble and fuelled by copious cups of tea and chocolate digestives, there are a few people who have helped me to realise my childhood ambition with this book.

The idea came to me one morning on the school run, but it was my time spent with the team at Curtis Brown Creative that helped to form it into an actual novel – particularly my tutor, Chris Wakling, who made me realise it was actually good enough, and Anna Davis, who gave me very helpful advice on what to do next when it was finally finished.

The people I met on the CBC creative writing course have become lifelong friends. To Alice Clark-Platts, Cath Benetto, Heidi Perks, Elin Daniels, Alex Tyler, Grace Coleman, Moyette Gibbons and Juliette Henderson in particular, I cannot thank you enough for your constant support and motivational emails, not to mention all the laughs and glasses of wine. Book launches will never be the same again. You are all talented writers and

DAWN GOODWIN

I am honoured to finally get a book on the 'Authors We Know' shelf in such esteemed company.

To the team at Bell Lomax Moreton, particularly Lauren Gardener for pulling my manuscript from the slush pile and falling in love with it, and my lovely agent Jo Bell, who has been an absolute joy to work with. Here's to sharing many more stories, dog-related or otherwise, Jo.

To the team at Aria, particularly Caroline Ridding, who saw the potential and took a punt on me and my stories with such enthusiasm.

To Mary, Kate, Sarah and Laura, because we all need a 'wingman' on a night out, mostly to help us remember what happened the next day so that I can put it in a story, and to Bear, because she'd be tickled pink to get a mention. You all love a good book, so I hope you like mine.

To my family – I told you I'd write a book one day – and to Ted, who has given me the support to follow my dream and always believed I could do it.

And finally to Paige and Erin. I hope I've made you a tiny bit as proud of me as I am of you. All you need is belief, patience, a smattering of sweat and tears, and a sprinkling of fairy dust for dreams to come true.

Hello from Aria

We hope you enjoyed this book! If you did let us know, we'd love to hear from you.

We are Aria, a dynamic digital-first fiction imprint from award-winning independent publishers Head of Zeus. At heart, we're committed to publishing fantastic commercial fiction – from romance and sagas to crime, thrillers and historical fiction. Visit us online and discover a community of like-minded fiction fans!

We're also on the look out for tomorrow's superstar authors. So, if you're a budding writer looking for a publisher, we'd love to hear from you. You can submit your book online at ariafiction.com/we-want-read-your-book

You can find us at:
Email: aria@headofzeus.com
Website: www.ariafiction.com
Submissions: www.ariafiction.com/we-want-read-your-book

f @ariafiction
𝕏 @Aria_Fiction
◎ @ariafiction